What Happened in Conroy

Elizabeth Rea

A Kate Jeffers Novel

What Happened in Conroy

READERSMAGNET, LLC

What Happened in Conroy
Copyright © 2018 by Elizabeth Rea

Published in the United States of America
ISBN Paperback: 978-1-947765-82-5
ISBN eBook: 978-1-947765-83-2

All rights reserved. No part of this publication may be reproduced, stored in a retrieval system or transmitted in any way by any means, electronic, mechanical, photocopy, recording or otherwise without the prior permission of the author except as provided by USA copyright law.

No lines, parts, and quotations were taken from other books or any previous publications.

The opinions expressed by the author are not necessarily those of ReadersMagnet, LLC.

ReadersMagnet, LLC
10620 Treena Street, Suite 230 | San Diego, California, 92131 USA
1.619. 354. 2643 | www.readersmagnet.com

Book design copyright © 2018 by ReadersMagnet, LLC. All rights reserved.
Cover design by Ericka Walker
Interior design by Shieldon Watson

This book is for Danny... and many others.

Contents

Kate	11
Kate	16
Conroy, Georgia	29
The Field House	36
Kate	41
Bayside Motel	46
The M.E.'s Office	53
Amy and Carlos	59
Amy and Sherry	66
Turley's Stables	71
Kate and Carlos	74
Bayside Motel	78
Kate and Gloria	84
Kate Calls Carlos	88
Kate	90
The Call From Carlos	96
Conroy High School	99
Sally and Kate	107
Clem	111

Kate	113
Sally	117
Clem	119
Kate at the Bayside Café	122
Papa's Lounge	125
Sally	129
Conroy Memorial Hospital	133
Kate at the Tysons' Home	137
Conroy Memorial Hospital	140
Kate and the Detectives at Mort's	143
Kate	145
Kate	150
Papa's Lounge	155
The Tysons' Home	158
Conroy Memorial Hospital	160
Conroy High School	164
Conroy Memorial Hospital	166
Conroy Memorial Hospital	169
Kate	173
Conroy Memorial Hospital	177
Kate and Sherry Johnson	182
Kate and Larry Tyson	188
Monroe Street Police Station, Atlanta	193
Prosciutto's Club	199
Kate	203
Kate	210
Kate	213
Kate: Back in Conroy	217
Lieutenant Whitaker: Atlanta	222

Conroy High School	224
Conroy High School Cafeteria	228
Tyson's Garage	232
Chief Hayslip and the Detectives	234
Tyson's Garage	237
Kate and Papa	241

CHAPTER 1

Kate

Sunday Evening

I'd barely gotten to sleep when Lieutenant Whitaker called me. "Kate," he began rather apologetically, "I really need your help."

I groaned into the receiver. I know that's not really professional, but hey!

I'd hoped to have at least a couple of weeks off before having to assist on another case. My goal had been to get some sleep, find out what was going on in my sister Emily's life and beg some cooking lessons from my brother and our grandmother. I guess that was going to have to wait.

My name is Kate Jeffers and I've been working with the Atlanta, Georgia police for a few years. For the past three I've been freelancing out of my home, just helping out when needed. You see, I'm a psychic. You may find that hard to believe, but there you have it. I *have* been able to help out on several occasions and have solved all my cases…so far. So when Doug Whitaker calls, I do whatever I can.

"What's up, Lieutenant?" I asked as I glanced at the clock. 10:00 p.m.

Doug proceeded to tell me a little about the current problem. "The head football coach out in Conroy dropped dead yesterday, and the medical examiner is suspicious. Can you come here to the station or meet me somewhere after work? I'll be finished here in about half an hour."

I suggested that he come to my loft apartment. It's close to headquarters. We could discuss the case and maybe order in some food. I could be sure he hadn't had dinner yet. I'd found some stale peanut butter crackers that I'd munched on before crashing into bed, but my stomach was already rumbling. Food sounded like a good idea.

"Sounds like a plan!" he said, and we disconnected.

I started a fire and turned on a few lamps. It was chilly in Atlanta—in the 50's—about what one should expect for an October evening. I fixed myself a cup of very strong tea—my grandmothers would have approved. I would rather have had a stiff bourbon, but I needed to stay awake. While waiting for Whitaker, I scrounged around in my "nasty" drawer—to find a take-out menu. Most of my favorite places are on my phone's speed-dial since fast food is all I exist on, but Doug doesn't like the same kinds of food as I.

I prefer ethnic food—especially Italian and Greek. Perhaps that's because the "love of my life" is Greek. But Lieutenant Whitaker prefers "good-old-American".

About an hour later, Lieutenant Doug Whitaker arrived at my mid-rise building, parked in the basement garage, said hello to Gloria, who was working the security desk, and took the elevator up to the top floor—my loft.

My loft is SO COOL! I've only lived here about four months, but I've fallen in love with the place! I have a living room, kitchen, eating area and a kick-ass office on the main floor. I put in a great fireplace and French doors that lead out to a garden/patio on the balcony. The upper floor houses my bedroom and bath as well as lots of storage space. It's gorgeous—just perfect for a single, twenty-five year old. I'd love to get a cat, but my work—sleuthing for the Atlanta PD—takes me out of town too much. Gloria, a.k.a. Glory, would be happy to come upstairs and feed, but sometimes she "helps out" on my cases. Actually, she's more in the way than anything and can be a pain in the rear at times, but she *is* a friend and to tell you the truth, she's a hoot! She makes my life fun—I have to admit.

Doug Whitaker arrived and I'd found a menu of which he would approve. I pulled a beer out of the fridge (for him) and finally poured my bourbon. Hey—I was awake from the tea and would probably need to hit the ladies' room every half-hour for the rest of the night. I *needed* the bourbon!

After deciding on food and placing a delivery order, Whitaker settled into a comfy chair next to the fire, and I opted for the sofa opposite. I have to tell you—I've been getting some weird vibes from Doug lately. His wife died about four or five years ago, and I get the feeling he's on the look-out for the next "Mrs. Whitaker". It makes me a bit uncomfortable…I'm crazy about "Papa", a Greek guy and here's my former superior and now co-worker—who acts like he might have designs on me! *Oh, boy!* "Uncomfortable" may not be a strong enough word!

You've probably guessed that my love life/social life stinks—and you're right. But more about that later. I need to tell you about this new case.

The Lieutenant briefed me on the information he had been given so far. The Police Chief in Conroy, a small town on the far eastern edge of Atlanta, had called and requested assistance. A "favorite" coach at Conroy High School had died. He'd been the head football coach. The results of the autopsy were still pending, but the preliminaries suggested that there might have been some foul play.

Gloria interrupted our discussion when she called to inform us that our dinner had arrived and she had allowed the delivery person access to the elevator. She requested any leftovers we might have. The girl loves to eat!

Over our burgers, Doug told me that our co-workers, Detectives Amy Stevens and Carlos Williams were already heading to Conroy, about a thirty minute drive (at least at this time of night). During rush hour it could easily take an hour and a half or more!

The deceased football coach was fairly young and was apparently healthy. *Not any more,* I thought and then admonished myself. With no sleep in the past week, I was feeling a little punchy! Police Chief Brian Hayslip, who heads the small police force in Conroy, said that the dead guy was practically revered as a god. He'd been there for many years and had winning seasons across the board. Well, that usually cinches the 'god' status—especially in a small town! His officers had nosed around, but no one was talking. That's why the police chief had called Doug.

Whitaker asked, "Would you be willing to go out to Conroy for a few days to lend a hand?"

The two detectives, Amy and Carlos, and I had worked on several cases together. They are really good people and hard working. The three of us had just wrapped up a kidnapping case and I knew they were as worn out as I. I'd been curious, lately, about their relationship. At first they'd been co-workers. Then they became partners after both becoming detectives. *Now,* they seemed really chummy, if you know what I mean. I'm sort of adept at psyching people out, even *without* having a vision. They'd make a nice couple—they respect each other and are very kind and supportive of one another. Don't we all wish we could find someone like that?! Oops…I caught my mind wandering again and tried to focus on what Doug was saying.

I suddenly remembered that Whitaker had asked me a question. So I grumbled, took a big swig of my drink and promised to head to Conroy first thing in the morning. Food eaten and mission accomplished, Whitaker said his goodbyes and headed home. I shuffled to the kitchen, programmed the java machine for *way* too early and made my way upstairs. I was glad *Whitaker's* social life hadn't been a topic this evening. Between being half asleep, half tipsy and completely lonesome, I might have done something I'd regret later on!

CHAPTER 2

Kate

Monday Morning

I slept like a log and woke up more rested than I'd been in days. I wished I could have stayed in bed for a few more hours, but a promise is a promise. Even on a *good* day I'm not a morning person, however, so I struggled into my fleece jammies and fuzzy slippers and managed to descend the spiral staircase and feel my way to the coffee machine without doing a face-plant. Don't laugh…It's been known to happen! Perhaps I should have installed a fire pole for caffeine emergencies such as this!

I congratulated myself for having remembered to program the coffee maker after Whitaker left the night before and poured myself a huge mug. The grandmothers would *not* have approved. They are both *very* proper. No mugs allowed—only dainty little china cups! Grandmas Jeffers and Phelps would also roll their eyes if they caught me propped up against the kitchen counter instead of "sitting like a proper lady".

My brother Dave, our sister Emily and I had been raised by our grandmothers after our parents were killed in an auto accident. I'd been twelve at that time. Dave is two years younger than I and Emily, two years younger than Dave. Considering we'd been orphaned, we had as good a childhood as you can possibly imagine.

My Grandmother Jeffers, Dad's mother, lived in a huge home on an estate in Buckhead. She had horses, a tennis court, a swimming pool and several acres of woods for us to play in. We spent most of our time at the estate. Now, Dave and his wife Sarah live in the big house and Grandma has moved into the gate house.

When we were young and school was in session, we spent the weeknights with Grandma Phelps, our Mom's mother. She lives in a house in the Emory area. We were fortunate to be able to attend a prestigious private school near her home. Her house and yard are smaller than the Jeffers', so there weren't as many distractions. In the evenings we sat in the kitchen and did our homework under her *close* supervision while she prepared dinner. I suppose that's part of the reason I'm such a lousy cook. I was always too busy doing homework to pay attention to what was on the stove.

Grandma Phelps still gets hysterical whenever she thinks about the time I asked if you had to boil water on both sides. Hey! I was just a kid back then!

The grandmothers set up trusts for each of us, so we'd be well-provided for no matter what else happened. The trusts were set up to be paid in installments on our twenty-first, twenty-fourth and thirtieth birthdays. I used most of my first installment to pay for college and to invest for the future.

Last year, when I received my second payment, I bought, renovated and furnished my loft. It is on the top floor of an old office building at the corner of 14th and Peachtree, right in the heart of Midtown. The location is perfect—it's close to everything—museums, shops and very importantly, restaurants and bars!

One of the Buckhead Life restaurants is nearby. I pop in for dinner to talk to Pano Karatassos, the owner, frequently. I have a very soft place in my heart for Greeks and for Greek food. Kyma is the only one of his restaurants that has strictly Greek food, but Pano's love of food and his hospitality are definitely apparent at all his restaurants.

Then there's my favorite bar—Papa's. Thomas Papadopoulos, a.k.a. "Papa" is the owner/barkeep. *He's* the love of my life that I mentioned earlier. But since I'm not Greek, our relationship probably won't progress any further than it already has. His family assumes he'll settle down with a "nice girl from the neighborhood"… ie, Greek. I have other ideas, which I (usually) keep to myself. The thing is, he's *really* crazy about me (I think…I hope)—he just fights it. I haven't given up on him yet, though I have tried dating a few other guys.

Recently, however, my "relationships" have ended up in disaster. Take the one that ended last week. The guy threw a twenty out his car window, told me to take a cab home and then sped off. How rude is that? Not to mention…humiliating. Did I leave the money in the gutter? Not a chance!

While I slugged down my first cuppa, I planned my day. Sipping on my second cup, I made up my plan of attack for the rest of the week and decided what to pack to take to Conroy. Besides work clothes, I chose some casual outfits—to fit in at the ballgames and hopefully have time to do a little riding at one of the stables! A girl can't work *all* the time. Little did I know what the week had in store for me.

After the third cup, I was wired and had to get moving! After a quick shower, I threw on some black slacks and a bright green turtleneck sweater. I ran my fingers through my hair and blew it dry. I grabbed a hair clasp and pulled my wavy, brown hair back, fastening it low on my neck.

How I ended up with brown hair is a mystery to me! Emily, now in her last year at the Art Institute, has gorgeous, long blond locks. All thick and luxurious-looking—makes me jealous just to think about it! She ended up with all the musical and artistic talent as well. But she's having a rough week. I was hoping to give her a lot of my time, but Conroy was calling.

I lugged my suitcase down the spiral stairs, again lucky to avoid falling. I grabbed my keys, my big black bag/briefcase, a black suede jacket, a bottle of water, and headed out the door to the elevator. While I was waiting for it, I remembered my cell phone and had just enough time to race back and grab it before the elevator doors slid open. There's nothing like starting the day off in a relaxed state of mind. I needed a massage already and hadn't even made it to the parking garage!

Gloria was off duty, so I waved hi to Pete, another security guard and threw my stuff in my car. I figured Glory would call me before too long, curious about Doug Whitaker's late-night visit. I don't know if Glory is nosy or just a good friend, but she sure keeps tabs on everything that goes on!

Once on the road, I pulled into the local waffle place for breakfast—their eggs and cheese are the best. I looked in the rearview mirror to apply some blush, mascara and lip gloss before going inside. No need to scare the servers!

After my eggs and raisin toast, I headed east towards Conroy. It was a beautiful fall morning. The sun was just coming up, but it was far enough to the south at this time of year, that it didn't blind me. Instead it reflected off the pretty leaves—red and gold. As I left the city behind, I began to notice small ponds and streams that sparkled in the sun. I smiled at the ducks swimming and diving for food. It was supposed to get to about 65 degrees, slightly cooler than average, but still perfect in my book.

I was in a zone and jumped a mile when my cell phone rang. I should have looked to see who was calling before answering, but since I was driving, I just pressed "talk". Mistake number one. It was Gloria!

"Hey there, girl," she chattered brightly. "What'cha doing? What was Whitaker doing at your place so late last night? Did he put the moves on you?"

I rolled my eyes towards heaven. Then I answered her honestly—to a point. I told her that Doug's visit was strictly business and that I was headed to Conroy on a case. Mistake number two, although I didn't find *that* out till later!

A huge sigh escaped my lips when I hung up. I adore Gloria, but sometimes she can be high maintenance! I realized that I was looking forward to a couple of days away from the big city.

Horse farms and pastures replaced office buildings, and exits from the highway became further apart. Before long, I saw exits to Conroy. I took the one that dropped me off in the center of the small town and proceeded to the police station where I was to meet Detectives Stevens and Williams and Chief Hayslip. The chief was going to brief us on the latest developments and then we'd decide where to go from there.

Police Chief Hayslip was already there with Amy and Carlos. The officer at the front desk waved me back when I showed him my I.D.—they were expecting me, he mouthed,—and continued his conversation with someone on the phone.

"G'mornin,'" said Hayslip. He motioned to a vacant chair, so I took the seat and listened.

"I want to thank you all for coming to help out with this," he began. "You see, small towns are different from the big cities like Atlanta. Everyone knows everyone else and all their business. Sometimes that's a good thing, but in a situation like this…it's a hindrance. People are tight-lipped. They thought Coach Johnson was perfect. Johnson has been…I mean, *had* been…the coach here for over fifteen years and was very well respected in the school system, in the community…heck, in the whole state! His football teams have won championships year after year."

Hayslip cleared his throat and wiped his eyes before continuing. He had obviously thought a great deal of Coach Johnson, himself!

"Of course, they're still completing the tests from his autopsy. It's impossible to think a man his age...he was just 40, and as healthy as he was...could just keel over.

"You see, he'd come here right out of college. Was the assistant coach for a couple of years and then took over as head coach. He was a great guy. Married a girl from here, Sherry Smith.

"It was like we all watched him grow up—he was only 21 when he came to Conroy. His death is a horrible blow to everyone here."

I thought, *Not to everyone. If the preliminary tests were right, someone wanted him gone.*

Brian Hayslip continued. "Poor Sherry! She was standing right close by when he collapsed. "I went to see her last night. She's hysterical...beside herself. Her parents are staying with her...with her and the kids, but they are almost as broken up about it as Sherry is! You know they have two kids and one on the way?"

We shook our heads. Sympathetically. The thought made me shudder. My brother, Dave, and his wife Sarah are expecting their first child. This incident made me think—what if this was my brother's family? How would Sarah cope? And the rest of us, too?

We'd already lost our mother and father when they were killed in an accident years ago. I'd recently discovered that a local drug guru and his South American contact had caused their deaths. They'd rear-ended my dad's car, pushing it through the guardrail and down into a ravine. The weather that night had been terrible and the car had burst into flames, both factors compromising any evidence from the scene.

I'd had one of my "visions" the day before and have had nightmares ever since. I always blamed myself in a way. I realize that as a twelve year old I didn't have credibility and I probably couldn't have prevented my parents from going out the next night, but I've always felt that if I'd understood the vision and had *said something*, things might have turned out differently.

It *is* somewhat comforting to know that my father had not been driving recklessly, as was reported in the paper, but nevertheless, both our parents are dead. Sometimes now I even have a hard time picturing what they looked like. And I'm sure it's even worse for Dave and Emily. Emily had only been *eight* when they died!

It must have been awful for both grandmothers too, now that I think about it. At the time I'd been too wrapped up in my own grief to consider their feelings. Both grandfathers had already died. And then Grandma Phelps and Jeffers had to deal with the loss of their two children. Not to mention that they had to take the three of us in and comfort us—when they were grieving as well!

Just thinking about it…if this were my brother instead of Coach Johnson…how our family and friends would react…I was getting a pretty good picture of the scene here in Conroy.

I shook my head to break my reverie…and focused on the continuing conversation.

"There is going to be an assembly at the school at 10:30 this morning and then school is going to be dismissed for the afternoon. No one can concentrate…there's no way they can carry on right now.

"I think it would be a good idea for all of you to attend the assembly. Maybe you can look around and get some ideas. Maybe you'll be able to notice things that my officers can't…you might pick up on something."

We agreed. It was decided that we should just go in as bystanders. Considering the mental state of the people in the community, no one would even notice our presence. That's how I wanted it…that's for sure. We planned to split up, each taking a particular section of the gymnasium during the assembly, to listen and watch. Then we'd compare notes afterwards.

After leaving the police station, I checked into the Bayside Motel, the same place Amy and Carlos were staying. Funny name considering there isn't a "bay" within two hundred miles of here! I suppose one could take into account Lake Sinclair or a couple other small bodies of water that might have a bay, but even those little lakes aren't really *that* close to the town.

It had been years since I'd been to the lakes or even to Conroy—probably not since my father had taken us all for a Sunday afternoon drive. I remember thinking those afternoons were sheer torture. My dad always drove at a snail's pace. It took hours to get anywhere! Granted, the highways are better now than they were fifteen or twenty years ago and cars today are more comfortable… And I much prefer driving to riding…but even so…I was surprised when I left the city and headed east that Conroy was actually so close to Atlanta.

I was sure that Conroy had changed, too, since we'd been there, but my main recollection was of dry, flat expanses, horse stables and dusty winds. I was anxious to check out the town again.

After I deposited my luggage in my room, we drove around in my car (didn't want to take the squad car) and scoped out the town. Amy and Carlos usually drive an unmarked vehicle since they often do surveillance work, but Lieutenant Whitaker had recommended a squad car this trip to make sure the local people considered them 'official'.

First we stopped at a small information/tourist booth and picked up a couple brochures about the area. Conroy has about twelve to fourteen thousand people. Pretty much a middle-class suburb. Some people commute to Atlanta to work, but most have jobs locally. The main streets of the town are lined with "mom and pop" businesses, little family-owned shops: a dry cleaner's, hardware stores, small coffee houses, an ice cream shop and a few small restaurants. We noticed two florist shops and commented on the amount of business they would get this week—with the coach's funeral a few days away.

On the outskirts of town we passed several horse farms. I was glad I'd thought to pack my riding boots.

After scouting out the town, we headed to Conroy High School and to the gymnasium where the morning's assembly was to be held. We arrived about thirty minutes early and did our split-up thing. Carlos hung around outside to watch people, mainly parents, as they entered the building. Amy went directly to the gym to get a handle on things in there.

I opted to roam the halls. In a word, it was awful! Kids, especially the girls were in the hallways, hugging each other and crying. The guys were a bit more stoic, but it was very clear that they were having a tough time of it as well. The teachers were in the halls too, keeping an eye on the kids. It was quite obvious that there was no way they would be able to have classes this morning.

One teacher looked at me strangely and I decided I'd better speak with her. I was certain she would keep very close tabs on anyone who looked like a stranger. I introduced myself and said, "I'm working with the Metro Police in Atlanta. A couple of us were asked by Chief Hayslip to come along to help out this morning. I have to admit, I'm curious. Why did you even *try* to have school today?"

"It's like this…we have kids from all over the county. Some of them don't have TV's, radios or phones. And since Coach died over the weekend, even though it was at a school event, not all the kids were here. There was just no way to contact everyone.

"There's another reason as well. In a small town, gossip gets out of control real fast. If people aren't told the facts, they just make something up! If we didn't have this assembly and didn't invite the townsfolk in as well, all kinds of rumors would be popping up! So far this morning I've heard that Coach had a heart attack, he'd been hit by a truck and that someone had shot him. I'm not sure what to tell the students, so for one, I'm *glad* to be here this morning so I can find out what *really* happened!"

"I appreciate you taking time to talk with me—it helps me get a better perspective on things. I'll probably see you later. Thanks," I said and headed off down another corridor.

The students were beginning to make their way towards the gym, so I fell in step and got swept along with the crowd. Amid the sniffling and blowing of noses, I could hear murmurs extolling

"Coach's" virtues. Everyone I overheard had nothing but praise for this man!

Maybe he *had* died of natural causes. I was really anxious to hear about the results of the autopsy. Whitaker had said "signs of foul play". Weird!

I found a seat among the freshman class. I thought that might be the most inconspicuous place. Not that I look that young. Oh no! At the tender age of twenty-five, I'm already starting to get an occasional gray hair!!

I just figured if someone noticed me in the crowd, they'd think I was a new student and that's why they wouldn't recognize me. Plus, face it. Freshmen girls are more apt to be weeping hysterically—it's just their nature. Hormones out of control and big crushes on teachers—especially the coaches. Yeah, okay, I was a freshman once, too. At any rate, I figured they'd be too caught up in the drama to pay much attention to me.

I looked around and listened carefully while waiting for the assembly to begin. While I was zoning out, checking out the crowd on the other side of the gym, something flashed before me. Puzzled, I blinked my eyes and gave myself a shake. I guess it was a vision, because as I looked around myself, I couldn't see what I thought I'd just seen.

My visions are strange sometimes. I can have them when I'm asleep or awake, if I'm working on something or just relaxing. They usually aren't this brief, though. Most of the time they are like very vivid dreams and occasionally they seem to last *forever*.

This time, I just had a very brief flash of an angry face. I was looking directly into this person's eyes and I sensed that this person was female. The eyes were squinted half-closed and there were furrows between her eyebrows. I couldn't tell how old she was or what color hair she had. But she didn't seem to be particularly young.

I searched the entire crowd looking for someone who could fit that description. No one. Nada. Zilch. *Crap!* Things are never easy—I don't know why I bother to get my hopes up.

Then my eye caught someone who appeared out of place—the guilty person? Not likely—it was Gloria. You know, Gloria, the security guard from my building! *What the heck is she doing here?* She caught me staring and stood up and waved. Both arms. Big arms! Then she yelled, "HI!" really loud.

I wanted to slither through the cracks in the bleachers and disappear into the hinterlands! But instead I waved, discreetly, and smiled at her as if to say, "Not now, I'm working!"

Fortunately, she took the hint and sat back down. And that's not an easy thing to do. You see, Glory is a *large* girl. And wears mostly spandex. And stiletto heels. I wondered how the heck she'd managed to get as far up on those bleachers as she had. Glory usually wears all black, but occasionally she'll put on another color—so people will notice her? Colors like fuchsia or chartreuse or neon blue. Believe me, people *always* notice Glory! This morning she was wearing glow-in-the-dark yellow…with feathers! Oh Jeeze!

"Just wait till I get a hold of you, girlie," I muttered.

"What?" asked the lady in front of me, turning around.

"Oops, sorry! Not you," I said apologetically. *Nothing like calling attention to yourself!* I thought.

The assembly was about to start, so the woman just shook her head, looked at me like I had three eyes and turned back to face the man who was climbing onto the stage at one end of the gymnasium.

The talking ceased as he approached the podium. Turns out the man is the principal at Conroy High. Another named Mr. Hayslip! *Wow*, I thought. *What's his connection to the Police Chief? Is everyone related to everyone else in a small town?*

He began to speak, comforting the students, calming the fears of the townspeople. Actually he was very eloquent. I was impressed. I wondered if he'd had help from one of the counselors or if he was always this good when dealing with people during a crisis. At any rate, by the time he'd finished, people were calmer, the hysteria quieted. Mr. Hayslip hadn't broached the subject of cause of death. I wasn't sure if he was aware of the possibility of homicide and I wished (again) that we had the autopsy results.

The principal announced the closing of the school until after Coach Johnson's memorial service, which was scheduled for Thursday afternoon. I wondered if the body would be available by then. He dismissed the adults in a somber tone of voice and then the students, by classes. It was very orderly and once again, I was impressed. The freshmen were dismissed last, so I was able to watch all the other people file out. I saw *no one* who matched the person in my brief vision.

I paid close attention when Gloria exited. She took the arm of a good-looking man who assisted her down the bleacher steps. She teetered on slim ankles and her four and a half stiletto heels. She reminds me of a horse—big body and tiny ankles—trying to tippy-toe over the ground. I doubt if I'll tell Glory of my comparison. She'd get stuck on the horse impression and then she'd kick my tail from Conroy all the way back to Atlanta!

Meanwhile, the man was in heaven! His chest was all puffed out and he held his head up as if to say, "Check *this* out, fellows." I could tell that she was thanking him and then she wiggled her yellow feathers at him and twitched her tushie as she hurried out of the gym.

I did a mental eye roll and made certain to leave by a different exit! I didn't want to meet up with her here at the high school. Instead I found Amy Stevens and Carlos Williams, and we made our way to my car.

Back at the police station, we again met in Chief Hayslip's office. We compared notes about the assembly and all had pretty much the same impression. I told everyone about my vision. The chief looked *very* skeptical as Amy and Carlos just nodded and looked thoughtful.

"I suppose I should explain," I began, noticing Hayslip's look. "I assist the lieutenant and the detectives with some of their cases."

"Yeah, Whitaker told me about you—I just didn't believe him. Ya really *see* things?"

I explained, for about the millionth time in my life, a little about the visions. The first one I can remember was when I was seven and in second grade. It was very vivid and I almost gave myself away in front of the entire class. A classmate had lost her ring and I'd had a vision of where it was. I'd never been to her house, so when I blurted out its location, half the people in the school decided I was a peeping Tom or a burglar or something else along those lines. I realized right then that I'd need to be very careful! After that incident I kept most of my visions to myself.

Several years later I'd had that vision of my parents' accident. I guess I still feel guilty about having "inside information" about some things. I'm certain that's why I ended up in police work. I needed a positive avenue for my talents. If I can help the police and thereby help others it might assuage my guilt over *not* being able to save my parents.

When I was finished explaining a bit about my visions, Chief Hayslip still looked like he didn't buy a word of it, but then I'm used to that. Most people react this way. To tell you the truth, I don't really understand the whole thing myself. But then the meeting continued.

"I talked to the coroner and the medical examiner on my way back here from the high school," Hayslip said. "They've found massive bruising on Johnson's right side and warfarin in his blood and some in his tissues. We don't know yet how he was bruised, but the M.E. knows all about warfarin. It's one of the drugs used to thin the blood. Warfarin is the generic form of the drug Coumadin. We'll do some checking to see if Johnson was taking it for high blood pressure or a clot or something, but I'd be real surprised. He's always appeared to be in perfect health. The M.E. hasn't been able to reach Johnson's regular physician yet, but is still trying. But it *could* turn out that someone's been trying to poison him."

CHAPTER 3

Conroy, Georgia

Monday Afternoon

The detectives, Amy and Carlos, and I sat very quietly while trying to digest this information. No pun intended!

"Wow," Carlos muttered, wiping a hand across his face. "Who'd want him dead? Sounded like they were about to make him a saint…"

We all agreed. We shared our comments about the morning's assembly. No one had overheard anything negative about Coach Johnson.

But still…I thought…*we must be looking at this all wrong—I need to come at this from a different angle.*

"You know what they say, don't you? Poison is a woman's weapon and the family is always the first place to look," commented Amy.

"His only really close relatives around here would be his wife, Sherry, and her family. There're their kids, Sean and Cory, but if you want to look at women first, they don't qualify," said Hayslip.

I thought *what a comment! We've really got a smart one here!* Sean and Cory are definitely boys! But I managed to keep my mouth shut. Maybe he was trying to lighten the mood by saying something funny. And the woman thing *would* go along with my vision. I glanced over at Amy who was trying hard to keep a straight face. She quickly averted her gaze—good thing or we'd both end up with the giggles. Not too professional!

We managed to keep ourselves under control until we'd left the station. Once we were safely in my car and en route to the motel, Amy let out a snort. "Gee, I guess the chief is pretty much convinced that the two sons aren't women. Go figure!"

"Yeah, I saw you two exchange glances," chuckled Carlos, "and figured we'd better wind up the meeting and get you two the hell out of there before you embarrassed me, yourselves and the entire Atlanta Police Force! Whitaker'd have our badges for sure!"

"Sorry," I replied as I turned into the motel parking lot. "But really…people should think before opening their mouths!"

"Oh, my god! Look who's here—speaking of people who should think before they speak…Did *you* tell her we were here, Kate?" Carlos shook his head and gazed at the yellow-feathered figure standing outside our motel. I just groaned.

Gloria wiggled her boa at us as we emerged from my vehicle. "I saw the squad car in the lot as I was driving around and figured it must be y'all's," she hollered.

"I thought Whitaker suggested we keep a low profile," Carlos muttered to Amy and me as we walked in Gloria's direction.

"Let me get her in my room—maybe I can talk her into going back home."

"Good luck!" said Amy.

"Fat chance!!" whispered Carlos. "We'll be next door writing down lists of people to interview. Don't be too long."

I glanced quickly around the lot to see how many people were staring—amazingly, no one—and dragged Gloria into my room.

"What the hell are you doing here?" I blurted out. I'm sorry to admit that I couldn't hide my annoyance. And the worst part was that I'd brought it on myself.

"I came to help," was her answer. She pouted and her eyes got real big.

Oh brother! I silently swore and reached way down inside myself to find a little patience. "Let's sit down and discuss this rationally," I finally said. Glory smiled.

I told her what I could about the case, which wasn't much. She'd already heard on the news that foul play was indicated in a coach's death. *Thanks a heap, media.* And so she had put two and two together and had driven out in her van to "help".

"I *am* going to stick around—I've never been to Conroy before—I might like it out here!" she added cheerfully.

I seriously considered having her arrested for interfering with and compromising a case! But actually, short of doing just that, there wasn't too much I could do. Finally, we compromised. She promised to get out of her ridiculous outfit and keep out of the way. I promised that we were still friends and I wouldn't arrest her—yet.

Glory went off to the Conroy Saddle Shop to purchase some "appropriate" outfits, and I went to Carlos's room where he and Amy were working.

"Well…?" they asked expectantly when Carlos answered the door.

I just shook my head and tried to convince them that it was *possible* that Gloria could be of some help. She is very out-going and easy to talk to. The guys in town might tell her things they felt uncomfortable telling us "cops". Amy raised her eyebrows and Carlos looked very skeptical. Can't imagine why!

We decided to split up again and interview some people. Carlos was going to drop Amy off in Coach Johnson's neighborhood and then head downtown to talk to some of the shopkeepers. I was going back to the school and the surrounding area to talk with anyone who might be lingering around. I still had a mental image of the "angry person" from my vision and was going to keep looking for him or her.

Tragedy is an interesting phenomenon. It brings people out of their own little worlds for a while. People who would normally not hang out with others do at a time such as this. People *need* to be surrounded with other people. They need to talk—they need companionship. Whether they feel like being surrounded with others will keep tragedy from striking them, or if it's a need to prove that they are alive, I'm not certain.

Whatever the reason, I was counting on human nature to bring people out of the woodwork.

My intuition was right! When I arrived back at the High School, there were still dozens of people milling around. They didn't want to go back home, just as I'd suspected. The majority were kids; students standing in small clusters, talking quietly. But there were also a few adults—probably some of the faculty and staff. I recognized the teacher I'd met earlier, waved and headed in her direction. I racked my brain trying to remember her name and couldn't. I decided perhaps she hadn't told me.

"Hey, y'all," the teacher said to the group as I walked up. "This is Kate Jeffers from Atlanta…a friend. Isn't it nice that she came out here today?" She smiled and shot me a conspiratorial glance as everyone else nodded and murmured their assent.

She started introductions: Alan the English teacher, Rose the school secretary, Carla the cook. "And of course you know me, Marta," she concluded.

Smiling and nodding to each, I expressed my pleasure in meeting them and my sincere sorrow over their loss. And then I thanked my lucky stars that Marta had mentioned her name. I'd look rather foolish not knowing my "friend's" name. *Marta,* I thought. *Easy to remember—just like the Rapid Transit System in Atlanta.*

Rose asked me if I'd been to the high school since it had been renovated and if I was a friend of Coach Johnson's. I hurriedly gathered my thoughts. I wasn't sure I should tell everyone about my real purpose for being here. But I also hadn't thought of what to say to people! Stupid, I know! "I'm sorry I didn't know the coach, he appears to have been a remarkable man," I began. "Of course I know Marta and Police Chief Hayslip as well." *Just a* little *lie!*

"Since this is such a sad time for your entire community, I thought I might be able to help—you know," I continued, floundering. "Uh…help with organizing, help people cope…" My voice trailed off. I wasn't doing this well at all! Fortunately Alan, the English teacher, saved my sorry self. "Oh, you're a counselor?" he asked.

I shrugged. "Of sorts," I replied and breathed a sigh of relief. "I'm a good listener and most people need someone to talk to during a crisis like this."

I could feel the perspiration trickling down my temples and brushed my hands across my forehead, swiping my face as though I was brushing the hair out of my eyes. Of course my hair was still pulled back by the hair clasp. But a few wisps had straggled out, so I hoped no one noticed my true purpose.

Alan nodded to a cluster of students close by, excused himself and walked over to them, leaving the three of us with little more to say.

Carla spoke up. "Well, I wondered what you were doin' here. You look like city—that's why I was wondering.

She continued, "I've got to get back to the kitchen—put the food away. No one told us there wouldn't be school today, so we set the breakfast things up real early this mornin'. Gotta go see what can be saved for later and what we may as well pitch.

"Made a big pot of coffee, too. It's still hot if anyone wants some." With that she turned and headed towards the building, still grumbling about wasting all that good food.

Rose, the secretary, decided she'd better get back inside, too. "I've got someone covering the phones for a few minutes, but she's most likely frantic by now. The lines have been ringing off the hook all day!"

Marta smiled wryly and commented, "Funny how everyone reacts so differently during a crisis. Rose takes control of the office, Alan helps the students cope and Carla worries about throwing away a few pancakes. And I just stand here in shock, not knowing *what* to do!"

After a moment, she sighed and said, "I guess I'll head back to my classroom and get my lesson plans re-arranged. It seems like the world should stop when someone dies…but life goes on, doesn't it?"

I smiled sympathetically and patted her arm, hoping to give comfort. "I'll leave you to it and go talk with some of the others," I said.

She smiled sadly and said, "My Social Studies papers are calling my name."

I told Marta I'd see her later and hurried to catch up with Rose. Secretaries often know more than anyone about the running of a business or school, so I picked her brain. First, I asked her about the principal's relationship to the Police Chief. She shook her head dismissively and replied that they were just distant cousins. I asked about Coach Johnson's relationship with his fellow teachers and the staff—especially the women. I must have reverted to "cop mode" questioning, because she glanced at me strangely.

"The coach was nothing but a professional," she answered stiffly. "He was adored by the faculty. I'm sure you noticed at this morning's assembly—no one could say anything but wonderful things about him.

"And he was devoted to Sherry and their kids. He was a great father," she continued, tearing up. She snatched a tissue from the pocket of her sweater and blew her nose. "Just imagine—those poor little boys having to grow up without their dad. And the baby…"

I felt so bad! Poor Rose dissolved into tears. What could I say? I patted her on her shoulder, murmuring condolences. Finally, I said, "I know it'll be hard on the whole family. But it does look like they have a wonderful support group—the school, the town, Sherry's family…"

Rose nodded in agreement and got her emotions back under control. I held the door open for her, and she led the way to her office. Her replacement looked thrilled to see her and jumped up, waving a fist-full of phone memos.

"Rose, I'm so glad you're back! I've got to run, but here are all the calls you need to return. I'm sorry, but I couldn't answer all the questions. But I was able to answer some…" Her voice drifted off as she saw that Rose had been crying. "Do you need me to stay longer? I can if…"

"No, sweetie," Rose answered. "You've been here way too long as it is. I'm grateful…thank you."

The lady looked relieved and practically mowed us down as she came from behind Rose's desk. She nodded to me, gave Rose a hug and fled from the office.

"She's a parent-volunteer," Rose explained. "Comes in on Mondays to help. Usually runs off the menus and staff memos and so on. When she arrived this morning, she hadn't heard about the coach…really knocked her for a loop!"

Rose kept talking, mostly to herself, with a dazed look on her face. She jumped when the phone rang again and looked up at me, startled, as though she'd forgotten I was there.

I sketched a wave, mouthed, "Talk to you later," at her and left as she snatched up the receiver and became the efficient office manager again.

CHAPTER 4

The Field House

Monday Afternoon

After leaving the front office, I wandered for a few minutes. The halls were mostly cleared out. I left the building by one of the back doors and took a path that led over to a large cement block structure that looked like it was still under construction. There were three teenage boys sitting on the retaining wall outside the building. As I got closer I realized that this must be the field house and indeed, it wasn't quite finished.

"Hey, guys," I said in a friendly voice. "Are they still working on this place?"

"Yes, ma'am," replied the boy sitting closest to me. "The inside is done—Coach wanted it finished before football season. I guess he figured the outside could be finished any old time."

I looked them over. I was pretty sure all three of them were on the football team. They were all built like it. I suppose I shouldn't have been surprised to notice that they had no apparent body piercings— no earrings, nose rings and so forth, but I did a double-take anyway.

I'm so used to seeing that and lots of facial hair on the teens in Atlanta. But then I thought of my own high school and the guys there. Only the real drugged out guys and the artsy ones had gone that route. The athletes were pretty clean-cut as a rule. If I remember correctly, piercings weren't allowed for safety reasons.

Two of the boys were relatively stocky, probably linemen or tackles. The third boy was taller and thinner, but broad through the shoulders. A receiver of some sort. They all looked as though they'd had better days.

"I'm so sorry about your coach," I began. They all nodded, but remained silent. "Were you guys here on Saturday when he collapsed?"

One of the shorter boys answered, "I was. It was so weird—he got this look on his face and then sort of…melted to the ground. You know? He went all rubbery and kinda folded up on himself. Weird…," he repeated, his voice trailing off.

"Yeah," said the other stocky boy. "My sister was there—she's a cheerleader. I was running late so I didn't get there till after…but I guess they'd just started the picnic. But she said pretty much the same as Keith here…Coach got real pale and just sort of went to the ground."

I turned my attention to the tall boy. "Are you on the team, too?"

"Yes, ma'am," he said, "but I wasn't here at the picnic. I was at home."

"Man, Clem," the second boy said to him. "You gotta do something about those headaches. You're missing out on everything!"

Clem nodded and kept looking at the ground. Then he looked up and said, "But I *did* go riding on Friday after school." He looked at me and continued, "Coach and a few of us went out to the stables after practice on Friday. We had a bye last week."

He noticed my confusion and explained, "That means we didn't have a game Friday night. Because of the scheduling, our school got a week off. So anyway, some of us went riding."

He looked off into the distance and I could imagine his thoughts. "That's the last time I saw him," he said.

"You were there too, right, Keith? At Turley's?"

"Yeah."

Clem then looked at the other boy whose name, I learned later, was Josh. He shook his head and said he hadn't gone.

A sad look came over Keith's face, but he almost smiled. "It was kinda funny…Coach was riding that squirrely gelding of Mrs. Turley's. Winnie was bouncing all over the place until Coach got 'im under control. And then…this is the funny part…you know how they don't like us to cinch the straps too tight? Well, so we all kept them pretty loose and when the horse turned real quick, Coach slid right off. It was a hoot! He was like in slow motion—just slid right off—like the saddle had been greased!"

"Was he hurt?" I asked.

"Nah. I mean, he landed on his feet and then kinda tipped over onto his side in the dirt, but he jumped right back up again. We were all laughing our asses off and he was more red-in-the-face than anything." Keith must have realized his faux pas, because he instantly blushed deeply and added, "Scuse my mouth, ma'am."

Josh looked aghast and said, "Yeah, Keith, Coach would be pissed if he heard you talkin' like that—in front of a lady!" And then he immediately turned red himself.

I covered my mouth to smother a snort, but couldn't help laughing. "You gentlemen are going from bad to worse!"

Changing the subject, I asked them about Turley's Stables and decided I'd better have a chat with the staff there. The incident on Friday might be able to explain the bruising on Johnson's body.

I thanked them for their time and excused myself. I decided I should touch base with the medical examiner and then head out to the stables. As I made my way towards my car, I heard and then saw Gloria's van heading my way. It rattled, worse than usual, as it chugged its way over the gravel parking lot, a plume of dust in its wake.

"Hey, Kate!" she cried, rolling down her window and then fanning the dust away. I have to say, she's one enthusiastic girl! It doesn't matter what the topic, she's right there in the middle. Even if she hasn't a clue what anyone's talking about. There's never a dull minute when Glory's around.

She slid down from the driver's seat and asked, "What do ya think of my new outfit?" She held her arms out to her sides and twirled around in a big circle so I could get the "full effect".

"It's uh…cool," I answered, at a loss for words. "Wow!" I added. I glanced over my shoulder towards the school and wasn't a bit surprised to see that I wasn't the only one who was speechless. The three boys I'd spoken with had disappeared, but there was a huge gaggle of football-type guys who had just come out of the field house. They were lined up near the building, staring, their mouths hanging open.

I smothered another laugh. First, I took in the cowboy blouse—white, tight and fringed in all the "right" places. She held a black hat with a black and white snakeskin band around the rim. The belt that cinched her waist matched.

"The jeans are kinda tight right now," she admitted, "but the salesman assured me that they'd stretch out some when I wore them."

"Did you need a shoehorn to get into them?" I asked.

Missing my joke, she said, "No, but I sure needed one to get these riding boots on. Man, they're tight!"

I hadn't gotten that far yet—my eyes were still glued to her hips. But it was true: she'd gotten new snake-skin boots to complete the outfit.

"Well, it's quite a fashion statement," I managed to say.

"Yeah—and the salesman was a real hottie! We're going out tonight." She smiled and winked at me.

How does *she do it?* I wondered. This girl has more dates in one month than I've had in two years put together! I was going to ask her what Ronnie, her new boyfriend in Atlanta, might think of her date tonight, but she changed the subject.

"What are you going to do now?" she asked, bringing my thoughts to the task at hand.

"I need to talk to the medical examiner. Then, if I have time, some other people."

"Well, I know you don't need me along for that—anyway, I don't like hanging around with dead bodies." She shuddered. "I think I'll just go have a talk with the guys over there before I need to get ready for my hot date. Maybe I can talk one of the cute ones into crawling under my van to see what's making that rattling sound. Just started on the way out here this morning. More than likely, I hit a pot hole and jiggled something loose. I've never seen such roads…but then we *are* out here in East Bejesus, ya' know!"

With that she lifted her chin in acknowledgement of the boys, smiled, showing perfectly white teeth, and sashayed in their direction.

I glanced behind me as I continued to my car. The boys had finally managed to close their mouths, but I swear that some of them were drooling!

CHAPTER 5

Kate

Monday, Late Afternoon

I stopped at the motel to freshen up a bit and phoned the medical examiner's office. Dr. Graves wasn't there; he'd gone to a conference in Athens for the afternoon and wasn't expected back until quite late.

I was headed out to my car when the squad car pulled up. Amy and Carlos had returned from town. We decided to compare notes. I guessed Turley's Stables could wait until morning. Besides…it was almost cocktail hour!

We chatted briefly and decided to talk over an early dinner—since none of us had remembered to have lunch. I realized I was starving! My cheese and egg breakfast seemed like it had been a lifetime ago.

Carlos suggested we try Mort's Restaurant. One of the shopkeepers he'd interviewed that afternoon said it had the best food in town. And it was within walking distance, so we could have drinks and not worry about driving.

The hostess allowed us to sit in a booth as isolated from other tables as possible. Our server, Shirley, took our drink orders and placed a basket of rolls and some butter on our table. We all dove for the basket as soon as Shirley had turned her back. My grandmothers would *not* have approved!

When we were growing up, it was required that we "dress" for dinner. Any type of pant was absolutely forbidden…for the ladies, that is. My younger brother, David, always appeared in at least a sport jacket. Emily and I occasionally wore long dresses, but normally a shorter dress or a cocktail-length dress was considered appropriate. Proper manners were second nature to all us children. I guess I can see the virtue of being brought up in such a manner. None of us ever had to worry about feeling out of place or socially inferior anywhere we went. We were comfortable in any social situation. Interesting that should occur to me at the moment. I guess knowing all the manners at least gives me the choice of whether to use them or not.

I choose not! I thought, and grabbed a hot, delicious-smelling, whole wheat roll. "M-mmm," I said as I tore off a little piece and watched the butter melt slowly before popping it into my mouth. "If the rest of the food here is as good as this bread, Carlos, you've made quite a find!"

We waited until Shirley had brought our drinks before talking business. In the meantime, Amy asked about Gloria, and both she and Carlos laughed out loud when I told them about her new outfit and her date this evening.

Our drinks appeared and were perfect! Both the detectives had ordered gin and tonics and I'd opted for some Woodford Reserve on the rocks.

I started by telling Amy and Carlos about my chats at the school—most importantly, about Coach Johnson's falling off his horse,—and they agreed that a trip to Turley's Stable would be on the list of things to do tomorrow. I ended by telling them I was planning to talk to the medical examiner first thing in the morning.

Amy had spent the afternoon in the Johnsons' neighborhood, talking with the families that lived nearby. She'd interviewed kids on the streets, elderly neighbors and people of about the same ages as Sherry and Coach Johnson. The consensus was that the Johnsons were a very nice family. They were friendly and helpful to the neighbors. Their two sons, Sean and Cory, played frequently with all the neighbor children and were sweet boys, always anxious to please.

The only item of note was something said by the next door neighbor, Sue Vanzant. She said she noticed that the coach and Sherry were strict with the boys: "the coach, perhaps more-so than Sherry". When Amy pressed her, she seemed to back-peddle. The coach was often at practices and games. She supposed he needed to be sterner with the children when he *was* at home. She did admit, however, hearing him raise his voice at the older boy more than once.

There had been several cars at the Johnson residence, so Amy had not tried to talk with Sherry or anyone else in the immediate family.

Carlos meanwhile had spoken with many people in the downtown area of Conroy. Both shop keepers and shoppers had only kind things to say about the coach. He *had* found out "Coach's" first name: Sam.

Amy giggled and said, "Wow, I figured he'd been named "Coach" from birth!"

Shirley came to the booth to see if we needed more cocktails (Yes!) and to see if we were ready to order (No! We hadn't even looked at our menus!)

She told us about the evening's specials and disappeared towards the bar. We noticed more chatter coming from that direction. The place was beginning to fill up.

Carlos and Amy were sitting facing the door. "Mondays are supposed to be pretty quiet, according to the owner of the hardware store," Carlos stated. "But it doesn't surprise me that it's getting crowded. Word on the street is that this could be a homicide. People downtown were whispering and giving each other furtive glances all afternoon. I was hoping to talk to more of the locals before it leaked out. Just didn't work out that way this time."

"Instead, everyone's come here tonight. Listen to them buzzing," added Amy, noticing that Shirley was headed our way again. "I suppose we should order."

We settled back with our drinks and talked some more while our dinners were being prepared.

Carlos had spoken with Lieutenant Whitaker and filled him in on our "progress". All three of us felt like we were just spinning our wheels. So far, no one had come up with anyone who could possibly be a suspect if this indeed turned out to be a homicide.

I thought about that brief vision I'd had of the angry face. Perhaps there was no connection at all.

We were pretty much bummed out by the time our meals arrived. But the food was delicious and it really helped buoy our spirits. Maybe we'd just been too hungry to think! We decided to splurge and order some Crème Brûlée for dessert before heading back to the motel. It was yummy, and we decided life wasn't as bleak as we'd earlier thought! We had the impression that Sam Johnson was a strict father. He did have a history of winning seasons. Perhaps he was as strict with his team members as he was at home. Could he perhaps have let one of the players or parents "have it"? At least it was somewhere to start!

We paid and plowed our way through the crowd and spotted Shirley, our server. We thanked her and told her she could have our table back. She looked grateful and commented that it was going to be a long night.

I was glad to be back at the Bayside Motel. We were all exhausted.

I noticed, as we headed along the outside corridor to our rooms, that Gloria's lights were on. I wondered if her date was with her inside…Neither Amy nor Carlos seemed to notice. They were too busy looking gaga-eyed at each other. *Am I becoming cynical?*

I'd just finished brushing my teeth when I heard a knock on my door. I peered through the window and got the surprise of my life! There were two men standing there: Papa and Gloria's boyfriend, Ronnie.

I was assaulted by conflicting feelings. First, my heart leaped into my mouth and I know I got a stupid smile on my face. I could tell, because Papa burst out laughing and motioned for me to open my door. But immediately another thought popped into my head. Ronnie! Where was Gloria? Was she still on her date? Was she *next door* with her date? What was I going to do? What could I tell him? *Oh my God!*

CHAPTER 6

Bayside Motel

Late Monday Night

I opened my door and let Ronnie and Papa in out of the chilly night. I've never been real good at masking my thoughts and feelings, so Papa was onto me even before I'd closed the door. I was silently thanking my stars that I'd only met Ronnie a couple of times. If he'd known me any better, he'd have picked up that I was nervous about something. Papa was standing slightly behind Ronnie and gave me a look that asked, "What's up?" and then proceeded to act normal.

"Hey!" I said, much too brightly. "Come in! What are you guys doing here?" *And what an unlikely pair you make*, I thought.

It's not that Ronnie wasn't attractive; he was, especially to Gloria. He's around six feet tall and stocky. Not flabby at all: all muscle! He'd been a bouncer, among other things, at a club that his mentor owned in downtown Atlanta. The bad news is that his mentor/ best friend/surrogate father had just been killed in a shoot-out a few days ago. So as far as I knew, Ronnie's plans, present and future, were still up in the air.

Papa, on the other hand, looked absolutely irresistible in my book. He's about four inches taller than I, has nice muscles and a trim waist. I know he works out, but doesn't come across as a body-builder, like Ronnie. And one of his most endearing qualities is that he has no idea of his effect on the ladies!

"Wait a minute," I said and stopped in my tracks. "You guys have never met!"

Papa laughed again, showing those gorgeous teeth. "There was this poor fellow that came into the bar this evening, moping around and all. So I started to talk with him. He told me that his new 'love' had come out here to Conroy. I told him that my girl had gone to Conroy, too. I started asking questions, put two and two together…and realized who he was! We decided Demetri could handle the rest of the night. Mondays are often slow and…Ron and I were lonesome."

He looked at me with those dark, smoldering eyes and my knees almost went out from under me. I chuckled and motioned for them to take the chairs. I was already in my flannel jammies, but what the heck. Papa had seen me in worse than this (and in *less* than this!), so I just sat cross-legged on the bed.

Ronnie didn't seem to notice me at all. His eyes were searching the room as though he was searching for something.

Oh, my gosh, I thought, tearing my mind from my own desires. *Gloria!*

"We had some business to talk over tonight, the detectives and I," I started, trying to think of something to say. "Um…I think Glory may have turned in early. Let me call her room and see if she's still awake."

"Just tell me which room's she's in, and I'll go surprise her," Ronnie suggested.

Ye, Gods! Oh, Holy Moly! I thought, panicking. Papa must have seen the fear in my eyes, because he came to my rescue.

"Oh, man, I'd hate to scare her, Ronnie," he said. "Let Kate call, it'll just take a second."

With that, I rolled to the other side of the bed, grabbing the phone as I went. I'd taken Tae Kwan Do (a long time ago, during police training) and I was trying to be graceful about this maneuver, but the mattress was squishier than I'm used to and the bed wasn't as wide. At any rate, I rolled right off the bed! I hit the floor and popped up, quickly, onto my knees. Papa stifled a guffaw, I turned beet-red and Ronnie just looked a bit confused. I'm sure he was beginning to wonder if I'm completely nuts!

I didn't say a word. I kept my eyes on the phone and punched in the extension to Gloria's room. "Hey, Glory, guess who's here in *my* room!? Right," I continued before she could say a thing. "Papa… and Ronnie!!"

She squeaked. How such a big girl could make such a tiny sound, I have no idea. I looked up at the guys and smiled sweetly.

"Are you shittin' me, girl?" came her voice through the receiver.

I just kept smiling at Ronnie and Papa and said, "I knew you'd be surprised…and pleased! As soon as you shake yourself awake, come on over, okay?" I hung us as she was saying something. I was too scared to listen to her any longer.

"She'll be over in a couple minutes. I think I may have woken her up," I lied. "Meanwhile, I wish I could offer you something to drink…" I continued, wanting to change to a new topic.

"I've got just the thing we need in the car," Papa said and got to his feet. In just a couple minutes, he returned, bringing an armload of bottles. "I mean, I *do* own the bar…and I wasn't sure what you'd be in the mood for…" He stopped talking, but gave me a *very* odd look as he made his way to the sink. He proceeded to set up his collection of booze bottles. "Bourbon for you, Kate?"

I mumbled my assent. I was a bit disconcerted about the look he'd given me, but before I had a chance to pick myself off the floor and ask him, there was another knock at the door.

Ronnie jumped up to look. It was Gloria and Ronnie's face lit up like a beam of light. He tossed open the door, picked her up and swung her around in a circle. (Not an easy thing to do!) "Well, don't you just look good enough to eat," he said and planted a kiss right on her lips.

She just burst into laughter.

Ronnie put her down and stood back to look her over. "Look at this get-up, Papa. Looks like she's right out of the Wild West! Is she a cute thing or not?"

Ah-hhh, I thought, *new love*. Gloria was still in her "cowgirl" outfit that she'd purchased earlier that day. I had an unwanted vision of them playing some kinky game later tonight.

Papa declined to answer Ronnie's question, choosing instead to pass out drinks to all. Ronnie took the armchair and Glory sat on his lap, all smiles. Papa sat in the desk chair. I ended up on the bed again and sat carefully with my drink, trying to avoid a repeat performance of rolling off.

We all chatted for a while. My eyelids were drooping, but I had no trouble paying attention to Ronnie's informative conversation. He told us that Lou Mancini's lawyers had been in touch with him and explained that he had inherited Lou's club, Prosciutto's, after Lou's death. The South American drug lord who'd shot Lou was behind bars, awaiting extradition to his homeland.

We'd learned, just before Lou was shot, that it had been Lou and the South American, Nick Escoba, who'd caused my own parents' deaths thirteen years ago. Escoba, who had been deported twice already, had been driving the car but escaped on foot. His plan was to blame Lou Mancini if anyone ever tracked him down. Highly unlikely, considering Lou was practically the only person who'd known Escoba was in the U.S. to begin with. But the crash had been ruled an accident and the case closed.

I'd never bought the decision that it was reckless driving on my father's part and had spent years trying to find out what had really happened. A part of me was relieved and pleased to have *that* case solved, but the larger part of me was still the young girl who continued to grieve for her mom and dad.

After drinks were finished, Ronnie and Gloria stood up to leave. Ronnie took their glasses back to my sink and Glory pushed the big chair back into the corner. While Ronnie still had his back to her, she mouthed to Papa, "I can explain!" and then smiled as Ron turned her way again. "See y'all tomorrow," she called out gaily and shut the door as they left.

I was so glad to get Papa alone…for several reasons! But my curiosity took control. "What was *that* all about?" I demanded.

"I was just going to ask you the same thing," he answered and I noticed he didn't look too pleased. "Good thing Ron didn't go out with me to the car. I found Gloria hustling some guy into his pick-up truck. Her teeth almost fell out of her head when she saw me."

I moaned. "I didn't know she had anyone in there. It was just a wild guess."

He raised one eyebrow.

"She *did* say she was going to see the guy who sold her the western gear tonight, but that's all I knew."

"So that's why you insisted on calling her, huh? To give her time, just in case? I don't like it at all," he added when I nodded.

We sat back down with another drink, Papa in the big chair, me propped on pillows on the bed, and discussed the fact that she'd said she could explain…and the fact that she seemed truly thrilled to see Ronnie.

Papa looked so sexy. He was slouched in the comfy chair, his right leg stretched out in front of him and his left dangling over the arm of the overstuffed chair. *Nice*, I thought and wished that I could be that comfortable in my own skin. But he wasn't thinking along the same lines as I.

He was not feeling comfortable. "She should be satisfied with just one guy. What's wrong with her?"

"Maybe we're jumping to conclusions," I said quietly, hoping the walls were thick enough that our neighbors couldn't hear what we were saying. "Perhaps it's nothing to get upset about."

Agitated, Papa got up and paced the floor. Finally, he shrugged and concluded that he wouldn't damn her for being unfaithful…yet. "We'll have to get the facts tomorrow. But, dammit, Ron considers her his girl! You should've seen him at the bar tonight. He deserves better treatment than this!"

I wondered if Papa considered me *his* girl. I hoped so, even though I'm not Greek. We'd dated on and off since high school but had never actually *discussed* our relationship.

"Come and snuggle with me," I said, patting the bed.

He smiled at me, a long, lazy smile and kicked off his shoes.

Of course, then my thoughts jumped to *his* mother's plan of hooking him up with a girl from their old neighborhood. My stomach felt very queasy all of a sudden. I wanted to ask him about it, but was too afraid. Afraid that I didn't really mean that much to him. Afraid that he'd tell me about the girl his mother had in mind. Afraid that after mentioning his views on people being faithful, he'd decide it would be wrong to stay with me tonight.

I'd felt abandoned when my parents died, even though rationally I knew it wasn't their fault. I was afraid to pressure Papa…I didn't think I could handle being abandoned by him, too.

We lay quietly in the dark for a while, our arms around each other. I was on the verge of tears for a long time. He asked me what I was thinking about…and I lied.

"Just about this case we're on."

He nodded and held me a little closer. I guess he can read my thoughts and feelings—even in the dark. He could tell I was upset and he knew it wasn't just this case.

"It's okay if you don't want to tell me. Get some sleep," he murmured, kissing my hair. "At least the walls aren't too thin. I can't hear a sound coming from Gloria's room. But then again, perhaps we could pick up a few pointers."

I giggled and snuggled closer.

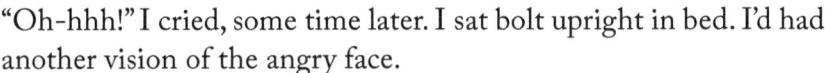

"Oh-hhh!" I cried, some time later. I sat bolt upright in bed. I'd had another vision of the angry face.

"What?" Papa said, jerking awake. "What's wrong? You okay?"

I nodded and breathed in slowly, trying to steady my breath. "Sorry, I didn't mean to wake you up. It's fine…I'm fine."

"A bad dream," he asked, "or one of your visions?"

"Vision," I began, and lay back down in his arms. I told him about the first one—seeing the angry face—and explained that this one was the same, only longer in duration and more detailed. I could also see more of the person's face and could tell that my initial impression of it being female was correct. "And she's got blue eyes," I added.

I felt comfortable telling Papa all this. We'd known each other for almost ten years and he was a good listener. He had never acted skeptical or shocked when I told him about my visions. His only comment had been that if people would open themselves up to receiving these "vibes", more would probably share my talent.

Sometimes he and I communicated on another level. *Why, then, do I have such a hard time actually talking with him?* My conclusion was that I was too afraid to hear his answers. *You're such a chicken,* I admonished myself.

Once again, instead of revealing my *true* thoughts, I told him a bit about the case. It was safer territory. He stroked my back while I talked. A while later, by the time I'd explained my strategy for Tuesday morning—seeing the medical examiner and then going out to Turley's Stables—I realized that he'd turned me onto my back and his hands were exploring my stomach and abdomen. *Talk about strategy!* I thought, smiling. I gave myself over to just feeling.

Some time later, in the wee hours of the morning, we finally fell into a comfortable, deep sleep.

CHAPTER 7

The M.E.'s Office

Tuesday Morning

I awoke consumed by questions. I really needed to speak with the medical examiner. I eased out of bed, being careful not to disturb Papa. He looked so relaxed lying there. His hair was tousled and he looked peaceful.

I tip-toed over to the desk, grabbed my cell and snuck into the bathroom, shutting the door behind me. First, I left a message on the M.E.'s office answering machine reminding him that I would stop by later in the morning and that I hoped to catch him. Then I made a "wake up" call to Carlos in the next room.

"This is your friendly desk-operator at the lovely Bayside Motel," I joked. "It's time to get up and enjoy the day!" I added cheerfully.

"Ugh-h-h," came through the receiver…and then some other unintelligible comments which most likely contained a few four-letter words!

I could also swear I heard a muffled giggle—definitely *not* Carlos! Amy's room was on the other side of Carlos's…and there was a door connecting the two rooms.

Hmm.

Then Carlos announced, "I know it's you, Jeffers, and you're gonna pay for this. You're going to be surprised one of these days when I decide it's payback time! What's up?" he asked and sounded anxious to talk *only* about the case.

"Can't sleep. Meet me for coffee in the lobby?"

Carlos grunted his assent and told me he needed ten minutes. I was already on my second complimentary cup when he staggered in.

"Rough night?" I asked with a huge grin on my face.

"Never you mind. I'm pleading the fifth…"

Amy straggled behind, pulling on a sweat shirt and trying to mash down her hair. What a sight! "Coffee me," she said. "And wipe that smile off your face…What time is it anyway? It's not even light yet!!"

We took our coffee over to a small group of chairs in one corner of the lobby, as far away from the desk as possible. We watched the sun rise as they moaned into their coffee cups and I briefed them of my concerns. "I plan to see Dr. Graves later this morning," I concluded, "and see what he can tell me about his findings."

We decided to go to the diner next door for some breakfast before heading out. As we left the lobby, Amy noticed a familiar car next to mine.

"Wait just a minute!" she cried, grabbing me by the arm. "You're teasing *us*? Whose car is that, I'd like to know?"

She'd spotted Papa's car. I felt myself blush. Carlos chuckled and muttered something about 'payback time' under his breath.

I used my cell to tell Papa where we were going. He said he'd catch up with us before heading back to the city.

We enjoyed a leisurely breakfast. After all, we needed to give people time to *get up* before we went pounding on their doors, asking questions!

Amy and Carlos had scheduled a meeting at the field house with the assistant football coach and the team members. We knew that Gloria and Ronnie would be "sleeping in". I know better than to call her before eleven—even as a joke! But Papa said he'd have to wake Ron up before too long.

I returned to my motel room and turned my attention to my ablutions, while Papa tapped quietly on Gloria's door. The showerhead was one of those massaging ones and the water was deliciously warm. I considered spending the entire day in there and was very tempted to invite Papa to join me, but then remembered why I had awakened so early.

I made myself get out and toweled dry. Papa had returned and wiggled his eyebrows at me as I emerged, wrapped in said towel (which was a bit skimpy, I admit). I, again, was tempted, but laughed and said, "Forget it! I've got work to do!"

Ronnie knocked and said he was ready to head back, so Papa kissed my wet hair and said he'd be in touch. He also whispered, "Find out what Gloria was up to last night!"

"Drive carefully," I called as he shut the door…and had a mental image of my parents' accident again. I shuddered and reached for the hair dryer.

Time to get to work! I headed over to the morgue, which is located right next to the Conroy Memorial Hospital. I didn't know whether its location was really good…or really bad! It was at the very least, ironic! Of course, the M.E.'s *name* was enough to bother anyone. Dr. Graves…I secretly wondered if he'd chosen his occupation because of it. I *have* heard of a chiropractor whose name is McCracken!

When I entered through the door labeled "MORGUE", a man sitting at the small desk jerked his head up with a snap. I apologized for startling him and introduced myself. "That's okay," he replied. "It's just that we don't get many visitors coming through that door. Most people read the sign and run the other way.

"I just heard from the doc. He got your message—had it forwarded to his home phone. Anyway, he said for you to stick around and he'll be here by 8:30.

"I'd show you around, but I don't like to go back in the autopsy suite myself! And besides, when the doc's working on a case, he locks everything up tighter than a drum. Even *I* have to wait till he's here to unlock the back."

"Oh, that's fine," I said. "I don't mind waiting.

"Did you know the deceased?" I queried.

"Oh, yeah. Everyone knew Coach. My boy who graduated last year was nose guard on the team. Loved the guy. Everybody did.

"I just can't understand how Doc Graves came up with suspicions of murder," he continued, shaking his head in disbelief. "Must be a mistake…has to be."

He continued to mumble, mostly to himself. I caught snippets such as "wouldn't happen" and "can't be".

I continued to stand since there weren't any chairs. The space was so cramped I couldn't have levered myself onto the floor without opening the outside door and crawling back inside on my hands and knees.

Fortunately, Dr. Graves arrived within minutes. I was glad to be out of that confining space. I've never thought of myself as claustrophobic, but I was finding it hard to get my breath.

He nodded to Stan Thomas (at least that's what the nameplate on the desk said), pulled a jangley bunch of keys from his pocket and unlocked the heavy steel door. We passed through and it creaked shut behind us as we moved down a narrow hallway. Gave me the shivers.

Dr. Graves was about sixty, I figured, with a thinning, but wiry crine of white hair. He was well over six feet tall and quite thin. At the same time, however, his kindly face and his carriage led me to believe he was a strong person, both mentally and physically.

"I apologize for keeping you waiting," he said as he unlocked another door. We went into another small room—obviously his office. "Things are tight around here—in more ways than one—at least I have a bit more space in here than Stan Thomas does at his little table! But that's the way it is in the real world. The politicians know that dead people don't vote, so our needs just aren't top priority."

He motioned to a folding chair. I carefully lifted up a pile of manila folders, slid them underneath and sat down. He moved around the desk and sat in a swivel chair.

Good thing he's skinny, I thought. *Any bigger and he would never be able to navigate in here.*

"Hayslip and I talked. I'll tell you everything I know so far. The first thing I noticed when examining the body was the bruising. It was subcutaneous—deep under the skin. I checked his gums. They displayed some signs of bleeding. Then when I examined the internal organs, there were signs of gastrointestinal bleeding. The liver was within normal parameters, but showed a limited amount of the enzyme epoxide reductase. I called his general practitioner to ask her if she'd prescribed an anti-coagulant to combat any sign of thrombosis."

I must have looked confused, because he stopped and then said, "Let me back up just a little. In lay terms the best way to explain this is to say that he was bleeding internally. His blood wasn't clotting as it should. This usually indicates a deficiency of Vitamin K. Normally anyone who is on a regular diet gets enough in their daily intake. And everyone around here knows how the coach harped about eating right. The boys on his teams joked about it. And he rarely drank, so his liver should have been in excellent shape. He and Sherry even gave up coffee a few years back. Instead the liver indicated a Vitamin K deficiency…very unusual.

"If, however, a person has a history of blood clots, they can be given injections of heparin or may be put on some type of medication (like Coumadin or Marevan) to thin the blood. But these medications are very tricky and it's difficult to establish the correct dosage. It's easy to over- or under-medicate the patient. So the doctor needs to constantly monitor the patient to be certain he or she is prescribing the correct amount.

"The testing is done with blood tests—twice a week, at least at the beginning of treatment. There is *no way* a patient could be on anti-coagulants such as these without his doctor knowing.

"Dr. Wright returned my call and left a message saying that she hadn't prescribed any anti-coagulants for him. She'll be in her office later today, so I'll give her a call and see what else she knows. Meanwhile, this is looking very suspicious."

"So what do you think happened? I don't want to seem dull, but how could something like this get into his system? Are you saying someone *gave* him something?"

"Perhaps. My first thought was of arsenic. Maybe someone got hold of some and put it in his food. But then I pretty much discounted that. You see, Coach Johnson was *very* particular. He'd have been able to tell something was off. Arsenic has a bitter taste to it. I doubt that he would have been able to eat enough to harm him.

"So I did more testing of his blood and noticed a very high INR level. (That stands for the International Normalized Ratio.) So I started thinking...What else could someone have slipped him?

"To give you a shortened version, I considered warfarin. It is an anti-coagulant similar to arsenic. It is used in some rat poisons. The big difference, however, is that warfarin is completely odorless and tasteless. So someone could have crushed it up and added it to Johnson's food and he wouldn't have been able to tell.

"And again, levels are watched very carefully if someone is prescribed it. Levels range between 2.0 and 3.0 and even though he died three days ago, Johnson's level is *still* higher than that."

"So that means that the level...the INR...must've been off the charts when he died?"

"Exactly! I could talk for days about the half-life of drugs, but just suffice it to say that it takes at least a few days for most meds to get out of the body, so even if he *was* supposed to be taking it, the INR would *never* be above 3.0 at this stage."

I sat in Dr. Graves's office and shivered. *Rat poison. My lord... anyone could get hold of it.*

CHAPTER 8

Amy and Carlos

Tuesday Morning

Tom Papadopoulos and Ron Walker drove home to Atlanta, Gloria was sleeping and Kate had already left for the medical examiner's office. Amy and Carlos found themselves all alone.

The two detectives went back to Carlos's room. Carlos reflected on his relationship with his partner while Amy showered. Theirs had been a slow-moving relationship, unlike Gloria and Ron Walker's. Ron and Gloria had met less than two weeks earlier—and began on very rocky terms! They'd met in the parking garage of Kate Jeffers' building when Ronnie, posing as 'Max the Painter', had tried to talk his way into Kate's condo to steal some files for his boss. He'd succeeded, of course, since Gloria had taken one look at Ron's muscles and had a complete meltdown—emotionally as well as physically! Ronnie had redeemed himself later by coming clean, switching sides to become a good guy, and even assisting in solving the kidnapping case on which Carlos and Amy had just finished working. Carlos always prided himself on trying to find the good side of others, but he wasn't quite sure about Ron. He decided to wait to pass judgment.

He and Amy had started out on the Atlanta Metro Police Force at about the same time, several years ago. They'd met a few times at meetings, but didn't get to work together until two years later. Carlos had arranged that.

Both he and Amy'd worked hard to become detectives and made a very good team. They'd spent hours together, in their vehicle, working on cases and at their office, completing paperwork. Over the past year, they'd begun to see each other socially. Carlos was very cautious about mixing work and play, he knew that Amy was hesitant as well. Just recently, however, things between them had heated up.

One late afternoon they'd been sitting in their vehicle in a bustling shopping section in Virginia Highlands, waiting to interview a shopkeeper about a recent rash of robberies. They were watching people closing up their establishments and heading home for the day. A couple walked out of their gift shop, locked the door and strolled down the street, hand in hand. Two middle-aged men walked towards them, chatting amiably and saying something about a party they were planning to attend the following weekend. Another lady was talking on her cell phone. He'd eavesdropped. She was speaking to her husband, asking him to stop at the grocery while she picked up his dry cleaning. Then they planned to rendezvous at their house. She ended the conversation by saying, "Love you, honey. See you in a few."

Carlos turned to Amy and asked, "Did you hear that?"

"Yeah," she replied wistfully.

"Do you suppose either of us will ever have a relationship like that?" he asked.

She sat silently, looking at him for a few moments before answering, "Maybe." And then she lowered her eyes and fiddled with her laptop computer.

After a few minutes of uncomfortable silence, Carlos cleared his throat. For some reason, his mouth had become very dry. He asked, "Do you think you and I should become more than just partners and friends?"

Carlos had never felt more nervous in his entire life! His palms began to sweat just remembering that afternoon! He'd interviewed murderers and been called to ghastly crime scenes that seemed easy compared to this. He valued his partnership with Amy more than anything else he could think of. If she said "yes", they would have some difficulties managing work and love, but he felt sure they would be fine. If, however, her answer was "no", it would probably ruin their entire relationship. He doubted that they could remain partners with the "love thing" hanging over them. He prayed that wouldn't happen—he didn't want to lose her—on any level. Depending on her answer, their relationship would be changed forever—for the better or worse. He realized that he'd been holding his breath. Maybe that's why he felt a little dizzy. He exhaled and forced himself to breathe evenly, but the dizziness didn't go away. He stole a sideways glance at his partner. She was looking straight at him. Slowly, he turned his head a little to the side, so he could see her face, but he couldn't bring himself to look directly at her.

"I wondered if you'd ever get up the nerve to ask," she finally answered and smiled. "I figured I'd have to make the first move... and the second...and the third..." She had actually chuckled at him!

What a relief!! He exhaled and realized he'd been holding his breath again. He felt the weight lift from his shoulders. He turned to look at her beautiful face as the tunnel vision he'd been experiencing seemed to vanish. "Really?!" he croaked. He felt like a thirteen year old boy—his voice had cracked! He coughed, felt himself blush and tried again. "Really, you really mean it?"

Amy closed her laptop, leaned over and brushed his cheek with a feathery touch of her fingertip. "I think it's a fabulous idea!" He turned to face her and she kissed him right on the lips, her tongue lightly skimming across them.

Carlos felt himself flushing again and getting warm in various regions of his body. Amy had taken control, thank goodness. She pulled back, smiled and said, "Now, let's go interview this shopkeeper fellow and then we can go to Lindy's to celebrate. How's that for a plan?"

He answered that he'd need a couple minutes to pull himself together before emerging from the vehicle. She laughed and exited the car, straightening her skirt.

Carlos heard the water turn off and went to the bathroom door. He knocked and asked Amy if she needed any assistance drying off.

"I think I can manage it all by myself, Ducky. But you'd better get your tail in here and take *your* shower. We're going to have to hurry to get to the high school by 9:30. We don't want to keep the assistant coach waiting."

"Darn it, I had visions of doing all kinds of wonderful things to your body."

"Save it till later." She breezed past him as she exited the bathroom and winked.

On their way to the high school, they reviewed the questions they planned to ask Johnson's assistant. They were to meet with him from 9:30 until about 10:15. Then the members of the football team (at least those who were able to get there) were going to meet with them in the field house. They were going to try to be finished there by noon. They hoped to be able to meet up with Kate and go with her to Turley's Stables.

The assistant football coach, Andy Menendez, was in the coach's office, going through papers when the detectives arrived. He looked overwhelmed, but cordially invited them in, shook their hands and offered them seats.

"I was just going over the schedules for the rest of the season," he said, sitting back down. "Sam was very organized, but didn't delegate much, so it's going to take me a while to catch up."

Amy thanked him for taking time to talk with them and promised not to take up his whole day. Carlos was always impressed by the way she put others at ease. She was able to get people to trust her quickly, thus smoothing the path for more pointed questions. That was just *one* of the reasons he was so fond of her.

The detectives proceeded to ask questions, first about the football program, then other ones—about Coach Johnson's personal life. According to Menendez, Sam Johnson truly liked the students, especially those on his teams. He was tough on them and expected a lot, but most of the kids rose to meet his expectations. Menendez stated only one concern, saying that he, personally, believed that Johnson sometimes went too far. That is, he went a little overboard.

When Carlos pressed for more details, Menendez said, "I really don't mean to criticize—I mean, we've been so successful over the years and I'm sure that Sam's methods are the reason—but I've always believed that you can respect the students and treat them like young adults rather than demean them, 'break' them and then rebuild them the way you like. I guess that was the biggest difference in our approaches." But he quickly went on to add, "Sam and I worked well together: you know, "good guy, bad guy" stuff. He wore the kids down and made them feel about this big (he indicated by holding up his thumb and index finger, about an inch apart) and then I built them up with encouragement."

He wouldn't give any specific details and clammed up on the subject. Carlos decided to delve into this "breaking down" routine some with the team members and tried to think of a way to get Menendez out of the room when he was talking with the team.

Amy and Carlos then moved on to questions regarding Sam Johnson's personal life. Menendez said that Sam and Sherry were very much in love, adored their boys and were very excited about the approaching birth of their third child. They were hoping for a girl this time, but would be very happy with another boy. Sherry was a local girl, very sweet and supportive considering the long hours that Sam was away from home at practices and games. She'd already graduated by the time Johnson had come on as the assistant coach, nineteen years earlier. She'd gone to college in Athens and had just returned to Conroy around that time. Sherry had taught school and was Cheerleading Advisor until Sam and she'd decided to have the kids. Menendez's statements supported Chief Hayslip's: no way would the coach have been romantically involved with another co-worker, staff member or student.

Hearing voices in the outer room, Amy suggested that perhaps Carlos wanted to speak to the boys without her—"Just guy stuff," she'd said wrinkling her nose—and that she'd maybe spend the time with Sherry Johnson if she could get hold of her. She skillfully guided Menendez out of the field house, asking him if he had Sherry's number and saying that her cell phone wouldn't get very good reception inside the building. Again, Carlos was awed by Amy's understanding of his desire to talk to the boys alone and her smooth way of getting people to do just what she wanted.

Most, but not all the team had assembled quietly on the benches in the field house, and Carlos introduced himself. The boys shared their concerns. Several of them had overheard that the coach had died "suspiciously" and they wanted to know what was going on. Carlos told them that their coach's death was under investigation, but tests were still being conducted and he really couldn't say anything until the results were in. He assured them that everything possible was being done to determine what had actually happened, that they would find an explanation and let the team know. He then proceeded to ask the boys about the football program, how often they practiced, the length of the practices, their relationships with coaches Johnson and Menendez, and their relationships with other team members.

The gist of the responses was that although Johnson was "into" his own family, football was pretty much everything to him. He didn't like it when outside activities interfered with practices. (Things like classes, work or farm responsibilities.) Coach Menendez was more realistic about the family and work obligations of the boys. But Johnson was "great"…and so on. The team members were careful to say absolutely nothing negative about the deceased coach…almost *too* careful, Carlos thought. He decided to try a different tack and hoped he could pull it off. He himself had never played football.

He talked to the boys about his own high school experience, however, and cited times when the upperclassmen were allowed, even encouraged to give the younger boys "the business". He described times when the freshmen were made to run extra laps by the older boys, mainly the seniors, and had to be their "slaves", getting the seniors extra food at lunchtime, and generally catering to them.

Carlos watched the faces before him carefully while he reminisced, and noted some looks of disgust (on the younger-looking boys) and sly smiles and some smirks on the faces of some of the others. *Oh, yeah,* he thought. He tried to get the boys to open up a bit about this, but the general impression he got was, "What goes on at practice, stays at practice." No one was going to open up, at least not in front of the others. He made mental notes of the boys he wanted to interview individually.

CHAPTER 9

Amy and Sherry

Tuesday Morning

Amy snapped her cell phone shut. She felt very lucky to have been able to schedule an immediate meeting with Sherry Johnson. Sherry's parents, the Smiths, had just taken the two little ones, Sean and Cory, to the nearby park for some fresh air and then with them to the store, "for things to go along with all the casseroles that friends and neighbors had sent". Amy took her leave of Coach Menendez, thanking him again for his time, and watched as he wandered toward the main school building, still looking a bit overwhelmed and distraught.

She hopped into the cruiser and drove quickly to the Johnsons' home. She wanted to have plenty of time to talk to Sherry—alone.

Sherry Johnson was watching through the front door as Amy pulled into the driveway. Amy hurried up the steps, noting that Sherry looked as though she'd been through hell. *But then, she* has! Amy thought.

Sherry was very polite, but appeared dazed and exhausted. Her face looked gaunt and had dark circles under bloodshot eyes. Amy's first concern was about the pregnancy. She was concerned that the stress of the situation could cause Sherry to lose the baby.

Amy had Sherry sit, a pillow supporting her lower back and her feet on a footstool. She proceeded to ask Sherry if it would be all right if she fixed them both something to drink and a snack. Sherry sat, unseeing, and nodded. "Wait," she called out as Amy went into the kitchen. "We don't have any coffee. We gave it up a couple years ago. But there's some tea in the canister on the counter… But at least there's some real food! All Sam allowed us to eat was healthy stuff."

When that task was finished, Amy placed a few tea sandwiches and a cup of tea on the end table next to Sherry and perched herself on the edge of a nearby chair. She leaned forward, taking one of Sherry's hands in hers. Sherry responded to her touch, and frowned at her as if she'd just realized Amy was there. Amy murmured condolences and then steered the conversation in a lighter vein.

Amy encouraged Sherry to talk more about the boys and the new baby. Sean, it turned out, was six and in first grade at the neighborhood primary school. Cory had turned three a couple months earlier and was anxious to "go back to school to see his friends". (He attended a morning play-group two days a week, but called it school so he could be big, like Sean.) Sean was able to understand that "something" had happened to his daddy, but Cory was just anxious to return to his normal routine. Sherry expressed concern that the boys wouldn't remember their father as they grew older, but appeared reassured when Amy pointed out that she could talk about the wonderful times they had together as a family and perhaps put together a photo album, especially of fun times that would help to jog the boys' memories. "Oh, yes," agreed Sherry, smiling wistfully. "We've video-taped so many of our times together. I'll put them all on a disc so they won't get damaged and then the boys can watch them whenever they want…Thanks. What a good idea! Maybe I'll get the boys to dictate some stories to go along with the photos."

Then Amy asked if the boys were excited about the new baby. Sherry ate a couple of little sandwiches, sipped her tea and became more animated. "Yes, the boys are SO excited! Now that the baby is moving a bit, they love to come up and rub my swelling abdomen, and they even "talk" to it.

"I wish I knew whether it is a boy or girl...I hate to call it "It", you know? But it's turned backwards in every single ultrasound! I think he or she wants us to be surprised!" She actually smiled. "I'm about five months along now...the baby's due in February. We planned it that way. I hate being pregnant in the summertime. It's so hot here and I love to swim. I can't imagine how awful it would be to be going through the eighth and ninth months in... like August!" She shuddered.

Amy hadn't really thought about that. Now that her relationship with Carlos was "progressing", albeit slowly, she began to consider the fact that maybe they would end up getting married and having children, themselves. *Wow,* she thought. She pulled herself back to the present, promising herself that she would explore these thoughts later.

They talked about Sherry's life as a coach's wife. "I met Sam the first year I came back from college. He'd just signed on as assistant coach and I was a first-year teacher...economics. The first year is so hard! Coming straight out of school...I really didn't know what I was doing and spent all my time planning and grading papers! I felt like I was only a half-step ahead of the kids all year! Sam and I saw each other at faculty meetings, but didn't really get to know each other until our second year. Things settled down for me. I felt like I knew what I was doing in the classroom, so I signed on as the Cheerleading Advisor. We ended up spending a lot more time together...at practices and at the games. One thing led to another and by Christmastime, we were dating. We were very careful in front of the students, but of course, they knew." Her eyes sparkled a little at the thought and Amy was able to see a hint of the normally vivacious girl that Sam Johnson had fallen for.

Sherry was like a fountain that had just been turned on. The words tumbled out of her mouth. "I taught and was the Cheer Advisor for several years and loved every minute! But then we decided to go ahead and start a family. Sam had become the head football coach in his fifth year, and we decided we could probably make it on his salary alone. If things got tough financially, I could always tutor, substitute teach or even go back to the classroom full-time if necessary. Sam doesn't have any family around here, but my parents live close. They volunteered to baby-sit if we needed them. I just think they were so anxious to have grand-babies that they would have done or said anything to encourage us!"

She continued, "But we managed fine—with my econ background I know a lot about finances and running of businesses and so on, so I figured I could certainly run our home and create a budget that we could live with. And I managed to save some money and have several investments that are doing quite well."

Amy sighed in relief. Sherry would most likely be okay. She was still in shock, but seemed to have a good head on her shoulders and appeared to be a pretty down-to-earth person.

As if reading Amy's mind, Sherry said, "Sam was really good about planning for our future. He made sure he had a big life insurance policy before the boys were born, so we'll be taken care of quite well. And as the kids get older, I can go back to work…I keep up on all the latest things in the econ world. So I can take whatever coursework I need online and I'll be fine." She absently rubbed the swell of her stomach. "But of course, I'd love to stay home with this one," she added, glancing down, "if possible."

Amy then turned the conversation back to her husband's affairs. Sherry said that she and her mother had begun going through some of Sam's things. Sherry normally took care of the bills, but they'd gone through Sam's desk in their home office, just in case he'd accidentally stuck something in there. He hadn't. The only thing of interest was a bunch of keys. Sherry knew what most of them were for: buildings at school, stuff in the locker room, his house and car keys; but there was one that she didn't recognize. She'd left them on top of the desk in order to ask Andy Menendez about them, so she directed Amy to the other room. When Amy returned, Sherry showed her the key and said, "I have no idea what it's to," and shrugged. "Probably something at school, but I don't know."

Amy told Sherry that she'd left Carlos at the school, talking with the football team and that she was headed back there in a few minutes to pick him up. Sherry asked her to take the keys with her and give the rest of them to Andy Menendez in case he needed them. Amy was hoping she'd ask! "I'd go and see Andy myself, but I'm just so tired," Sherry said.

"I don't want to keep you any longer," said Amy, taking the car and house key off the ring and handing them back to Sherry. "And you really need to rest before your kids get back. I'll be glad to give these to Andy. Perhaps he'll know what this little one is for." Amy refreshed Sherry's tea and left the plate of sandwiches within her reach. "No, don't get up. I'll let myself out. It's been so good to talk with you. I'm certain we'll talk again. And if you think of anything else, please give me a call. My cell number is on my card," Amy added, placing one on the table next to the front door. "Take care of yourself and your little surprise!" Amy nodded to Sherry's tummy. Both women smiled and Amy went on her way.

When Amy arrived back at the field house, the team members had left, but Andy Menendez hadn't yet returned. Carlos and Amy looked around to see what the key might fit, but didn't see anything. So they left a note about the keys for the coach, telling him they'd be in touch soon, before hurrying back to the motel. They didn't want to miss Kate.

CHAPTER 10

Turley's Stables

Tuesday Afternoon

I joined Amy and Carlos in the cruiser, and the three of us headed out of town in the direction of Turley's. First, we swung through a fast-food restaurant for sandwiches and drinks. On the way, I commented, "I feel like a prisoner sitting here in the back seat! Like you guys are carting me off to the jail. It's a *very* uncomfortable feeling!"

Carlos's retort was, "I'd let you sit up here with us, but you'd have to sit on my lap and Amy might get jealous!"

We all chuckled. "Speaking of which, y'all," I continued, "I don't get the impression that there's any jealousy thing going on here with the Johnsons. Do you?"

We discussed the morning's interviews and concluded that the Johnsons' personal lives seemed to be on the up and up and that there was little chance of either being involved with anyone else.

Amy said, "And I can't see Sherry being a suspect if it turns out that Johnson *was* poisoned. She just doesn't have it in her. I'd have picked up on it if that were the case."

"Yup," Carlos interjected. "It sure doesn't sound like it. I still want to talk to some of the boys privately, though. And it would be good to find out what that key belongs to. Maybe Menendez will know."

Before long we pulled into the stable yard. The day was sunnier than we'd expected. We all shed our jackets, stepped out of the cruiser and stretched in the warmth.

"Man, this feels great," Amy stated. Carlos and I agreed as we headed to what obviously was the office.

Mrs. Turley was there. After some minutes of polite small-talk, she insisted we call her "Mrs. T." and we got down to the business at hand. Carlos explained the reason for our visit, and we noticed concern written all over Mrs. Turley's face. She sank thoughtfully into her chair and wiped a hand over her face when Carlos mentioned the bruising on Johnson's body and the possible connection to his riding incident the previous Friday.

After a few moments, she looked up at us. She was ashen. "You think it happened here?" she asked, her voice shaking. "I was close by. I'd given him Winnie—the same horse he always rides. Winnie's a bit skittish at times—'til you let him know who's boss—but Sam knew how to handle 'im…firm, but not rough."

I said, "Some of the boys who were here at the time said that Johnson slipped off the horse…"

"Oh! Well…yeah, I *do* remember that, now you mention it. Sam said something about showing them how to barrel-race and took off on Winnie. I won't let them keep the girth too tight. If you're a good rider, you don't have to," she added for our benefit, in case we didn't know what she was talking about. "You can control your horse just fine. But when you're barrel-ridin', you'd better know what you're doin'. Winnie cut real sharp and the saddle started to slip sideways. Sam just slid right off into the dirt." She closed her eyes and frowned, trying to remember. "Yep, he jumped right back up. His boys were laughing and teasing him about it—you know, like kids do. I think he was embarrassed, more than anything."

"Try to picture it in your head, Mrs. T. When Sam Johnson fell off, what exactly happened?" I asked.

Mrs. Turley's eyes remained shut. "He was riding away from us." She used her hand, turning it back and forth, plotting his course. "Then he turned to go around the barrel—turned to his left. The saddle slipped to the right and Sam slid off." She opened her eyes. "Of course, at that point the horse was in between him and us, but I'm sure that Winnie didn't step on him or anything. I'd have noticed.

"Now, he landed in the dirt—on his side—his right side, that would be. In a cloud of dust. But by the time the dust had cleared, he was already up, telling the kids to…I think he said, 'Cut it out,'… but he was laughing, too." Mrs. T. looked up again. "And then he caught up with Winnie, cinched the girth a little tighter, and got back on." After a few more moments she added, "Nah…he wasn't hurt at all. They went on out for their ride and that was that."

"Did they have a guide with them?" I asked.

"Normally, I send someone out with all the groups," said Mrs. T. "But two of the boys work here as trail guides sometimes, so I figured they'd be fine. Anyway, Matt (he's the guide that was here Friday) was out with another group. They'd have had to wait a half an hour. No sense in that."

We thanked Mrs. T. and I told her that I hoped to be able to get in a little riding before returning to Atlanta. Mrs. Turley said we'd all be welcome and she'd even give Amy and Carlos a free lesson since they were helping out on the Johnson case.

Our little group headed back to the motel in Conroy, agreeing that Mrs. T.'s account of the incident mirrored the football players'.

CHAPTER 11

Kate and Carlos

Tuesday Afternoon

We returned to the Bayside Motel and dropped Amy off at her room. She was going to type up a report of the day's activities, check on Gloria and call Lieutenant Whitaker to update him on our progress—or lack thereof.

Carlos and I headed back to Conroy High School. Our plan was to try to locate Mr. Menendez to ask him about the keys. We checked in the field house first. There were a couple of athletes working out on the weight machines who volunteered that Coach Menendez had gone over to the main building for some coffee.

Leaving the boys and following the sidewalk from the field house to the main building, we cut off onto the path that led directly to the cafeteria. The door was locked, so we skirted around to the back where the deliveries were made and where the dumpsters were kept. Someone had propped the door open, so we stepped inside— into a maintenance room. We allowed our eyes to adjust and started to walk towards another door that led to the cafeteria kitchen, but

Carlos put a hand on my arm to stop me. He put a finger to his lips and then he cupped his ear with his hand. I strained forward and could hear two people talking in the kitchen area.

"What do you mean, 'Oh, rats'?" said one voice. "We don't have any rats. We only have mice…and they've been wearing combat boots!"

"I dropped a pan on my foot," the second voice said. "I wasn't talking about rats, literally."

The two were calling out to each other as if they were in separate rooms. We edged closer to the door and Carlos peered through the crack. He then stepped back and motioned to me to come away from the door. I did, and he told me what he'd seen. The first voice had come from an interior office and was probably the Cafeteria Administrator. The second voice came from a person standing on the other side of the cafeteria, in front of the sink. It was she who'd dropped the pan and was leaning against the counter, rubbing her injured foot. There was no sign of Andy Menendez.

We crept near the door again and continued to eavesdrop. "Speaking of mice," the second voice said, "this is the time of year when they try to get inside—away from the cold nights, but I haven't noticed any lately. Is it because that new stuff you got is working better than what we used to use?"

"You know, you could be right," commented the administrator. "I really hadn't thought about it, but I haven't seen any mice or droppings in the past few weeks. The exterminator said the mice had most likely become resistant to the rat poison we'd been using. So he told us to get rid of it and sent us some of the new…I can't remember what it's called. But I guess Carla put it out and it must be working better."

"What happened to the old stuff?"

"Carla said she pitched it."

"Will Carla be here tomorrow?" asked the kitchen worker.

"I don't know for sure. Her boy's still having trouble, so she may have to take care of him. Doesn't matter, though…we've got nothing going on here until school on Friday—"

"Hey, Andy," the second voice interrupted as Carlos and I heard another door open and close. "You need more coffee? I just made a new pot. Several of the teachers are here this afternoon, catching up on paperwork and wanted some…but I admit…I just made decaf. I don't want to be accused of causing everyone to be awake all night!"

"As long as it's hot and wet, I don't care," Andy Menendez replied. "Just the smell of coffee—even decaf—helps keep me awake."

Carlos and I shrugged and nodded at each other. The conversation had switched from rat poison to Carla's troubles to chit-chat, so there was no longer any reason not to show ourselves. Carlos ran back and rattled the outside door as though we'd just arrived and I called out, "Yoo-hoo! Anyone around?" We passed back through the maintenance room and pulled open the door to the kitchen.

"Hey, y'all," Carlos said. "Great! Look Kate, it's Coach Menendez—just who we were looking for. The boys at the field house said we might find you in here." He nodded to the cafeteria lady who had stopped rubbing her foot and shook hands with Menendez. I followed suit. The administrator emerged from her office, holding a sheaf of papers with both hands. She smiled and nodded to us, but from the look on her face, she hadn't heard that we'd be around. We introduced ourselves to both women and accepted the pro-offered Styrofoam cups of decaf. I was happy it wasn't the high-test stuff—I needed to get a good night's sleep one of these days.

"I got your note this morning," Andy said to Carlos. "I'm just heading back to my office. Walk with me and I'll show you what I found."

The three of us went back through the maintenance room. Menendez was careful to keep the door propped open. He shrugged and offered, "Smokers. We're supposed to be smoke-free, but the state hasn't officially passed the law yet, so there are still a couple of people who hide here to catch a puff…stupid, if you ask me."

I wondered if he thought it was stupid of the people to be smokers or if he thought the law was stupid, but decided not to pursue the matter. As we walked to the field house, Menendez said, "I looked over those keys you left. All of them belong to the doors here at school and to Sam's desk. I did, however, find a lock box in his bottom drawer. The little key that Sherry showed you might fit it, but I didn't try. I admit I was curious, but decided to let y'all check it out first. Sam didn't normally lock his desk, even the bottom drawer. Both it and the lock box itself were locked when I looked."

Menendez held the door open for us and followed us in. It took a few moments for our eyes to adjust from the bright sunlight. Then Andy said to follow him. He led us into Sam Johnson's office. Andy went around and sat in the chair. He unlocked the bottom drawer and removed the contents. Coach Johnson's day timer was there, stuffed with all sorts of papers and held together with a rubber band. Menendez pushed the calendar across the desk, saying, "Don't know if you'll be able to tell much from all this, but here it is. And here's the box."

He placed it on top of the desk and turned it around to face Carlos. Carlos took the keys and opened the fireproof lock box. The box held Johnson's Social Security Card, his passport, some insurance papers and two business cards. One was the name of a football equipment supplier and the other was a card for a Dr. Sanchez in Atlanta. The card said that Sandra Sanchez was a doctor of internal medicine and gave the address and phone numbers for her office. Carlos showed me the back of the card, on which was written, 'Thurs. 3:00 pm'. He raised his eyebrows at me, but all I could do was shrug. I'd never heard of Dr. Sanchez, nor had anyone mentioned an appointment for Johnson or anyone else on a Thursday afternoon. But I was definitely excited. Perhaps when we went through the calendar we'd find out.

We thanked Andy Menendez for all his help and took the calendar and box with us. Menendez announced that he'd had enough for one day, locked up the field house and followed us out to the parking lot.

Carlos and I sped back to the Bayside Motel, anxious to pour over Johnson's day timer and go through the receipts and papers stuffed inside.

CHAPTER 12

Bayside Motel

Tuesday, Late Afternoon

Carlos and I stopped at Amy's room to let her know we were back. She gathered her laptop and followed Carlos next door to his room to compare notes. I noticed that she went through the connecting door which they'd left standing open. I smiled to myself. Amy said she'd seen Gloria, though not to talk to.

"I'm going to talk with Gloria for a minute and then I'll be back," I said, heading down the corridor. "I'm dying to find out what Johnson had locked away."

But I'm also dying to find out what's going on with Glory! I thought. She answered at my first knock. "Come on in," she said, "I saw y'all pull in, so I've been waiting for you. I've got some stuff to tell you… but first…what was the deal with Papa and Ronnie? Did you know they were coming?"

"No," I answered honestly. "But I called you as soon as they showed up. I was afraid your date was over in the room with you."

It takes a lot to make Gloria blush, but she did anyway. *"He was!"* she cried, "But it's not what you think. And I'm so glad that he took off before Ronnie saw him!

"I can't believe that Papa saw him get into his truck. I'll tell ya', the look he shot me was unreal! I was so afraid to come into your room—I figured Papa'd already blabbed everything to Ronnie... but I guess he hadn't."

I agreed that Papa hadn't said a word, but that he'd shot me a look that would kill, too. We sat and Gloria continued.

"Let me tell you what happened! Arnie (that's the guy's name) and I just met for Happy Hour at that bar down on the corner. They had two for one drinks and free appetizers until 8:00 pm. He was a cutie and all that, but we started talking and I realized that I was telling him all about Ronnie! So I thought, 'Girl, you must be stuck bad on this guy.' (I *never* talk about one man in front of another...it's just not right!)"

Good policy, I thought. *I'll keep that in mind in case I ever* know *two guys at the same time!* "So, what happened?"

"We talked and drank and ate some stuff and I couldn't get Ronnie off my mind. So when Happy Hour was over, Arnie drove me back here. He was sweet and walked me to the door. He came in and had a look to make sure there were no bad guys waiting in here for me. That's when you called! I pushed him back to the door and told him he needed to get out of here, *like now!* And we were still standing there when Papa came blasting out of your room. He scared the bejesus out of me! I freaked when I saw him, 'cause I figured he'd call Ronnie outside and I'd never be able to explain. So anyway, Arnie jumped in his truck and took off. Papa got something out of his car and I ran back in my room till I stopped hyperventilating!"

We both took a couple of deep breaths. *What a tale,* I thought. *And probably true!* We do manage to get ourselves into messes!

"As soon as I walked into your room, I knew Papa hadn't said anything. I could'a kissed him! But then Ronnie grabbed me and swung me around. I guess it's lucky that we didn't take out a couple of lamps, as crazy as he was acting!"

I had a mental image of Gloria kissing Papa, and was a bit disconcerted about my feelings. She's had lots more experience with men than I've had. She's probably got better techniques, too! Would I be upset? Jealous? But I suppose she didn't really mean it. I said, "I'll need to tell Papa something when I talk to him next. His curiosity was about to eat him alive!"

"That's fine. I already told Ronnie all about Arnie so go ahead and tell Papa. I just don't want him giving me any more of his 'looks', ya' know! Those eyes of his can go right through a person."

I nodded in agreement. "I need to get back over to Carlos's. We found some interesting papers that we need to go through.

"You want to do something together for dinner?" I asked, my hand on the doorknob.

"Sure! No more 'dates' for me," she added emphatically. "I'm a one-man woman from now on!"

I didn't say a word, but wondered how long this 'one man' thing would last this time. I've heard her say that before…

"Oh yeah," she added. "I saw those football players again. You know, the ones that checked out the underside of my van?" She waited till I nodded my head. "I saw them downtown this afternoon. I'll tell ya' what they said over dinner. Catch you later," she said as I left.

I popped back into my room to freshen up a little. As I splashed water on my face, I had a vision. There were lots of guys and they seemed all hot and sweaty. Their faces were red, sort of like the lady in my previous vision, except that the guys didn't look angry…just tired. I could even *smell* the sweat! Yuck! Made me gag. The vision disappeared. I sat down for a minute, closed my eyes and tried to visualize everything I'd just seen. Jerseys…they were wearing black and orange jerseys…Conroy's colors. *Were they football jerseys?* I asked myself. Couldn't tell. I tried to recall the background. It took place indoors. The field house, perhaps? Or a similar location. There were some boys standing, talking. A couple others were sitting on what must've been a bench. One guy had his head in his hands and another guy was leaning over towards the first, his hand on the guy's shoulder. I realized that it was *not* the Conroy Field House—unless someone had re-arranged the benches. Then I remembered that the new field house wasn't even finished yet—so perhaps my vision was of the *old* one. Or somewhere else altogether. I sat a minute longer and concentrated. I'd heard voices, but I wasn't able to make out what the boys were saying. Nothing else came to me, so I dried my face and went next door to Carlos's room.

Carlos and Amy were sitting together with their heads bent over the pile of papers and receipts that had come from Johnson's calendar. They said they were sorting them into categories: gasoline purchases, restaurant receipts, and so forth. Another stack held an assortment of brochures: vacation rentals, hiking trail maps and one other pamphlet that caught my eye.

'DVT...at a Glance' was its title. "What's this?" I asked. Amy kept sorting and Carlos looked up at me and smiled.

"I thought you'd be interested in that! DVT stands for Deep Vein Thrombosis...and...when I looked at the back..."

I quickly turned the pamphlet over. Sure enough...there was Dr. Sandra Sanchez from Atlanta. My eyes locked with his and we both murmured, "Ah-ha!"

I plunked myself on a chair and glanced through the brochure. As I'd correctly remembered, a thrombosis is a blood clot. And often patients are put on blood-thinners to try to dissolve a clot, rather than opting for surgery. It followed exactly what Dr. Graves had told me earlier. But why didn't Dr. Wright, Johnson's local doctor, know about this? Maybe Johnson had gotten the pamphlet because of someone *else's* health problem. Pregnant women have been known to have leg problems...maybe Sherry? But I kept my thoughts to myself for a few minutes. "If this was Johnson's," I began, "and if he were on medication for DVT, then his death really *could* have been accidental, right?"

"Right," Carlos said. "But we need to talk with this Dr. Sanchez. I called her office a few minutes ago. The receptionist said the doctor had a speaking engagement this afternoon, but also said she couldn't give us any information about another patient anyway. So I scheduled a meeting with the doctor for first thing tomorrow morning. Amy and I will probably go back to Atlanta tonight. We won't have to fight the traffic that way. Then we'll hook up with Whitaker and call you if we find out anything interesting."

"Do you suppose I should stay here?" I told them a little about my vision and how I got the feeling that something was going on—something other than the possibility that Johnson was fighting a blood clot. I also mentioned my idea of Sherry having circulation problems connected with this pregnancy, but Amy remembered having Sherry put her feet up while they visited, and said she hadn't noticed any swelling at all.

Amy answered my question about sticking around. "The funeral is just the day after tomorrow. Even if this turns out to be an accidental death, it wouldn't hurt to stick around. And who knows? You might figure out the connections between your visions. Why don't just the two of us go back and you and Gloria can stay here and scout things out some more. Carlos told me about the conversation y'all overheard this morning—about the rat poison—it wouldn't hurt to find out more about that."

What Amy said made sense. I suppose if the truth were told, I was anxious to get back to Atlanta—back to Papa, that is…But work comes first, I reminded myself. And it was very possible that the detectives' meeting with Dr. Sanchez would turn out to be a dead end. I also remembered that Gloria had things to tell me about her chat with the football players. Maybe they could enlighten me about my most recent vision. And, I thought, I'd like to talk with the cook again—Carla. She'd been the one who'd replaced the rat poison and had disposed of the old. And we'd overheard the Cafeteria Administrator saying that Carla's son was having trouble. I wondered what that was about. How old was Carla's son? Had we met him yet? I also wanted to go through Johnson's calendar. Amy finished organizing the slips of paper and paper-clipped them all together. She stuck the groups back inside the calendar and handed the whole thing to me.

"Maybe some of the things in the calendar will jive with some of these receipts," I said. "I'll go through them tonight. Be sure to call me after you talk with Dr. Sanchez. Hopefully we'll all have found out some more info by then."

Amy went to her room and Carlos began packing his belongings as I stood to leave. "Gloria and I are having dinner and then I'll work on the calendar. If I find anything earth-shattering before morning, I'll call you. Um…where'll you be?" I asked, trying not to look directly at Carlos. If he and Amy were having an affair or a fling or whatever, they hadn't said anything about it yet—at least not to me. And I didn't want to pry.

"Call my apartment," he answered. But he *didn't* mention whether Amy would be there with him.

CHAPTER 13

Kate and Gloria

Tuesday Evening

We decided to walk to Mort's again. They served great comfort food and Shirley had started treating us like locals. The sun was getting lower in the sky, but the evening was still warm enough for a stroll. And it wasn't that far. I figured if Glory sprained an ankle (she was back in high-heels again), I could get her back to her room without too much trouble.

Shirley ushered us back to our 'regular booth' so we could talk privately. She winked at us. We ordered drinks, which she brought immediately. Then Gloria told me about the guys she'd met. They'd felt comfortable talking with her and told her that things were going to be a lot different now that Mr. Menendez was going to be the head coach. The boys weren't sure if Menendez would stay in that position next season or if another head coach would be hired. But for the remainder of the season, Menendez was 'the man'. When I asked how they felt about it and what sort of things would be different, she said that one of the boys had said, "No more yelling at us like we're little kids—you know—like we're idiots."

"I asked them who had been yelling," Gloria said, but the other guy had elbowed the first one and they both shut up.

I considered what Menendez had said about his approach to dealing with the boys as compared to Coach Johnson's. I also remembered what the neighbor had told Amy—she'd heard Sam Johnson yelling at his elder son, Sean. Perhaps Sam Johnson shouldn't be canonized just yet!

I told her about the football players that I'd met earlier in the week—Keith, Clem and Josh. Gloria hadn't met any of them, but said that one of the boys she'd talked with had mentioned the name Clem. She couldn't remember what had been said about him but remembered the name since she'd never known anyone by that name. "What's he like? Is he cute?"

"Gloria! He's a *kid*, for Christ's sake! You can't start messing around with a *kid*! And anyway, I thought you were a 'one-man-woman' now."

Gloria laughed, "Oh yeah, I forgot."

Our food came and we ate companionably, talking about this and that. Gloria said that she'd love to go riding with me at Turley's. Amy had mentioned something to her about free lessons. I had a bit of difficulty picturing Gloria on a horse, but what do I know? We agreed to check it out if we had time.

After dinner and another drink, we started walking back to the Bayside Motel. As we passed the ice cream shop Gloria stopped me, saying that the fellow behind the counter was the one who'd said something about Clem. We decided to go in. I found a spot to sit while Gloria asked him if he could talk to us. She came back with a Butter Pecan ice cream cone and offered me some. I shook my head. She told me the kid was supposed to have a break in ten minutes and had asked if we'd mind waiting.

Mike, the ice cream server, came towards us a few minutes later wiping his hands on his apron. Gloria had just finished her cone and was licking her lips. I was hoping she was just getting the sticky ice cream off—not licking her lips about Mike (although he was pretty well-built!).

"Good evening, ladies," he said. He extended his hand in my direction and said, "I hope I got all the stuff off them. This job can be really messy!" We shook hands and I assured him they were fine. Gloria introduced us and Mike said he had about fifteen minutes before he needed to be back at work. He looked over his shoulder and smiled at the girl who'd taken his place. "The assistant manager," he said. "Just making sure I'm not in trouble with you." We both smiled reassuringly and waved to her.

"Um, I'm not real sure what to ask you, Mike," I said. "I guess I'll just begin and see where it takes us, okay?" Mike nodded. "I met Clem the other day and talked to him and a couple other team members. I've heard others mention his name, too. What can you tell us about him?"

"Uh…" he thought for a minute. "He's a senior this year; is a tight end. He runs the ball," he added. I guess he thought perhaps we didn't follow football. "Umm…he's lived here all his life. I moved here four years ago and have known him and his girlfriend ever since. Her name's Sally Kim. They're both real nice. Sally's dad teaches Art at the High School. He's a potter. Makes really cool stuff. Oh yeah, Clem's mom's one of the cooks at school. Mrs. Tyson."

"Is there a Mr. Tyson?" Gloria asked.

"Yes, ma'am. He owns the garage over on Miller Street. He's a mechanic. I haven't seen him lately. He and Clem seem to get into it whenever we're around, so I've kinda been avoiding going over there."

"Do you know what's causing their disagreements?" I asked.

"No, ma'am, not really. The last time I was there Mr. Tyson called him a lightweight. I guess he wanted Clem to do something and Clem had this real bad headache, so didn't want to do whatever it was." Mike shrugged.

It dawned on me at that moment that one of the boys I'd met, either Josh or Keith, had said something to Clem about his headaches while we'd been talking. I asked Mike, "Has Clem always had headaches?"

"I don't know. I can't remember him having them during last year's season, but he could've and I just don't remember. We're good friends, 'cause we're on the team and all, but I'm not his best buddy. That'd be Keith…and of course, Sally."

"I'd better get back to work," he said, standing. He nodded to both of us and went to wash his hands one more time.

Gloria and I were almost to the door when something occurred to me. I dashed back to the counter to ask Mike one more question. "Do you happen to know Mrs. Tyson's first name?"

"Oh…yes ma'am. Of course we'd never actually *call* our friends' moms by their first names, but I know hers…it's Carla," he answered.

I thanked him and we left. My mind was spinning. Clem had headaches and was arguing with his father. Carla was Clem's mother and a cook at the High School. Carla was the one who'd replaced the old rat poison with the new and had disposed of all the old poison. I tried to make a connection among all of this, but I was missing something. But I felt like maybe I was on the right track.

Gloria said she was going to call it a night and go to bed early. It turned out she hadn't slept all morning—she'd been out and about—and talking with Mike and his pals. But first, she admitted, she was going to call Ronnie. She 'missed' him, she said, and became teary.

I left Gloria at her room and went next door to my room to work. I was most anxious to see if there was anything suspicious in Sam Johnson's calendar. And I wanted to mull over the Tyson family in my mind.

CHAPTER 14

Kate Calls Carlos

Late Tuesday Evening

I hesitated to phone so late. I could picture Carlos in several different scenarios in my mind's eye. One was that he'd be sound asleep…by himself. Another was that he was asleep, but not alone. And a third was that he was neither alone *nor* asleep! But I really needed to share what I'd found in Johnson's papers…before he met with Dr. Sanchez. So I pressed the key on speed dial.

"Williams," answered a sleepy voice.

I began by apologizing for waking him up and he muttered "It's okay," even though I know he must've wanted to kill me.

"This is really important, so if I tell you stuff, will you remember it in the morning?" I asked.

"Yeah, I'm awake. Go ahead." I could hear him rustle around, probably turning on a light. I also heard another voice in the background…Amy's?

I was excited about what I'd found out, but tried to be calm and give Carlos time to take down some notes. During several weeks before Johnson's death, he'd made entries about meetings in Atlanta. His gasoline receipts were always from stations in Conroy, but they were made on the days of the meetings. The interesting thing was that he'd also purchased more gasoline shortly *following* these meetings, so if he hadn't made the trips, he wouldn't have needed to buy more gas.

"Hang on," Carlos said. "Let me make sure I have this straight: What you're saying is that a tank of gas would have lasted several days if Johnson had just been driving around Conroy, but since he'd had these meetings in Atlanta, he'd used his gas up much more quickly."

"Exactly! I guess you *are* awake," I answered, and then continued. "The card you showed me today had 'Thursday, 3 pm' on it. It looks like he had appointments on Tuesdays and Thursdays, starting back at the end of September. I have gas station receipts for four visits. There were notations in his day timer for last Tuesday, last Thursday and also for today. But there were no gas receipts. Tuesday's meeting was scratched out, as was Thursday's. *And* I found another card from Dr. Sanchez's office folded in half and stuck inside the day timer. It was for that Tuesday at 3 pm: the one that had been scratched out on this month's calendar. So…if I'm right, these 'meetings' that were listed were for him to see Dr. Sanchez. He'd gone to the first few, but not the last three. (Natch, he couldn't have gone to today's, since he died on Saturday.) But he'd also skipped the two previous appointments." I ended our conversation by saying, "Call me *the second* you get out of your meeting with Sanchez in the morning. I'll be pacing the floor until then!!"

He assured me I'd be the first person he called, and we disconnected. I turned out my light. Carlos is one of the fortunate ones who can go back to sleep instantly. Not so for me. I lay in bed staring at the ceiling for hours! So much for getting a good night's sleep.

CHAPTER 15

Kate

Wednesday Morning

I jerked awake early Wednesday morning with a terrific headache. I suppose it was from lack of sleep. I wished I could have forced myself to sleep in a bit later, but I was too antsy. I looked at the clock: only 6:00. I groaned and got up.

My shower helped a little, but it wasn't caffeine. I quickly dried my hair and threw on a clean outfit. My 'dirty' pile was growing larger. I'd have to either get back home soon or break down and find a Laundromat. I groaned again.

I opened my door to a very chilly morning and reached back for my trusty suede jacket. I've had it for years and it's beginning to look ratty, but it's so comfortable, I'll probably never give it up. I visualized myself, years from now, sitting in the old-folks' home with Gloria. I'd be there in my threadbare jacket listening to her tell stories about all her men and the good old days! (I hoped this was merely my imagination and not a real vision!) I wondered, as I made my over to the restaurant next door, if I could find a tailor in Atlanta who could take the old jacket, make a pattern and sew a new one for me. Of course I could! But it would have to wait till spring. I'd need it all winter, first. *Kate, you're brilliant!* I thought. *A wee bit distractible, but brilliant! Now, just get 'brilliant' on this case!*

I appreciated the warmth of the restaurant as I slid into a booth. I could smell bacon frying and the coffee brewing. I began to salivate. The server must have noticed because he brought me a large coffee without even asking. I laughed and then smiled at him.

"We're trained to pay attention to our customers," he volunteered. There were only a couple others in the café, so after he put in my order, Danny (according to his name tag) and I chatted for a few minutes. He was twenty-eight, married and had one child, a little girl, Becky, named for his wife. Danny and his wife had both attended Conroy Senior High School. They'd gone to the old school, not the new consolidated one. He said he'd probably get lost if he tried to find his way around in the new complex. His younger brother was a senior this year and had assured him he'd get used to it just like everyone else, but Danny wasn't so sure.

"Has your brother said much about Coach Johnson's death?" I asked.

"Oh, yeah! Everyone's talking about it. It's all we've heard about since Saturday. Don't tell anyone I said so, but there will be some people that'll be glad he's gone. I don't want to say anything bad about someone who's dead, but he could be one bad-ass guy! I didn't play football, so I never had Johnson as a coach. But I had him as a P.E. teacher and in Health Class."

"What was your impression?" I asked, hoping he'd be a bit more forthcoming than the members of this year's football team. He was!

He said, "As long as you did everything by his rules, things were fine. But if you didn't…look out! Johnson would make your life miserable. I gave him some lip once and I thought he was going to tear me in half! My life wasn't worth living from then on, not till I graduated. I was never so glad to get out of anywhere in my whole life!"

Very interesting, I mused. "And you say there are others who have 'felt his wrath'?"

"Yeah, but nobody's going to say anything. And now that he's dead, he can't bother anyone any more, so there's no reason to."

"I'd be interested to know what kind of stuff he did. Was he abusive?" I asked.

"Nah, not really…unless you mean verbally. I mean, as far as I know he never shoved anyone or anything like that…but he sure could make you feel like crap. He'd belittle you and call you a pussy and stuff like that…in front of your friends. That's real hard for high-school-age kids to take. If he gave me a hard time now, I'd probably be able to take it—even stand up for myself, but not when I was that age."

"How did he treat your brother?" I wondered aloud.

"Oh, okay, I think. I told Josh to watch out for Coach way before he joined the team."

Danny brought my breakfast and more coffee, checked on the other patrons and then returned. We talked a bit longer and I found out that his brother Josh was the same 'Josh' I'd met earlier in the week, a friend of Keith's and Clem's. Josh had told Danny that he'd managed to get along with Coach Johnson, but that Clem and the coach had really gotten into it during summer camp. *Bingo!* I thought. *Another piece to the puzzle?* But unfortunately, Josh had failed to elaborate.

The sun was shining when I left the café and my spirits were a bit sunnier, too. I was trying to kill some time while waiting for Carlos's call, so I decided to find out where the Tysons lived and pay a visit to Carla and son.

The phone book in my room showed three entries for 'Tyson': the first was for the garage on Miller Street and two others for residences. I jotted down the address and phone number for the garage. Then I phoned one of the residential numbers which turned out to be Clem's grandparents' house. I spoke with the grandmother who was very chatty and said that her husband, Old Mr. Tyson, as he was called, was the original owner of the garage, but that Young Mr. Tyson, Clem's father, had bought it from his dad several years earlier. The elder man still helped out most of the time since

Larry, her son, 'had nervous disorders' and was on medication for his condition.

I thanked her for her and hung up. I smiled to myself, amazed at the things complete strangers will tell other people. Then I called the third number. A young man answered. It turned out it was Clem himself. He and his mom were just sitting down for breakfast and, yes, it would be okay if I came over for a few minutes.

I grabbed my big black bag and hurried to my car. My bag holds my life, it seems. I keep notebooks, files, my cell phone (when I remember to grab it) and usually a change of clothes in there. It's my office, tool box and suitcase all rolled in one. I'd be lost without it!

Conroy isn't that large, so I made it to the Tysons' in just a couple of minutes. Clem answered the door and greeted me warmly. He didn't appear to have a headache at the present time. He showed me to their kitchen where Carla was just pouring another cup of coffee for herself and offered me one. I accepted gratefully, and joined them both at the table.

We chatted about things in general for a few minutes. They seemed tentative at first, understandably, but soon loosened up. It seemed that both were hesitant to say anything disrespectful of Sam Johnson, but when I asked Carla about the football program in general, she voiced several concerns.

"I guess I see more than most people, since I'm always at school. I've tried to get the other moms to speak up, but no one will. I have to tell ya', I'm not fond of the football program. I think they expect too much from the boys. For one thing, they run them too hard, especially when it's hot out.

"The names I've heard the boys called would make your hair stand up on end!" she went on. "And they've even allowed the older boys to say *awful* stuff to the younger ones!

"I've been telling Larry this for years and he just says I'm too easy on kids, but it's true." She was on a roll. "And now that Clem's been on the team—this is his fourth year on varsity—I know it for a fact! I couldn't even treat a dog like that! Clem never says much, but a mom can tell." More to Clem than me, she said, "You can't tell me that something didn't go on at that camp! I can tell you—that man probably *molested* someone or something!"

"Mom," Clem said, warningly. "Mom, that's enough."

Carla took a couple of deep breaths and appeared to regain her composure. "Well," she said and pouted at her son, "it's true and you know it.

"But listen, I've got to get to school." She stood up and shrugged on her jacket. "Feel free to stay here if you need to talk more to Clem," she said to me. "And help yourself to more coffee."

And then to Clem she said, "Honey, when you're through here, I could use your muscles to help restock the pantry over there. We've got a delivery truck scheduled for this morning."

"Yes ma'am," Clem answered politely, but he didn't make eye contact with her.

"Your mom's very opinionated, isn't she?" I asked after Carla'd left.

"Yeah…sometimes she goes too far. And as for the coach molesting anyone…well there's no way that happened!" he said. "Mom means well, but she doesn't understand what happens when Coach gets wind of anyone bad-mouthing him."

"Tell me, Clem. Just what *does* happen?"

He rubbed his temple and took a swig of his orange juice. "Oh nothin' much. He just comes down real hard on you if he thinks you're saying stuff about the program or the way he runs things."

I got the impression that he might be about to clam up. *'Clem the Clam'*. "Do you think Coach Menendez will do things differently?"

"Probably, ma'am. He understands us guys a little better, I think. He won't make fun of us, at least." Then his head jerked up and there was fear in his eyes. "I'd better get over to school to help my mom," he announced, standing up.

"Can you tell me more about Coach Johnson?" I prodded.

"No, ma'am," he answered, looking down at his hands. "And I don't mean to be rude, but please don't ask me anything else. There's nothing more for me to tell you." He picked up his keys from the table and waited for me to gather my things. He locked up after we'd walked outside and escorted me to my car. He held the door open for me and smiled before turning towards their driveway.

I quickly rolled down my window and called to him. "Clem? Just one more thing…" He turned and started to walk back in my direction. "How long have you been getting these headaches?"

I was glad I had the protection of my car when he answered. I was actually afraid for my safety! I thanked goodness he wasn't carrying a weapon. Instantly, Clem had become another person. Gone was the quiet-mannered, polite young man I'd just interviewed. Instead, the person in front of me was seething. His rage was palpable. His face became red and I thought the vein in his neck would burst. He glared at me for a few seconds, hatred in his eyes. His fists clenched and he screamed, "Shut up, bitch!" He shook as he bellowed, "Leave me alone!" He fled to his truck.

I sat, dumbstruck, as he scrambled into his truck and roared backwards out of the driveway. Gravel flew as he took off up the street.

I sat there a few more minutes, shocked, wondering about Clem's sudden personality change. *Is this guy a schizophrenic?* I wondered. *Or are these outbursts connected to his headaches? Could it be possible he has a brain tumor?*

I was no longer concerned about myself, but for Clem and any person he might see before he calmed down. I decided I should tail him and followed him to school. While driving, I tried to sort things out. Why had he refused to give me any more information about Johnson? Was my question about the headaches really enough to set him off? As I pulled into the school parking lot, I saw Clem's truck parked near the cafeteria. Fortunately, it appeared he'd made it unscathed. Just then my cell phone beeped.

CHAPTER 16

The Call From Carlos

Wednesday Morning

Maybe it's Carlos! Breathlessly, I answered, "Hey!"

"Hi, Kate. I just left Dr. Sanchez's office and am heading to my car. I wanted to fill you in. Very interesting!"

I felt impatient. *Get on with it,* I thought, squirming in my seat. I heard him fumbling with something and then heard his door slam. He sighed. I rolled my eyes.

"Okay," he began. "I'm finally in my car. Let me put all this stuff down and then I'll be able to talk."

Impatiently, I counted to ten. Finally, he talked. He said that Sandra Sanchez had been terribly concerned when Carlos arrived. She'd been trying to get hold of Sam Johnson for several days. He'd missed a couple of appointments…appointments that were crucial to his health. When Carlos had informed her of Johnson's death the previous Saturday, she'd gone white as a sheet! "I'm certain she's concerned about a malpractice suit, but her first concern, of course, was about Johnson. I told her what I could about the case. She's calling the medical examiner as we speak, so Dr. Graves will know what's going on."

Carlos looked through his notes and confirmed the information I'd gathered from Johnson's calendar. He'd been seeing Dr. Sanchez for over three weeks. Several years ago he'd had knee surgery for a football injury he'd gotten during his high school career. Dr. Sanchez had told Carlos that sometimes clots form after these surgeries. Johnson had been experiencing a bit of pain and swelling and had contacted her. Dr. Sanchez had gone on to say that Johnson had come in once for a consultation and she'd done some tests. At his second appointment she'd prescribed Coumadin as a blood thinner. She had stressed to Johnson the difficulty in regulating the medication. He had returned three times over the next two weeks and assured her he'd come back twice the following week so she could check his INR level again. But he had cancelled the appointments scheduled on the 16th or 18th. And he hadn't shown up again yesterday. He'd forbidden her to phone him at home and hadn't answered any other numbers she'd tried.

Carlos had asked her what could happen to a patient whose INR level was too high. Dr. Sanchez explained that if the patient has too much of the medication in his system, he could overdose. The symptoms could include excessive bruising, bleeding from the nose or gums, or the presence of blood in the stool or urine. If this occurred, the patient would be treated with massive doses of Vitamin K. In severe instances, transfusions might be necessary, as well.

Dr. Sanchez and Sam Johnson had considered injections of heparin, but had agreed the oral medication would be better in his case. Johnson had expressed concerns about anyone in Conroy knowing that he was on any medication. *Including his wife and local doctor*, I thought.

"What's that about, Carlos?"

"I don't know," he answered. "I guess it's a 'guy thing'. We macho types can't admit to any illnesses. It might make us look weak!" I rolled my eyes again.

"What are you working on this morning?" he asked me.

I told Carlos about the debacle with Clem that morning and that I was at the high school. Among other things I wanted to see if Clem was back to his normal self again.

Well, I thought after we'd hung up. Johnson's autopsy had shown some of the signs mentioned by Dr. Sanchez: bleeding from nose and gums, excessive bruising, off-the-charts INR levels. Maybe all this was caused by the Coumadin and we were all just wasting our time here.

CHAPTER 17

Conroy High School

Early Wednesday Afternoon

After talking with Carlos, I headed toward the cafeteria. Carla was there, working in the pantry.

"Hey, Kate!" she said and looked pleased to see me. "Is that boy of mine with you?"

I answered in the negative, but said I had noticed his truck parked outside. She didn't seem concerned and replied, "Oh, he's around somewhere. Sally was here earlier. She's been helping her dad in the Art Room. Clem probably saw her car and went off to find her. I'm sure he'll be here in a few.

"In the meantime, do you want a sandwich? I've made a bunch for the faculty who're working today. Everyone's trying to catch up on their work. Not too many distractions…and it keeps their minds off Coach Johnson."

I realized that my stomach was rumbling and accepted gratefully. Not exactly my grandmother's cooking, but it tasted great! Any time that someone else is doing the cooking, I think it's good. I was reminded that my brother Dave had offered to give me cooking lessons this week. (Wasn't going to happen!) I looked around the cafeteria and the pantry. I wondered if Dave would be green with envy. Twelve burners on the stove…walk-in refrigerators and freezers…I couldn't even identify all the gadgets and supplies. My hat's off to anyone who can manage such a huge place! Carla blushed when I told her this. "It's nothing," she remarked humbly, but I could tell she was pleased.

The back door opened and a very pretty young girl with long, straight dark brown hair entered. "Hey, Mrs. Tyson," she began and then stopped short when she noticed me sitting on a nearby stool.

"Hi, honey. Oh Sally, don't worry, this is just Ms. Jeffers. Come on in." Carla dusted her hands off and gave Sally a big hug. "Is Clem with you?"

"No, he's doing a few laps around the track. Then he'll be in." Sally looked as though she wanted to say more and glanced my way. I wished I could melt into the woodwork. But then she continued… "Um, how did Clem seem to you this morning, Mrs. Tyson?"

Carla was unloading another box onto the counter. "Call me Carla, honey." Then she glanced up at Sally and frowned. "Clem seemed fine…he was okay," she answered slowly. "Why?"

"Oh, it's nothing. He just seemed a little upset, that's all." Sally wouldn't let her eyes meet ours.

"Ms. Jeffers? Was he okay with you?" Carla looked my way.

Gulp! "Right as we were leaving, I may have upset him," I admitted. "I asked him about his headaches…" and I grimaced as their eyes locked.

"A touchy subject," said Sally. And then she looked at me again. "So *you're* the one he'd been talking to." It was more of a statement than a question, but I nodded anyway. He'd obviously told Sally of my early visit.

"I didn't realize. I'm sorry, I would have been more careful if I'd known."

Carla waved a hand. "Don't worry 'bout it. He'll be fine…he'll get over it. But Sally and I have been talking. We're both worried about him. He started getting these things late this summer. I want him to go to the doctor, but Larry won't hear of it. (Larry's my husband.) He says there's nothing to worry about."

"It wouldn't hurt to take him to a neurologist," I suggested. "If nothing else, it could rule out some things." *Like a tumor.*

"You're preachin' to the choir," Carla agreed but reminded me again that Larry was dead set against it. I decided I needed to meet Larry Tyson and check him out for myself. *Could he really be that proud and pig-headed?* I also thought it would be a good idea to talk with Sally—by herself. Before long, an opportunity presented itself. Sally announced that she was going back to the Art Room to continue helping her father. And Carla said she was going to stick her head out the door and give Clem a shout. She needed him to help lift things onto the top shelves.

I walked through the main cafeteria with Sally and we scheduled a time later that afternoon to get together for a talk. Then she took the corridor to the Art Room and I headed toward the main offices.

It was beginning to look like Sam Johnson's death was accidental. He had been on an anti-coagulant and had missed two appointments. His levels could very easily have gotten out of control and no one would have known: neither his wife nor his local doctor knew he'd been to see Dr. Sanchez. And his fall from Winnie on the previous Friday had probably caused his internal bleeding.

I'd almost convinced myself to give up the search for any more clues…but then I remembered my visions…first, the ones of the angry woman. I needed to remember to look for anyone with blue eyes. *What color are Carla's?* I asked myself. *How about Sally's?* I hadn't noticed. And then there was my vision of the sweaty guys in the orange and black jerseys. *Why would I have these three visions if they weren't connected with this case?* I was missing something!

I realized that I was standing outside the counselors' offices and had been there in a 'zone' for quite a while. I wondered if one of the counselors would have any words of wisdom for me. I knocked on one of the doors. A Mr. Jinks looked up from his work. The counselor was a thin man, about forty-five, I guessed, with longish brown hair and a thick, rather good-looking mustache. I don't usually like facial hair, but on him, it worked. It made him look friendly. He must have recognized me because he smiled, stood and we shook hands. "I figured you'd be coming to see me before too long," he said and waved me to a chair.

I sat down saying, "I'll try not to take too much of your time and I'll also try not to ask any confidential questions."

He smiled, but said, "That will be almost impossible!"

I nodded in agreement, but decided to forge ahead anyway. I explained the situation as best I could. Then I explained what information I needed.

He frowned when I told him about Carla's fears of something happening to Clem or one of the other boys at football camp, maybe even sexual harassment or abuse. And he stroked his mustache when I briefed him on Clem's violent behavior earlier in the morning.

We sat in silence for a few moments. I knew he was trying to decide how much he could tell me. Mr. Jinks' face twisted into something between a smile and a grimace. "I'll try to be of some help," he said, "but you know I can't tell you anything about any of our students or faculty."

"I understand," I answered, although I really didn't. I mean, I understand the confidentiality issues, but it's not like I wouldn't keep my mouth shut. And if there were any chance of some type of abuse, he'd be legally bound to speak up.

"I *can* tell you that I've known Clem Tyson for a good many years. I've never known him to complain about headaches before. And I've never witnessed him having 'an outburst' as you put it. I've always been quite fond of the boy. He's been an upstanding member of our school and the community. His grades are top-notch and he's a conscientious student.

"As for the football program, I've never been privy to much information about it. I will say that I've overheard some general comments about the methods that some of the coaches used with the boys. I can't be any more specific than that. And no one has mentioned any sexual harassment to me…ever.

"It appears that you've already gotten more information from Andy Menendez than I've given you. He's probably your best bet...unless you can talk to some of the team members and they choose to open up to you."

I thanked Mr. Jinks and left his office. As I'd figured, he wasn't at liberty to tell me much at all. However...his choice of words stuck in my mind. He'd said that Clem had never complained of headaches...BEFORE. And then he said he'd never WITNESSED an outburst. What he *didn't* say was that Clem was NOW complaining or that OTHERS had witnessed them. *Hmm.*

I decided to pop back into the kitchen before meeting with Sally Kim. Clem was on top of a small stepladder, hoisting some heavy-looking boxes onto the top shelves in the pantry. He turned beet-red when he saw me.

"Ms. Jeffers, ma'am...I'm very sorry about what I said this morning. I-I don't know what happened...I just lost it."

Carla was standing at the base of the ladder and gave him a strange look.

"Don't worry about it, Clem," I said, silently breathing a sigh of relief that he appeared back to normal. "We all have our moments!"

"To tell you the truth, Ms. Jeffers, Mom and I have been talking." He backed down the ladder and looked at me with red-rimmed eyes. "I'm kinda scared, I guess. This stuff comes out of nowhere. Sometimes I can tell that I'm getting out of control, but I can't seem to stop it. Ya' know?"

I felt so bad for the kid. He blinked his eyes and looked at the floor. "I'm sure there's an explanation," I began. "You may want to see a doctor. He or she'd run a few tests and maybe have you get a CAT scan."

He shook his head, still staring at the floor. I had to strain to hear him say, "What if it's something really bad?"

"Clem..." I had to clear my throat and blink a couple of times before I could continue. "The worst thing is not knowing. People tend to let their imaginations run away with them and they start thinking the worst. Then they psych themselves out and become too afraid to ask for help. Maybe that's what's going on here?" I phrased it as a question and he nodded slowly.

"Even if it *is* something serious, the sooner you find out, the easier it will be for you to cure whatever it is. Can you tell your mom and me anything about this? Like when the headaches started or if you can remember anything that happened to you?"

He stood very still for at least a minute. "I'll think about it," he finally said. Then he took the box that his mom had been holding, climbed back up the ladder and went back to his work.

Carla and I looked at each other. We both had tears in our eyes. She looked at me pleadingly and mouthed, "What am I going to do?"

There wasn't much I could say. We stepped out of the pantry. I patted her arm and whispered, "He's making progress. He's starting to talk—bits and pieces. It'll be okay." I was trying to reassure myself as much as I was her.

I left the cafeteria wanting to cry. I'd try to find out more when I talked with Sally. Then, suddenly, it occurred to me that Carla's eyes were very blue—and I'd seen them before! "Oh, my God," I groaned aloud.

I walked outside to the area where the students liked to gather during off-hours. I sat at one of the tables and waited for Sally, soaking up the autumn sun and trying to get my emotions back under control. It wasn't easy. I couldn't stop thinking about Carla's eyes. Was she really involved? And Clem and Sally…it's so tough to be young.

I remembered so well being a teenager and trying to cope with things that were happening in my life. I felt guilty about my parents' deaths. The fact that I'd had a vision and was too unsure of myself to speak up about it. If only I'd said something! And then later in high school when I admitted my visions to my best friend, she'd scoffed and called me a weirdo and made fun of me in front of several of the other girls. *Some friend.* She'd never spoken to me again. I'd left school that afternoon, mortified, and headed to Grandma Phelps' house to lick my wounds.

That's when I'd met Papa. His real name is Tom, but no one besides his parents calls him that. He'd caught up with me before I'd gotten even a block away from campus. "Wait up," he'd called. "Kate! Hold on."

I stopped, but didn't turn around. I was furiously blinking the tears from my eyes. I didn't know who was calling out to me, but I was sad and embarrassed and didn't *really* want to be alone. I had no one to turn to. So I stopped.

He came up behind me and asked, "You okay? I saw that back there. Don't mind that Brenda-girl—whatever her name is…She's nuts." I still hadn't moved.

He continued, speaking in a soft voice—one with an accent I couldn't place. "You headed home? Come on, I'll walk with you."

He came up beside me and I turned my head to look into the darkest, most beautiful eyes I'd ever seen. I thought at the time that they were jet black, but really they were a very dark brown.

I stood there like a total fool. I'm sure that my mouth dropped open. I was such an idiot! He wasn't much taller than I, I noticed. And he had black curls that should have looked feminine, but didn't at all. His face was quite angular and not gorgeous, but he was very handsome in a way…and nice…and he knew my name. Then he smiled and I about lost it. White, even teeth and his eyes began to sparkle.

I thought my knees would buckle, but somehow managed to stay upright. He walked slowly on and I scurried to catch up. We walked on, close together, but not touching. Never in my life have I ever wanted to reach out and take a stranger by the hand! It was so tempting! My heart was pounding. I'd never had this feeling before. *What's going on?* I remember asking myself. *I don't even know who he is. This just isn't proper.* (That was my Grandmother Jeffers talking inside my head.)

Grandma Phelps wasn't quite as much the stickler for these sorts of rules, but even she would have keeled over, I'm certain!

I rationalized this urge to grab hold of him as a defense mechanism. After all, my best friend had just turned on me. I feared I was looking for a quick replacement. But this guy was such a sweetie…and HOT, too! *WOW!*

Trying to be cool and use my best manners, I said, "I know you know my name, but I'm sorry to say that I don't think I know yours…" I glanced at him out of the corner of my eye. He glanced back at me, but walked steadily on. "I'm Tom, but everyone calls me 'Papa'."

"As in someone's dad?" I squeaked.

He laughed. "Nah, as in short for Papadopoulos. That's my last name."

"Oh," I said and then *completely* forgot my manners. "That explains your accent." Still to this day I blush, thinking about how impossibly rude and politically incorrect that was. "I like it," I added, trying to cover my faux pas. I'd looked down at my feet wondering how in the world they were still functioning.

But he just chuckled and agreed that his accent was pretty thick. He went on to explain that his grandparents and parents had emigrated from the old country just before he and his sisters and brother were born and that they all lived together still. They spoke only Greek in their home.

As he talked, I began to relax. We talked about other things and pretty soon we were at Grandma's. I asked if he wanted to come in, but he said that he needed to get to work. He asked if he could walk me home again the next day. I was too dumbstruck to answer. I just nodded and backed into the front door. I reached around and grasped the handle, still staring at him. I know he must've thought I was crazy! Somehow, I managed to open the door and get inside before sinking to the floor.

Grandma's startled eyes looked at me from where she was sitting in the next room. Then she jumped up and came running. "Sweetie! What's wrong?"

"Nothing…," I answered. "I've just met Mr. Right."

CHAPTER 18

Sally and Kate

Wednesday Afternoon

I smiled as I remembered the first time I'd ever seen Papa. It had taken several days to convince him my grandma wasn't behind the door with a 12-gauge shotgun—just waiting for him. He was so shy! But Grandma Phelps fell in love with him when he finally got brave enough to come inside.

I looked up to see Sally Kim walking towards me. I brought my mind back to the present, and wondered if her relationship with Clem was anything like mine had been with Papa.

Sally sat next to me at the table and wrung her hands. "I'm glad you wanted to talk," she said. "I've been so worried, but didn't know who to talk to. I can't talk to Mrs. Tyson…I mean Carla. She insists that I call her by her first name, but it still feels weird, you know?" I nodded and she continued. "Clem and I started going out when we were sophomores. He's always been so great, but lately…" her voice faded away and she frowned.

"You probably know him better than anyone," I said and then remained silent in order to let Sally get her thoughts together.

Sally nodded and whispered, "He needs help…Please help him."

The sun was still warm, but my arms were covered with goosebumps. Poor kids! They were suffering so badly!

I asked Sally about their early relationship, concentrating on what she said about Clem's personality and his temperament. She relaxed a lot and obviously enjoyed reminiscing. Basically, Clem had always been a low-key kind of guy. I asked what her parents thought of Clem.

"Oh, my dad really likes him. He spends a lot of time at our house and Clem is sort of like the son he never had. Dad's real artistic, but not much of a handyman. He gets into the middle of a project and then gets stuck. But then Clem comes over and helps him out and gets him through the tough spots. Clem's no artist; he's more like his dad in that he's mechanically inclined. But they work well together. And Clem says he doesn't mind helping out."

Sally went on to say that Mr. Tyson occasionally had a bad temper and that Carla could get real angry, but not that often.

"Tell me about your mother," I said.

"She liked Clem, too. She met him a few times when he came over. But she was pretty sick that year and then died during the summer between our sophomore and junior years."

I expressed my sympathy for her loss and told her about my own mother being dead, too. I didn't go into the fact that *both* my parents had died when I was a teen. She didn't need to be burdened with the thought that she could lose her dad, too.

We began talking about Clem again, and his more recent behavior. Sally admitted that for the first time ever, she'd begun to feel scared sometimes. "He just like turns into someone else. I can't explain it. Sometimes it goes along with the headaches and other times it's something that someone says or does that sets him off. And sometimes it just happens. I've been thinking about breaking up with him," she continued, and brushed away a tear. "I don't want to, but he scares me when he gets like that! I try to help, but I'm not sure what to do. Maybe if I threaten to break it off, he'll go to the doctor."

She looked so sad when our eyes met. I had trouble keeping myself together. "You know, he's scared too," I told her. "I think he's so afraid that there's something seriously wrong, that he doesn't want to be told. I suggested to him that the not knowing was worse than anything else."

Sally nodded and said she had tried to tell him the same thing. She'd asked him to go to the doctor and even offered to set up the appointment herself and go with him, but so far he'd refused. "Maybe it's even worse since we watched my mom die that year. He doesn't want that to happen to him—nor does he want me to have to go through it again with him."

Insightful young lady, I mused.

"You know, his grades are dropping, too," she added. "He's always been a good student, but he says he can't remember stuff like he used to. And he's distracted. When we study together, his mind is somewhere else. And he gets dizzy once in a while. He's never fallen over, at least not that I know of. But sometimes he reaches out and grabs a chair or something to steady himself. How strange is that?"

All this began in late summer, after the boys had returned from summer camp. Clem hadn't told Sally much about camp this past summer. He'd just said "it was just all the usual stuff" when she had asked him. But she remembered that it had been very hot that week—in the high 90's—and she'd wondered how the guys were getting along.

I was reminded of my vision of the sweaty guys in their jerseys. When I asked, she told me a little about "two-a-days", when the boys were required to wear their full uniforms, pads and all, for the afternoon practice. *Maybe,* I thought, remembering the vision.

Then she said, in an excited yet embarrassed voice, "You know, I just remembered something." She turned red and let her long brown hair cover her face like a security blanket. "We were making out the first night after he got back. My dad had gone to bed—he's pretty aware of what goes on with high school kids. Anyway, I put my hand around his head and started to pull him toward me, and he winced and jerked back. I remember now because it surprised me. I asked him what was wrong and he said that he'd fallen at practice and had gotten a lump on his head and it was still sore. I felt real carefully and there was a little bump, but it wasn't that big. And it must've gone away 'cause he never mentioned it again. Do you suppose that could be what happened?"

"I don't know, but it's certainly something to check out!" We were both excited and decided to do some more sleuthing. Sally was going to talk with Clem and his mom, and I was going to try to find some of the other football players to ask if they remembered anything about Clem's fall. We parted, both feeling encouraged.

CHAPTER 19

Clem

Wednesday Afternoon

Clem finished storing the last box for his mother in the school's pantry and told her he was heading back home. Carla kissed him and told him she would be home later.

"Love you, mom," he said on his way out the door. Carla smiled at her son and wondered what *that* was about. He'd been going through a phase the past couple years that made him embarrassed to express his emotions (at least with Larry and her). *Maybe he's over that now,* Carla thought and smiled again. She turned back to her work.

Clem drove home slowly, his thoughts troubling him. Things were *not* going well. He'd been so furious earlier in the day. That Jeffers woman—poking her nose into things. *Not really*, he admonished himself. *She's just trying to help.* But it was like she could see right inside him and that made him uncomfortable. She'd really sent him over the edge! He had never had these rages before.

If she'd been standing outside her car, he'd have strangled her with his bare hands! *And I called her a bitch—I can't believe I did that!*

And then when he'd arrived at the high school—he didn't even remember driving there—Sally had taken one look at him and started to back away. She'd been *afraid* of him!

That's why he'd decided to run some laps. Just pound the hostility and anger out of himself. And it had worked pretty well. By the time his mother had called to him to help in the cafeteria, he'd felt back in control. But Sally had backed away—she'd been afraid. He couldn't bear that. "What's wrong with me?" he asked aloud.

He entered the house through the back door and just stood for a couple minutes, looking around the kitchen. He wandered through the rest of the downstairs, touching the god-awful knick-knacks that his mom loved to put around. He smiled wistfully and headed to his parent's bathroom. He'd made his decision. And he started to feel a little better.

CHAPTER 20

Kate

Wednesday Afternoon

I was encouraged, but still troubled after Sally and I talked. I decided if Clem had fallen and bumped his head, it was possible that was the contributing factor. He could have had a concussion or something like that. I didn't really know too much about head injuries, but know that they can mess a person up pretty badly.

Sally was going to ask Carla about it, and I was going to try to find some of the football players. There were very few people at the school, and the field house looked deserted. Many of the staff's cars were already gone, so it appeared as though people were calling it a day.

I got in my car and decided to head downtown to see if any of the guys were around. As I drove that direction, I remembered Larry Tyson, Clem's father. I'd been planning to touch base with the man…now would be as good a time as ever. He'd probably still be at work over at his garage on Miller.

The garage looked like it had been in use, *hard use*, for many years. It had probably been white at one point, but the color had peeled and flaked off for the most part. It looked pretty tired, but it was kind of cool-looking. There were lots of old signs: Pure (the white sign with blue letters and that blue zig-zaggy stuff in a big circle), a Sinclair sign (with the green dinosaur), old oil advertisements for Penzoil and Marathon and a couple of old red Coke signs. There were two posters, as well, advertising Black Jack Gum and Skybars. I remember Grandmother and my dad talking about these old products. I hadn't thought of them in years! I smiled at the memories of Dad.

There were a few cars in the lot waiting for their turn to be repaired. I could see through the windows that there were several cars up on racks. *The place looks ratty, but business must be pretty good,* I thought as I walked towards the building.

I opened what looked to be the main door and got the surprise of my life! The inside of the place looked like the workshop out of a race-car driver's magazine! The place was huge, spotless and as brightly lit as an operating theater! Countertops and cabinets were pristine stainless steel. (Dr. Graves, the M. E., would love this place!) The mechanics wore dark green coveralls and were concentrating on their work. They didn't notice me.

I'm sure my mouth was hanging open and I looked awfully stupid as I gazed around the interior. A large man stepped out of what was probably the office and laughed. "Quite different on the inside, isn't it?" he asked.

I was totally impressed and said so. He smiled affably and came over and shook my hand. "Want a Necco Wafer? I've eaten all the black ones but there are other colors."

My father had made me taste all the colors when I was little. I hated the black ones—even back then! Now they taste too much like Ouzo! I thanked him and took a couple of the round, pink discs he held out to me. They taste like wintergreen.

"I decided to keep the outside rustic-looking. You know, more in keeping with the rest of the neighborhood. Decided to keep the high-tech stuff in here."

He introduced himself as Larry and asked what he could do for me. I told him my name and watched as the smile left his face.

I guess he'd heard of me. And he probably figured I wasn't there because my car needed work. He was polite, however, as he invited me into the office and offered me a chair.

I explained briefly why I was in Conroy and then broached the subject of Clem. *May as well get right to the point,* I figured.

That's when things got nasty. His blood pressure must've skyrocketed, by the looks of him. He started sputtering, stood up and placed his beefy hands flat on his desk. He leaned forward and stared at me. He told me in no uncertain terms that we were meddling in affairs that we didn't need to be worried about. "My son and wife are of no concern of yours, young lady. They had nothing to do with Coach Johnson's death if that's what you're implying. You're not to speak with either one of them again…Do I make myself clear?!" He raised up, lifting his hands from the desk. I noticed that they were shaking—sort of like my knees. *I should have brought Chief Hayslip with me,* I thought belatedly.

"Now, get the hell out of here and leave me and my family alone!" he boomed as I quickly stood and inched backwards to the door.

I know I'm a chicken and that I probably should have stood up to him, but I couldn't get my mind to work. I was truly flabbergasted! I just wanted to escape with my life.

Needless to say, the crew in the dark green coveralls *did* notice me this time as I hurried out the door and scrambled into my car.

I sat still for a few moments, trying to calm my nerves. Man, what an awful day I was having—screamed at by two guys—from the same family!

After I calmed down a bit I thought about going back in and asking him if Clem had mentioned falling at summer camp. That had been my main reason for going there in the first place. I decided against it and figured I'd get more (and probably better) info from Clem's teammates.

My knees had stopped knocking by the time I got back to the Ice Cream Shop. I really needed a drink, I thought, but a Fudge Ripple cone would have to do. Mike was working again and pointed out some others from the team who were sitting in a couple of the booths. I paid, thanked him and made my way in their direction. Three booths along the wall were filled to capacity. All guys except for one girl, whose back was turned.

When I got close the girl faced me, winked and said, "Hey there, girl! Come sit and meet the boys!"

I should have guessed—Gloria! Completely surrounded by teen-age boys! *Oh, my God!* I stood by as the boy at the end jumped up and dragged over a chair from a neighboring table for me. I thanked him and sat down, licking my cone.

Glory was all bubbly—as only she can be. She pointed to each guy in all three of the booths and introduced me. She remembered all their names and the positions they played on the team! She never ceases to amaze me.

They were very friendly. I recognized Josh and some of the others. But when I asked them all if they knew if Clem had some sort of fall at summer camp, they all but turned hostile. Most of them glared and a couple looked down at the table. "No ma'am," said one boy, spokesman for the whole group. "We don't know anything about that."

"Okay. Thanks. I just wondered," I said lightly and decided I'd better leave before I was beheaded. "I'll see you back at the motel, Gloria." I smiled at everyone and hurried out the door. I'd just managed to infuriate every male in Conroy. Not my day. But I'd hit a nerve, of that I was certain. I must be making progress.

CHAPTER 21

Sally

Late Wednesday Afternoon

Sally felt somewhat relieved after her talk with Kate Jeffers. She thought about concussions as she made her way back to the cafeteria. Concussions were just bumps on the head. She supposed there could be complications, but she remembered hearing that for the most part, the side-effects didn't last too long—unless the concussion was *really* bad. Sally decided she'd look up head injuries on her computer when she got home.

Carla was gathering up her belongings when Sally entered the cafeteria. "Hi, Sally. I'm just heading home. You want to come over for dinner tonight? Larry's got to work late, so it'll be just the three of us…unless your dad wants to come, too."

"I promised my dad I'd stay home this evening, Mrs. Tyson… uh…Carla…but thanks anyway. I think Dad's worried after what happened to Coach Johnson. I'm all he's got now that Mom's gone. I think the coach's dying kinda spooked him, you know? So I promised we'd stick together tonight—just the two of us. I'm going to stop at the store and get something to make for dinner before I go home. But thanks. Another night, okay? And if I can find a good dessert, I'll make extra and bring it over when I come for dinner."

"That sounds like a good deal to me," Carla replied and she smiled.

"Oh! I almost forgot: the reason that I came back inside! Ms. Jeffers and I were talking and I remembered that Clem said he fell at summer camp and hit his head. We wondered if he'd gotten a concussion. Did he ever say anything to you about it?"

"No, honey, he never said a thing to me. But then he wouldn't, would he? His dad's always after him to be tough…manly. He'd never say a thing."

"But, just think. If he *did* get a concussion, maybe these headaches will go away after a while. Wouldn't that be wonderful?!" Carla smiled and hugged Sally tight.

"Yes, ma'am, it sure would! I think I'll stop in and see Clem before I go to the store. He'll be so excited and relieved if that's all that's wrong with him!"

Sally ran to her car, brushing tears out of her eyes. *God, let it just be a concussion,* Sally prayed as she drove.

"Oh God, What have I done?" Carla wailed after Sally left.

CHAPTER 22

Clem

Late Wednesday Afternoon

Clem checked the medicine cabinet in his parents' bathroom. "These yellow ones ought to do the trick," he said aloud. There were only ten left in the bottle. "You could've left me a few more, Dad. Thanks a heap."

He carried the bottle with him to his bedroom and sat down at his desk. He pressed a key on his computer and it came awake. *Notes are for weenies,* he thought, but began to type anyway:

Dear Mom, Dad and Sally,

I know this will be hard to understand, but maybe after you read this, you'll be able to. There is no reason for me to go on living and you'll all be better off when I'm dead…

 I'm not feeling sorry for myself. I've given this a lot of thought and this is the only answer. I know that there's something really wrong with me. My brain just doesn't work like it used to. I can't remember things. I'm flunking Math—and I've always gotten A's before. My headaches are killing me.

And even worse than that, I've scared you, Sally, when I get mad. I did it again today. I never want to hurt you—or anyone else, either, but I can't control myself. I know that one of these times, I'll really hurt someone.

Mom and Dad, I heard you arguing again the other night. You thought I was still out. If I'm not around, you won't have to argue anymore. I'm not the macho son that Dad wants, but I'm not the little boy that Mom wants, either. I heard what you told Dad about Coach Johnson, Mom. I want you and everyone else to know that I was the one who killed him. Show this to the police and then they'll stop investigating.

If you're wondering why I did it, here's why: I hated him. He's had it out for all of us guys on the team and said he'd 'ruin' anyone that ever said anything bad about him. So I know that none of the other guys will say anything. But I will. He screams at everyone, especially the freshmen. He calls us pussies and makes fun of you in front of all your friends. He makes you do extra stuff in practice if you show any signs of slowing down. And if you're sick, he makes you run up and down the bleachers for twenty minutes. He's sick and twisted. And if someone can't take it, he laughs and then yells at him some more.

The other day, Coach called me a retard because I'd forgotten a play. And he was right.

I know no one will believe what I'm saying, but it's true. He's just got everyone so afraid of him, that no one will say anything bad. He got away with almost killing me—he'd really kill someone else if I didn't stop him. I know that Keith and Josh and the others will hate me for telling you this, but something had to be done.

So that's why I did it. Tell the police. I guess that's all I can think of to say. Except that I love you all and will miss you. But you'll all be better off and so will I.

Your son and boyfriend,

Clem printed out the note, signed his name, folded it carefully and laid it on his desk. He took the bottle of pills to his to his bathroom and poured a glass of water. He spilled the tablets into his hand and counted them one more time. Looking at himself in the mirror, he said, "Down the hatch," toasted himself by raising his glass and smiling, and took the pills. He carefully poured out the rest of the water, wiped his mouth and went back to his bed to lie down. He turned on his radio and said to the little yellow tablets, "Do your thing."

CHAPTER 23

Kate at the Bayside Café

Late Wednesday Afternoon

I returned to the Bayside Motel and parked the car near the café. I was hoping Amy and Carlos had returned from Atlanta as they'd said when I'd spoken with them earlier. But the cruiser wasn't in the lot. As I walked towards my room, my cell phone beeped. It was Gloria. She said I'd really made the football team mad. (Those were *not* her exact words. The Grandmothers wouldn't have approved of the ones she used!) It had taken her some time to get them calmed down again. Then she told me she'd decided to go back to Atlanta. Ronnie had called and asked her to 'come home'. "He's lonesome," she added. I rolled my eyes as we rung off.

I'd just inserted the key into my door when I heard a man's voice calling, "Lady! Ma'am? Uh, 'scuse me. Ma'am?" I turned around and saw Danny, the server from the café waving and looking my way. I looked around. No one else was around, so I figured he was yelling at me.

I headed his direction as he scurried out of the café door and continued to flag me down. By the time he caught up with me, he was out of breath. "Hey, I'm glad I saw you. I've been watching out for you since my shift began." He took a couple of deep breaths and continued. "My brother—Josh—he wanted me to give you this note. I read it...I know I shouldn't have, but I did anyway. I think it might be important." And he shoved a piece of paper at me.

"Thanks, Danny. What's all this about?" I asked.

"I've got to get back inside," he said turning around. I trotted after him. Over his shoulder, he said, "Something happened at summer camp. Here," he said, indicating a stool at the counter. "Sit here and I'll get you a cuppa coffee."

I'd already glanced at the note from Josh. "Better make it high test, Danny. This might be a long night."

I read Josh's note and then read it again. It made me want to get sick to my stomach...or go bust open a few heads. Johnson's for a start. But someone had already taken care of him.

Josh's note told a bit about the two-a-day practices. The weather had been scorching that week and everyone was throwing up, especially during afternoon practice. He said that Coach had laughed and told them they were a bunch of pansies and they needed to toughen up. Clem had collapsed as they had been running around the track. Johnson had yelled at Josh when he'd stopped to help Clem: Had told him to keep on going. Josh had. He said that he'd never seen anyone that red in the face—that Clem looked like he was about to die from the heat. But that Josh had left him there and kept running. Coach had come over and dragged Clem off the track. He'd towered over him as he sat at the side of the track and had yelled a lot. Josh had been on the other side by then and couldn't make out Coach's words. Then Coach had made Clem run up and down the cement bleachers. Clem had made two full trips, up and down, in pretty good shape. Then he'd started to stagger. Johnson was still there, yelling and calling him names. Clem had struggled halfway up again and then had sat down on one of the steps. "Nobody stops when Coach is in one of his moods," Josh had written. Clem had then removed his helmet and wiped his face. He had said something to the coach, who had turned from him and waved dismissively, shaking his head and looking disgusted. The boys had held their collective breath to see what would happen next (my words, not Josh's). Johnson had stomped back down the steps. When Clem stood up to follow, his legs had given out and he'd fallen forward, tumbling head over heels, all the way to the bottom. Keith and Josh had run to his side. Clem had been knocked out for a few seconds, at least. Josh was pretty sure he'd hit his head a couple times on the way down the cement steps. "There's no way he couldn't have," he added.

Practice was pretty much over by then and Johnson wasn't around since he had stomped off, so Assistant Coach Menendez had told everyone to hit the showers. He'd walked over to the three friends. Clem had come out of it, so Menendez said Clem'd be okay and for the other two to help him back to the changing room. After their showers, Clem had seemed pretty much back to normal, except for a few bruises that were beginning to show. He'd been pretty quiet that evening, but by the next morning he'd seemed fine.

Josh's note ended by saying that he'd noticed a difference in his friend ever since, though, and since Coach was dead, he thought it would be okay to speak up now.

I folded the note and stuffed it into my pocket. Briefly, I closed my eyes. *That son of a...*, I thought. When I opened them again, Danny was looking at me, knowingly, and shook his head, his lips compressed into a thin, straight line. I drank deeply from the cup of coffee, barely noticing that it was lukewarm. I left a couple dollars on the counter and heaved myself off the stool. Danny looked up from the table where he was delivering food. "Thanks," I called out. "I'll be in touch soon."

CHAPTER 24

Papa's Lounge

Late Wednesday Afternoon

"Hand up that Pinot, would you, Papa?" Demetri murmured his thanks as Papa hoisted the case of wine up in the air. Demetri balanced himself on the ladder as Papa stood holding the case straight up over his head.

"Be quick, man, this is going to get real heavy—real soon."

"I thought you had some muscles! Anyway, I'm going as fast as the law allows—you wouldn't want me to drop these, would you?"

"Knowing you, I'd get my head split open by one of them on its way down!"

"Well, at least then you could call your sweetheart and have her come over and console you…"

The two friends bantered amicably while they re-stocked the bar before the evening rush began.

"Speaking of sweeties, mine's still out in Conroy," Papa grumbled. "I don't know *when* she's getting home! This job she's working on is sort of nasty.

"And," Papa continued, "I've never even *met* your girl! When are you going to introduce us? She could pop in here and say hello, couldn't she?"

"One of these days, you'll get to see her. I'm taking it pretty slow with her. She's from the old neighborhood. And she's real shy. Her family keeps her on a very short leash. You know what I mean…I don't know if she's even dated anyone before!" was Demetri's reply. "I've only met her parents once—and that's just the *first* step in a relationship. We've never even been out on a real date!"

"Wow! And good luck to ya," was all Papa could think of to say, at first. Then he added, "I guess that means it's not too likely that she'll be coming in this place some night for a quick drink, huh? What's her name, anyway?—"

The two were interrupted by a middle-aged Greek gentleman who walked in at that moment. "Good evening, gents," he said in a friendly voice. It was Mr. Mercouri. "Well, it's almost evening, anyway. I understand congratulations are in order!"

"Oh, yeah?" both Papa and Demetri said and glanced at each other, shrugging.

Papa shrugged again. "You got me. Enlighten us, please!"

The man looked at Demetri and winked. "He's keeping this close to the vest, I see." When Demetri looked puzzled, he added, "You mean he hasn't even told you…his best buddy?"

"Come on, friend, I've got no idea what you're talking about," Papa said and began to feel unsettled.

"Pour me a shot and I'll fill you in", said the man as he pulled himself up onto a stool.

Papa grabbed the Ouzo and poured a shot for each of them. He had a sinking feeling in his gut—and it wasn't from the Ouzo. He had an idea that he might need more than just one, so he left the bottle on the bar.

The man got himself comfortable in his seat and appeared to be hunkered down for the evening. There was a twinkle in his eye. "Here's to you, men," he said and downed his shot. He banged the shot glass on the bar and grimaced. "You know, I love this stuff, but the first shot always makes me shudder! Can't taste it after that—mouth's all numb!"

He laughed out loud as he saw Demetri and Papa do the same thing when they'd drunk theirs. Then he looked at Papa and announced, "I've just been talking to your momma, son!"

"O-kay-y…" said Papa, slowly. His stomach began to clench—again, not from the drink.

"Yep, saw her at the butcher's down on Briarcliff Pike. She told everyone in there that she's going to officially announce your engagement on Saturday at the Community Center over on LaVista Lane. I know the little lady, too. She's quite a girl; and pretty, as well. Goes to St. Constantine's.

"Better give me another one of those," he said, scooting his glass closer to the bottle. "Then I'll be off. My wife will want to hear all the latest gossip from 'round the neighborhood."

Demetri poured, more puzzled now than he'd been before. "Kate doesn't go to St. Constantine's", he murmured.

Papa didn't hear what his friend had said. He was in shock. His mother had finally gone off the deep end! What in the name of heaven did she think she was doing? He hadn't even seen Anna in eight or ten years—if that's the one his mother had in mind. He closed his eyes and put his head down on the bar.

"What's a matter? You mean to tell me this is news to you?!" Mr. Mercouri burst out laughing. He tossed some bills on the counter, slid down from the stool, laughing and shaking his head. As he turned toward the door, he sketched a wave and cried, "My wife's gonna love this!"

Demetri looked at his friend and boss. "What's going on?"

Popa groaned and poured them each one more shot before restoring the Ouzo to its proper place.

"You look a little pasty, Papa," Demetri said. "You need to sit down?"

"No, I need to go kill someone! Or at least call and yell about this. I don't know which one to call first—Mama, Kate or…or Anna!" And Popa stomped off to the back room, cursing under his breath.

Demetri vaguely heard the bar door open and subconsciously saw someone come in from the street. In the back of his mind he knew he was supposed to make whoever just walked in feel welcome and find out what they wanted to drink, but he was in a stupor. He just stared after Papa. He tried to get his mouth to work, but couldn't. All he could think of was "Anna". Papa had said Anna. There couldn't be that many girls of marrying age named Anna in the old neighborhood! *What if Mrs. Papadopoulos was talking about my "Anna"!!*

CHAPTER 25

Sally

Late Wednesday Afternoon

Sally left school feeling better than she had in weeks. She couldn't wait to tell Clem that she'd figured out what might be wrong and that he'd be better soon. Then she'd stop at the store and pick up something for her dad and her for dinner. She smiled and began to put together a menu in her head.

Clem's truck was pulled way back in the driveway, so she knew he was home. She remembered that Carla was coming too, so Sally pulled into the drive, turned around and backed onto the street. She checked in her side mirror to make sure she was close enough to the curb and nodded in satisfaction.

Sally assumed the back door would be unlocked, so she walked around. She knocked on the door and then tried the handle. It was open. She peeked in and called Clem's name. Nothing. Walking in further, she called louder and let the door shut behind her. When she got to the living room and stood at the base of the stairs, she could hear Clem's radio. Following the sound, she made her way up the steep steps and into his room. He was on his bed, sleeping again. *He's been sleeping so much, lately,* she thought. *Maybe that's another thing that goes along with concussions.*

"Clem? Wake up, sleepy!" she said, sitting on the edge of the bed. "Hey, wake up…Clem? CLEM!"

Sally shook him hard and began to panic. "JESUS!" she cried and her eyes searched the room, as though someone might magically appear to help. She saw a bottle on the counter of Clem's sink and ran to his bathroom. She grabbed it and shook it. Empty. Clutching the bottle, she hurried back to Clem's side, grabbed the phone on his nightstand and punched in 911.

"Shit…come on…" she muttered, waiting for someone to answer and looking at Clem's pale skin.

After only two rings, a male voice answered, "Is this an emergency?"

Sally talked as quickly as she could, "My boyfriend. He's unconscious! He took a bunch of pills…um, Valium, it says. I've got the bottle here. It's empty! Send someone…quick!"

"Ma'am, calm down. I'm sending help now. But you've got to talk to me. What's your name? What is your location…the address? How old is the victim and do you know how many pills he took? Look at the bottle. How many milligrams are the tablets? And what is the date on the bottle…when the prescription was filled? If I know that, I may be able to figure out how many pills were taken."

Sally was shaking, but just talking to someone helped. When the man took a breath, she interjected, "Are they on their way?"

"Yes, Miss. You're doing just fine. Just stay on the line with me. You should hear the sirens soon. Is the door unlocked?"

Sally could hear the siren, even over the radio. "Oh, god," she cried. I've got to unlock the front door!" And she dropped the receiver and raced to the stairs.

Grabbing the handrail, she slipped and slid the length of the steps, cursing them as she went. She landed at the bottom, twisting her ankle. She hobbled to the door as the paramedics pulled into the driveway. "Hurry!" she yelled, opening the front door. "He's upstairs and I can't wake him up!"

Two men wearing uniforms brushed past her and looked where she was pointing. They dashed up the stairs. One carried a medic bag, the other, a radio.

Sally couldn't hold still. "Hurry," she said again, turning away from the door and following the two medics up the narrow stairway.

When she got to the top of the stairs, she realized there was no more room in Clem's bedroom. She stood at the door and asked if he was going to be all right.

"We're working on him, ma'am. Just stay back if you would. He's breathing and we will be transporting him to the hospital shortly."

"Bring up the backboard," the first man said. "We'll have to strap him. There's no way the stretcher'll fit up those stairs."

"You got it," the second EMT replied and squeezed past Sally saying, "Ma'am, you will need to come downstairs with me and keep out of the way."

Sally tried to get another glimpse, but her vision was blocked by the medic who was still working on Clem. She limped down the stairs and waited in the living room, wringing her hands and silently urging the medics to hurry up.

The medics met each other halfway up the steps, and the first asked his partner to back the truck up to the front door. Then he grabbed the backboard and hurried back up the stairs.

It seemed to Sally that it took forever, but in the back of her mind, she knew it was only a minute before the man had moved the emergency vehicle, rushed back upstairs and the two medics came down the stairs, sliding Clem between them. She followed them out to their truck which was now next to the front steps of the house. Sally stood by helplessly as they attached Clem's board onto a regular stretcher. Then they slid the whole contraption back inside. Sally started to climb in too, but one man stopped her. "Are you kin?"

"What?" Sally asked. She shook her head, uncomprehendingly.

"If you're not family, I can't let you in here." He looked sympathetic, but firm. "That your car?" he asked, nodding to the car parked at the curb. When Sally nodded mutely, he added, "Then just follow us."

The driver was already in his seat, on his radio with the hospital staff as the other jumped in with Clem and slammed the doors. Off they went, leaving Sally standing in the Tysons' front yard, dazed.

As the ambulance rounded the corner, Sally noticed the car that had pulled over to let it pass. Carla's car. "Oh, my God, Carla!" Sally breathed aloud. She raced to the curb and flagged Carla down. Scurrying around to the other side of the car, Sally yelled, "Turn around! Turn the car around. That's Clem! They've got Clem!" She jumped into the moving car as Carla made a U-turn in the front yard to head back the opposite way.

"What happened!" screamed Clem's mother as she and Sally roared after the ambulance.

CHAPTER 26

Conroy Memorial Hospital

Wednesday Evening

They sat in the waiting room. Several people were there. Carla and Sally were holding hands, both perched on the edges of their chairs. Sally's eyes were closed. Carla was rocking back and forth, looking from Sally to her husband, who was sitting on her other side. She had called Larry at the garage as soon as she and Sally had gotten to the hospital.

Josh and Keith had been downtown when they'd seen the ambulance go by. They hadn't thought too much about it until they'd seen Carla's car speed past. They'd gotten to the hospital only thirty seconds after Sally and Clem's mom.

Sally told them what had happened, and now the pair was seated side by side across the room from Sally, their eyes glazed over.

Josh finally leaned over to Keith and whispered, "I'm a day too late. I finally told my brother Danny what happened at camp and told him to tell that other cop…the one who keeps coming into the café. If I'd said something yesterday, Clem would be all right. I f-ing blew it!"

"Shut up!" Keith hissed back. "He'll be fine…He's got to be."

Sally looked up when she heard the boys whispering. They'd gotten quiet again. Mr. Kim appeared in the doorway of the waiting room. Sally jumped up and raced into his arms, ignoring her throbbing ankle. "Oh, Daddy!" she wailed. He wrapped his arms around her and hugged her tight.

"Have they said anything yet?" he asked into her hair. She shook her head. "Let's sit. Tell me what happened. Then maybe the doctor'll come out." Sally, still in shock, mutely followed her father.

A few minutes later, Carlos and Amy walked in. They had just returned from Atlanta. They asked if anyone had seen Kate Jeffers and that's when everyone realized that she probably didn't even know what was going on. No one had seen her. Amy hurried back outside to use her cell phone.

"Jeffers…where are you?" she asked as soon as Kate had picked up. She listened and then asked, "Well, will you be coming to the hospital? Okay. We'll still be here, I'm sure."

Amy returned to wait with all the others, running what Kate had said over in her mind.

At long last, a doctor appeared at the door. "Are you Clem Tyson's relatives?" he asked. When everyone looked at him and nodded and Mr. Tyson had stood up and approached, the doctor went on. "He's a lucky young man. We believe he only ingested ten of the Valium tablets. That's enough to render him unconscious, but for a boy his size, it's not enough to kill him. It's really too early to tell, but it's quite possible he'll be all right. But I'm telling you this with all due caution. The first twenty-four hours will tell."

Mrs. Tyson burst into tears, sobbing loudly. Amy rushed to her side, a box of tissues in hand. Josh and Keith gave each other 'high fives' and stayed seated, grinning like fools. Mr. Tyson shook the doctor's hand and clapped him on the back, thanking him for helping his son. The color drained from Sally's face and her father grabbed her arm in case she fainted. He asked the doctor for smelling salts.

Sally waved him away. "No, Dad. I'm okay. I'll be all right now." But she was still worried about Clem and still looked quite pale.

She asked the doctor, "Can we see him?"

The doctor pursed his lips and looked thoughtful. He rubbed a hand across his tired-looking face. "I'm still concerned about him. He *did* just try to take his life. He's still quite groggy. For his own safety, we've got someone with him at all times. He's under a suicide watch until we can get to the bottom of all this. I don't think it would be prudent at this time to have any of you in to see him. I'm going to ask for your cooperation and understanding about this. Until we know exactly why this incident occurred, he would be better off not to speak with anyone, I think." He thought, but didn't verbalize, *It's likely that one of you people sitting here did or said something that pushed this kid over the edge.*

"My suggestion to you all is to go home and get as much sleep as possible. Your boy's in good hands here and he'll need you much more tomorrow than he does right now."

Carla stood and pleaded with the doctor. "Can I just look in at him? If I could just see him…" Her eyes filled with tears again.

"I think that can be arranged, Mrs. Tyson," the doctor relented. "He's sleeping at the moment. You can see him, but I don't want him disturbed."

She nodded and followed him out the door. As Carla and the doctor headed to ICU, everyone else took deep breaths and stayed right where they were, too weak to move.

The nurse was standing close at Clem's side and looked up when Carla's head appeared around the door. She mouthed, "He's asleep," and motioned for her to come closer. She whispered, "I know you're worried to death about him, ma'am, but his vitals are good and I'll be right here with him until the night nurse takes over at midnight.

He's a strong boy and we all pray he'll be okay. If he wakes up, there'll be someone right here to reassure him."

Before Carla turned to go, she reached out and touched Clem's pale hand and whispered, "Oh, Son, I'm so, so sorry." Tears sliding silently down her cheeks, she found her way back to the others.

CHAPTER 27

Kate at the Tysons' Home

Wednesday Evening

I felt weighted down. It was all I could do to put one foot in front of the other as I left the Bayside Motel Café. I've never wished for anyone to die, but I was *not* sorry Johnson was dead. Instantly, I was consumed by guilt. Sherry and the children would have to go on without a husband and father, and I'd never wish that on anyone, but…

As I walked, I absent-mindedly reached for my keys and got into my car. Before I knew it, I was headed to the Tysons'. I hoped to find someone at home.

I knew something was wrong when I pulled into their drive. A brief vision had flashed before my eyes on my way over there, but I would have known it anyway. The front door was wide open and there were tire tracks on the front lawn. Absently, I looked at the tracks and decided that the Tysons must have a sprinkler system for their lawn. I couldn't remember it raining for a long time. I sat for a minute, collecting my thoughts and reviewed my vision. I'd seen an ambulance in my mind. It was speeding down a side street—this one, perhaps? I groaned.

I grabbed my trusty bag, jumped from my car and ran to the front of the house. Standing at the front door, I called, "Anyone home?" There was no answer, so I proceeded slowly inside. The house felt deserted. I pulled a pair of laytex gloves from my big black bag and tugged them on. I glanced into the kitchen at the back of the house and that's when I first noticed the music coming from upstairs. I crept slowly up the steep steps, hoping that there was no one up there, waiting to jump out at me. There was an annoying beeping noise, too. Both sounds came from one of the bedrooms.

First, I scanned all the rooms and looked behind doors and in the closets. When I was certain I was truly alone, I went back to the room where I'd heard the noises. The beeping sound came from the handset of the telephone. Someone had dropped it on the floor and it had gotten shoved under the bed. Clem's bed, by the look of the room. The bedcovers were rumpled. The room was painted a medium shade of blue and the walls were covered with posters. Shelves filled with trophies lined the wall above the desk.

I pressed the red 'end' button on the phone and blessedly, the noise ceased. I then switched off the radio and was enveloped by quiet. I was still on my haunches next to the bed. Slowly, I turned 360 degrees, taking in everything else. I looked through to the bathroom. I scanned the desk. A screen-saver was scrolling across the monitor, so I went closer to have a look. I jiggled the mouse and the computer came to life. I played around for a few seconds and was able to pull up a screen with an icon for 'recent documents'. The last one had been saved almost two hours earlier. It was saved as: "Dear Mom, Dad…"

"Oh, man…" I said aloud and raked my fingers through my hair. My worst fears were becoming realized! That's when I noticed the folded letter on the desk next to the computer. *Duh!* I handled it carefully, even though I was wearing gloves. My heart broke as I read it.

I pondered the contents for a few seconds. Then I pulled my cell out to call Carlos and Amy. But before I flipped it open, the phone beeped. It was Amy, calling me. She told me who all was at the hospital. She also said that everyone was on pins and needles waiting for some word of Clem's condition. I informed her about the two notes—the one that Josh had given to his brother, Danny. And the second one—Clem's suicide note, giving his reasons for his actions and confessing to Sam Johnson's murder. We both agreed that it was odd that he hadn't said *how* he'd killed the coach. When someone confesses, they usually want people to know everything. He was so specific in all the other details of his note—why would there be this inconsistency?

After I hung up, I looked around the bedroom and bathroom carefully. I noticed the bottom of the glass still held a trace of water. I thought it was unlikely that someone else had written the note or perhaps forced Clem to take an overdose, but I didn't want to take any chances. I carefully lifted the glass and took it and Clem's note to the kitchen. I scrounged around and found some zip-lock bags. I put each item in a separate bag and sealed and labeled them both. I checked the house again, locked the back door and made sure the front door was closed tightly. I headed quickly to my car, shaking my head and wondering how life could get this crazy.

I sped towards the hospital. On my way there, I had the strangest vision—so out of place. It was of a bride, and church bells were ringing. It didn't last very long. I concentrated on the girl. Could it have been Sally? Gloria? Amy? Whoever it was had dark hair, but I couldn't tell the length. It was either pulled up in a fancy hair-do, or it was short. The bride was wearing a veil, so it was impossible to tell. I tried to recall her face. She was pretty but didn't look familiar. Very odd. For sure, it wasn't *me* standing there!

I parked quickly in a visitors' slot and dashed inside to see how Clem was faring.

CHAPTER 28

Conroy Memorial Hospital

Wednesday Evening

I met Amy and Carlos in the hallway outside the ICU. They'd just gotten the news on Clem and said he was probably going to make it, but wasn't out of the woods yet. There was someone with him at all times since he was under a suicide watch. The doctors and staff were taking this very seriously, I was pleased to note.

We made our way back to the waiting room and noticed that Clem's parents were walking down the corridor in front of us, headed towards the parking lot. I motioned to the detectives to let them go. I didn't want to talk to them right away. I hadn't mentioned, when I'd spoken earlier with Amy, my run-in with Mr. Tyson at his garage. I imagined I was the *last* person he wanted to see right now. This was *not* the time for a confrontation!

Mr. Kim and all the teenagers were gathering up their personal belongings when we entered the waiting room. They looked totally wiped out. Mr. Kim shook our hands and repeated what the doctor had told them.

I was dying to tell everyone, especially Josh and Sally, about the note Clem had written, but I bit my tongue. Carlos, Amy and I needed to mull things over first and then get hold of Chief Hayslip. I was happy that he and Clem's parents had all left the hospital before I'd arrived. If they'd still been there, I'd have felt obligated to share my information with them. As it stood, I could buy a little time to decide the best course of action.

Josh and Keith left, leaving the three of us with the Kims. Sally sat back down and announced that she was remaining at the hospital. She knew that they would let her go in to visit for a few minutes each hour. She wanted to be there just in case Clem woke up. Mr. Kim agreed to let her stay. I guess he understood what she was going through, having lost his wife such a short time ago. He offered to get her and the rest of us something to eat. "And," he added, seeing his daughter propping her foot up on a nearby chair, "I'm bringing back an elastic wrap for your ankle."

We thanked him for his kind invitation, but declined. The three of us needed to share our respective information, so we left the hospital and headed for our usual table at Mort's.

Carlos and Amy drove the cruiser, and I followed in my car. I turned my cell back on and noticed two voice messages. The first one was from Gloria. "Oh, girl, you'd better call me quick," it said. Her voice sounded worried as she added, "Have you talked to Papa?" I groaned and deleted her message. The second one was from Papa. I listened as I drove. It said he had to talk to me 'now'—it was 'urgent'. His voice was strained. I went over a list of awful possibilities in my mind as I followed behind the cruiser. I planned to call him back as soon as I'd parked. But before we'd gotten to Mort's, my cell phone rang again. I answered and asked the caller to hold for a second. We pulled into the parking lot and I rolled down my window. "Guys?" I shouted to the detectives. "Go on in. I've got to take this call. Order me a drink. I'll be inside in a few minutes," I added, holding up my cell phone and wiggling it for them to see. They nodded and turned toward the restaurant.

I looked at the phone in my hand, took a deep breath and tried to keep my voice steady. "Hey, Papa," I said as I stared out over the parking lot. "What's going on? Are you okay?"

CHAPTER 29

Kate and the Detectives at Mort's

Wednesday Evening

A few minutes later I staggered into Mort's. I was dazed. Shirley grabbed my arm and guided me back to the booth where Amy and Carlos were sitting with our drinks. I swung into my side and grabbed the glass of Bourbon that was in front of me. I slugged it down in a single gulp. I realized that all three were looking at me strangely, frowning. But instead of telling them anything, I politely asked Shirley for a refill.

Her eyebrows went to her hairline, but she turned from our table and headed towards the bar. Amy reached out her hand and jiggled my arm which was still attached to the empty glass. "Kate? What's up?" she asked worriedly.

"Was it the phone call?" asked Carlos. "Who was it?"

"Papa."

"What's wrong?"

I know I was rambling when I finally answered. I mumbled something about how he had to call me because he couldn't call his mother. She was still at Vespers Services. She goes every night. He couldn't call Anna, whoever the heck *that* is. He hadn't seen her since she was thirteen and didn't know her number. So he had to call me.

"Kate, you're not making any sense," Amy stated. She gratefully retrieved my second drink from Shirley and pressed it into my hand. "Here. Drink this and start over."

Finally I was able to function. I told them the saga and ended it, saying, "Papa's mother announced his engagement…to Anna! He's getting married!" Then I dissolved into tears and hiccups.

When I lifted my head from the table, Amy and Carlos were sitting stone still, their mouths open. Amy finally blinked and said, "There's got to be some kind of mistake. He's crazy about you!"

I frowned, replayed the phone call in my head and then admitted that Papa had told me not to worry. He'd called because he didn't want me to hear it from anyone but him. (He'd already seen Gloria and knew she'd call me right away.) He'd also said he was going over to his parents' house and straighten things out. I admitted I'd short-circuited and had forgotten that part of the conversation.

"Well then," Carlos sighed. "Everything is cool. You've got nothing to worry about."

Amy and I exchanged glances. I can't say that I was as optimistic as Carlos, but I *did* feel somewhat better. Maybe Carlos was right and that's why I felt better. Or maybe it was the booze.

After dinner the detectives suggested I go back and try to get some rest. They volunteered to drop the two notes off at the Police Station before returning to the motel. I didn't argue, even though I wanted to get Brian Hayslip's take on things.

CHAPTER 30

Kate

Thursday Morning

I need a vacation! And a massage. And some mind-numbing drugs so I can sleep at night. I woke up Thursday morning feeling as though I hadn't slept at all. I must have, because I woke up. But I know I'd tossed and turned all night thinking of Papa. It occurred to me at some point in the middle of the night that the bride in my vision might be the Greek girl (oh yeah, *Anna*) that Mrs. Papadopoulos had in mind for Papa. Yuck! Even though I hadn't recognized the girl, I remembered that she was pretty (the bitch!).

    I dragged myself into the shower, my self-esteem at its lowest point ever! Man, I just wanted to finish this case and get back to Atlanta. The steam shower helped a little. I at least was able to work the kinks out of my neck and shoulders. While I was standing there I thought about Doug Whitaker, our lieutenant who'd recently been acting as though he'd like to start something up with me. If Papa really *did* get married to Anna what was I going to do? End up with someone like Doug?

I mentally kicked myself. That's not very nice of me to put it that way. The 'end up with' thing. Doug's really a very nice, kind person. He's a little more than ten years older than I am and that's not *that* old. We've been friends for several years, so there wouldn't be any surprises. He'd had a tough time coping with his wife's death. I'd felt so bad for him. He was wracked with guilt about her getting caught in the crossfire of a sting operation. It hadn't been his fault! It wasn't anyone's. It was coincidental that she happened to be there. Margo had come out of a shop, noticed Doug across the street and started towards him to say hi. Of course, she (and anyone associated with the police) knew better than to approach a cop when he was on duty. But she just didn't think. She walked right into the line of fire. She didn't die immediately. Whitaker rushed to her and threw himself over her until the shooting was finished. Then he held her, rocking her back and forth, knowing she didn't have a chance. She'd apologized for getting in his way, he told us later. She kept saying she was sorry.

Doug had taken some time off after that, but was stir-crazy and depressed. So he finally came back and worked in the office, behind the scenes for a while. He gradually began to cope better and went back to work as a detective, out on the streets until he was promoted to Lieutenant about three years ago.

As I said, he's a really nice guy and no one should feel like they're 'ending up' with him. He'd make a very good husband. He's thoughtful, understanding, supportive, stable, hard-working, reliable and not too hard on the eyes. Anyone would be lucky to be with someone so…safe. *So what's your problem?* I asked myself.

By that time I was all pruney and my skin was lobster-colored. I shut off the shower. I couldn't spend any more time worrying about Whitaker. Today was Sam Johnson's Memorial Service, and I hoped to talk to Danny at the Bayside Motel Café before having to get ready.

I stuck my head out the door of my room and was pleased to see that the day was going to be warm and sunny. I threw on some comfy clothes and headed towards the café. I figured I'd have time to grab a bite of breakfast, get to the hospital, check on Clem's condition, maybe talk to Sally and still have time to get back to the motel to change before going to the service.

Danny wasn't working this morning, but was sitting in a booth and waved me over as soon as I entered. "Hey! Join me, okay?"

I said sure and slid in across from him as he waved to the girl behind the counter to bring us more coffee.

"I'm glad you showed up. I wanted to talk to you. I figured maybe you'd be in here. I saw Josh last night. He told me about Clem. Man, what a bummer. Have you been to see him this morning?" I shook my head, no. "Josh felt real bad about not saying something to y'all sooner," Danny continued, shaking his head sadly. "Or maybe if I'd seen you just a little earlier you could've figured out what had happened at camp. Maybe this suicide thing could've been headed off, ya know?" He looked up at me, needing reassurance.

"Well, the good thing is that Sally found him right away and the paramedics were there in no time. They did a great job and the last I heard the doctors think he'll be fine. Sally stayed all night at the hospital so she could go in for a few minutes every hour. I'm heading there as soon as I grab a bite to eat. Meanwhile, you can't beat yourself up about this. You and Josh *did* speak up and that's the important thing." I tried to be as kind as possible.

The waitress came to take our orders and poured more coffee. "Can't stay away, huh, Danny?" she teased.

"Nah, I love this place too much!" he answered, giving her a weak smile.

After breakfast, I paid the tab since this was really a 'business' meeting. Danny went back home to see his wife and play with little Becky. I drove to the hospital.

Sally Kim was just outside the ICU door. "They're going to let me in again in a minute," she said with a tired grin. "He's been pretty much out of it all night, but they told me he acts like he'll come around soon."

A nurse motioned for us to come in. "He's more lucid than before and he's mumbling some. Maybe you can understand him better than I can."

We both went in and stood, one on each side of his bed. We leaned in really close to try to make out his words and Sally stroked the back of his hand while he talked.

After a few minutes he stopped and drifted back to sleep. I motioned to Sally to step back outside with me.

"Could you make out much of what he said?" I asked.

"Some. He kept repeating something like 'You shouldn't have done it.' Or 'Why'd you do it?' or something like that. How about you, Ms. Jeffers?"

I rubbed my chin. "I couldn't make out much at all," I admitted. "But he kept shaking his head and I could understand 'no' when he said that."

"I wonder what he was talking about," Sally said. "*Who* shouldn't have done *what*? If he'd been talking about taking the pills, he'd have said 'I shouldn't have…' right?"

I just nodded. I wondered again about his suicide note. He'd not said any specifics about killing the coach. Could it be possible that he found out who really *had* killed him and then decided to take the blame to protect that person? Who would Clem want to protect? His family? Sally? That was a new thought. I hadn't considered Sally before.

I looked over at her. She was staring at me, a look of curiosity on her face. It was as though she could see the wheels turning in my head. Could she have blamed the coach for Clem's personality changes? Would she have been so angry as to try to harm Sam Johnson? I felt like asking her straight out, but decided to give it bit more thought. Instead I said, "I need to think this over. I'm not sure what's going on, but I have some theories."

"What?" she asked excitedly. "Tell me."

But I shook my head. "Not quite yet. Let me do a little checking. I'll let you know as soon as I possibly can. Are you staying here, Sally, or are you going to go home and rest?"

"I'll stay here for a while longer. Can I have your cell number in case Clem starts talking again?"

I thought that was a brilliant idea and jotted it down for her. "I know you can't use your phone inside the hospital, so I won't try to call you," I said, "but I'll leave mine on vibrate so even if I'm somewhere I can't answer right away, you'll be able to get me. I'll call you back as soon as I can.

"Oh," I added, "are you planning on going to the memorial service?"

"No, ma'am. I can't do anything for Coach, but I might be able to do something for Clem."

"I understand completely," I said…and meant it.

CHAPTER 31

Kate

Thursday Morning

I left the hospital mulling things over in my mind. I just couldn't picture Sally Kim being involved in any sort of nefarious plot against Coach Johnson or anyone else, for that matter. She was the picture of innocence. She couldn't be that good an actress. I know that we need to look at the facts in every case, but in the past my intuitions about people have almost always led me in the right direction. So I was going to trust myself again and concentrate on other suspects—if, indeed, there were suspects at all!

I still had a couple of hours before the memorial service and didn't want to think about Papa, so I decided to keep busy. First, I needed to touch base with Police Chief Hayslip. Luckily, he was in his office when I arrived at the station. I was waved back by the officer on duty at the front desk.

"Glad you stopped by," he began. "I was just going to have somebody track you down for me. I've been going over those notes that Detective Williams dropped off last night—you know, the one written to you from Josh and then Clem's note..." he added, his voice trailing off. He shook his head. "I'm going over to the Tysons' before I go to the memorial service. I'm going to show them the notes. I want to watch their reactions. I was hoping you'd come as well."

"Sure!" I agreed. "I'd like to be there. I noticed a few inconsistencies in Clem's note and would like to be there when his parents find out he confessed to killing Johnson. What time are you going over?"

We decided on a time to meet, then poured over the two notes a couple more times.

It was a beautiful morning, so I drove to the high school and sat outside at one of the tables in the courtyard. I pulled my notes out of my trusty black bag to look over again.

The thing that kept bugging me the most was Dr. Graves' findings. Johnson's INR levels were so high—even after his death. Could that possibly have been caused merely by the Coumadin that Dr. Sanchez had prescribed? Or had someone here in Conroy 'helped it along' by trying to poison him?

The other issue I kept coming back to was Clem Tyson and his family. Had Clem really poisoned Sam Johnson? Or was he trying to protect someone else? Why had Larry Tyson become almost violent towards me? Did he know something? He'd supposedly been very supportive of Johnson and his football program. I found it hard to believe that he would have been involved. If he *had* done something to the coach, I doubt that he'd have tried to poison him. It just didn't fit Larry Tyson's personality. He'd have beaten him up or something like that! Mr. Tyson was volatile and impulsive. No way would he have secretly planned the coach harm.

So—who's left? Carla. Clem's mom. I considered the situation from her point of view: Her son had been having headaches and violent outbursts. She didn't like the football program all that much to begin with. She'd stated that she saw things she disapproved of at the school. She'd also commented that when she tried to get others involved, they'd refused to speak out against Johnson or his methods. She certainly hadn't received any support from her husband. Carla Tyson had access to the school's supply of rat poison—and the coach's food. *Hmm. And she does have blue eyes!*

I wondered what I'd have done had I been in her position. For starters, I'd never kill someone. But would she have? Could she have been *that* distraught?

Just then I saw her emerge from the back door of the cafeteria. I glanced at my cell to check the time. I only had a few more minutes until I had to meet Chief Hayslip and go to the Tysons' house. I wondered if Carla was aware that Hayslip was on his way to her house. I didn't have enough time to get into a heavy discussion with her, nor was I sure of what I wanted to say. But I quickly stuffed all my notes back into my bag and hurried after her. She'd reached her car by the time I'd caught up with her.

She just shook her head at me, saying, "I can't talk now. I want to stop by the hospital again before I go home and Larry just called to say the Chief wants to talk to us. Then I've got to get ready for the service."

"But—" I began, but she interrupted.

"Anyway, Larry won't let me talk to you anymore. He's furious about this whole thing. He told me to stay away from you." She jumped in the car and started it up. She didn't allow her eyes to meet mine.

"Okay, Carla," I said. "I'll back off. I don't want you to have to deal with any more than you already are. Go ahead and go." (Like she would have stuck around if I'd wanted her to.) She nearly took off my toes bombing out of the parking lot. I watched her go, thanking my lucky stars I wasn't in her position.

I headed to my own car, calling Carlos's cell as I went. I filled him in on the situation. We decided perhaps *he* should go to Tysons' with Chief Hayslip. Carlos promised to be there on time. I slid into the seat and punched in the Chief's number. He was just leaving his office and agreed that I should make myself scarce for a while. He and Carlos would let me know the results of their conversation after Johnson's memorial service.

My nerves jangled as I headed back to the motel. I wished I could make myself invisible so I could witness the discussion at the Tysons'. I *really* wanted to see their faces! I'd tried to impress that point on Carlos and I knew how good he is at his job. He'd tune in to their body language. But it really *bugged* me not to be there, too!

I muttered all the way back to the Bayside Motel. Amy was waiting outside her room when I pulled up. "Oh good, you're here. Carlos just left, so I'm going to ride with you. Hurry up. Change and meet me back here a.s.a.p."

It appeared that everyone in Conroy was at Sam Johnson's Memorial Service. Everyone that is, except for the Tysons and Sally Kim. I was sure that Carla and Larry had been blown away by the notes that Brian Hayslip had shown them. I'd seen Carlos and the Police Chief slip into the school gymnasium after the service had started. Both had looked grim. They'd had to sit way across the gym from us and didn't look our way. Amy and I both sat there wishing we could read their minds. We were dying to find out what had gone down at the Tyson home.

The entire floor of the gym had been littered with baskets and bouquets of flowers. I remember thinking I'd be lucky not to have an allergy attack before the day was over! I drummed my fingers on my knees and listened to over two hours of funeral directors, ministers and friends extolling Sam Johnson's virtues. My back was killing me and I was beyond relieved when the uneventful service finally came to an end!

I felt (somewhat) guilty and knew that I'd have felt differently if I'd known the guy, but man, these things drag on forever! *Now* most people were going to the cafeteria for a reception! Part of me felt like I should be there, but more of me wanted to escape! More importantly, Amy and I needed get together with Hayslip and Carlos! I also figured that the reception would go on for *hours*. We could always go later, if necessary.

We finally caught up with the two men and hustled them into one of the empty offices near the gymnasium, closing the door firmly behind us.

CHAPTER 32

Papa's Lounge

Earlier Thursday Morning

Demetri was already at the bar when Papa arrived Thursday morning. That was unusual, but Papa didn't think too much about it as he began to restock the bottles before doing the books.

Demetri leaned on the counter, arms crossed, silently watching his friend and boss. Papa finally looked up and asked, "What? What's with you?"

"That's what I want to know!" Demetri said heatedly. "What's with *you*?!"

Papa wiped his hands on a bar cloth and set it on the counter. Then he pulled up a bar stool and sat down, waiting for his friend to continue. Demetri glared at him for a few moments. Suddenly, he said, "You don't know, do you? This is incredible!" And he ran his fingers through his curly black hair.

Papa looked so completely baffled that Demetri finally continued. "Your Anna is *MY* Anna!"

"WHAT?"

"You heard me. I talked to Anna last night. She told me all about her father and your mother's plan to marry off the two of you! So what do you have to say for yourself?"

Papa was dumbfounded. He stared at Demetri for a few seconds. He grabbed the bar towel and rubbed it over his face. "I don't believe this! Anna is the girl you were telling me about yesterday?" Papa scrubbed his face again with the towel.

Demetri nodded. "I called her after I left here last night. She was crying. Nothing I said made her stop. I offered to go over to her house, but she said no. I felt useless!"

"Well, I *couldn't* call her because I can't remember her last name! I haven't laid eyes on Anna for years! And I never *did* get hold of my mother! I think she must've been hiding at St. Constantine's. Instead, I paced the floor, drank too much and Kate was the only one I got to talk with!"

Demetri felt a little better after realizing his best friend wasn't actually plotting behind his back to steal his girl. So to lighten the moment he said, "I'll bet Kate was pleased."

Papa swore—very loudly. Demetri hadn't heard such a string of four-letter words since they'd been learning to swear—way back when they'd been kids. Papa hadn't lost the knack.

"Kate didn't have a lot so say. She sort of mumbled and I'd overheard her asking Amy to order her a drink. Sounded a wee bit shocked, if you get my drift. I imagine her night was pretty bad. She *did* say that she'd try to finish up on the Conroy case and get back home soon so we could talk. I guess if I'm smart, I'll give her another call real soon.

Papa continued, "At least I know that Anna will be in good hands. Yours! It won't be like I'm ditching her at the altar. I was up half the night trying to figure out how to let her down easily. Sounds like she feels the same way I do about this. Hot damn—that's a relief! Now that you and I are on the same page, I know she'll be taken care of."

"What about your mother—and Anna's father?"

"Hmm," Papa groaned. "Several times last night I considered slitting my mother's throat. Short of that, I don't know. You know how she is when she gets something stuck in her head. But, the good news is that she really likes you, so if I can convince her that you're the better man…"

The friends looked at each other, nodded and smiled. Papa added, "Then we'll only have to worry about Anna's dad."

Demetri grunted and the two men began polishing glasses again. "Uh, Papa? You might want to use a clean cloth," he added, eyeing the sweaty bar towel in Papa's hand.

CHAPTER 33

The Tysons' Home

Thursday Afternoon

Carla and Larry Tyson watched through their front window as Police Chief Brian Hayslip and Detective Carlos Williams walked back down the steps and got into their vehicles. Carla slumped onto her husband's chest as he pulled her closer and put his arm around her shoulder.

"What was the kid thinking?" Larry asked his wife. "Saying he'd killed Johnson. Why do you suppose he wrote that?"

Carla began to weep again. "He was trying to protect me. Remember in the note when he said he'd heard us talking? He must've meant when I told you about the rat poison. I only gave the stupid man just a little of it—only once before the picnic and then again that day—it shouldn't have been enough. I looked it up. You have to use a bunch of it before it works. I don't know what happened!" She broke down, sobbing.

Larry helped her over to their couch. The two of them sat side-by-side in shock. Carla was the first to recover. "I'm not going to that bastard's funeral!" she announced. "He can rot in Hell!" She turned to face her husband. "You saw that note that Josh wrote! I *knew* something had happened at camp. Why didn't Clem say something? Why didn't he tell us?"

"I've been doing a lot of thinking lately, Carla. He didn't say anything because I wouldn't have believed him. I would've said the same thing as the coach. I'd have called him a pansy, too," Larry admitted sorrowfully. He leaned forward and rested his elbows on his knees. "Don't worry, honey, we'll get through this somehow. And…I'm really sorry, Carla. I should have listened to you." His eyes welled up.

Carla buried her face in her hands and wailed, "I can't let Clem take the blame for this. I've got to tell them what I did."

"No, honey, not yet. Don't say anything yet. I agree that we can't let Clem be blamed. We won't let that happen. But…just let me think about this for a while, okay?

"And you're right. We're *not* going to the service. Come on, get yourself pulled together and we'll go see our boy."

CHAPTER 34

Conroy Memorial Hospital

Thursday Afternoon

"Hey," Sally greeted the Tysons as they came towards the ICU Unit. "I thought y'all were going to the service. But I'm so glad you're here. There's a neurologist in with Clem—Dr. Sanders. Clem woke up just after you left this morning, Mrs. Tyson, so they called the doctor and he came just a little bit ago! The nurses made me wait out here since I'm not really family. But they'll probably want you to go in. Let's ask, okay?"

Sally felt giddy as she led Clem's parents to the nurses' station. The one nurse jumped up when she noticed them and exclaimed that yes, they should go in to hear what the doctor had to say. Sally was glad that the emergency room doctor from the previous night wasn't anywhere around. He would have probably objected to all of them traipsing in there.

Dr. Sanders was just finishing up with Clem. He offered to step outside while Clem's parents cried and hugged their son for a moment, but he requested they join him shortly since he had other patients to see.

A minute later the Tysons hurried out into the hallway. Carla squeezed Sally's hand and said, "He smiled at us…" and then turned her attention to Dr. Sanders.

Sally wanted to hear what the doctor said too, but slipped back into Clem's room. Clem was groggy, but awake. "Hey," Sally said tentatively. They'd removed most of the tubes so Clem was able to talk a little, but his voice was still raspy. Sally poured a small glass of water, added a bendy straw and raised the top of Clem's hospital bed.

"You're pretty good at all this nursing stuff," he said and smiled. His voice was still scratchy, but it was a lot easier to understand than it had been earlier.

"I've had quite a bit of practice, you know," Sally answered. "Clem, I don't know what all this is about or what is really going on, but…" She had to stop for a moment. She wasn't sure she could get through this. She took a deep breath and continued, "I'm sure glad there weren't very many pills in that bottle. I don't think I could've gone on without you."

Clem had been looking at her, but then turned his head away. "I'm sorry, Sal. It's just that I can't seem to do anything right these days—not even kill myself." He swept a hand around the room. "Just look at this. It's pathetic!"

That made Sally mad. "Just stop it! Don't talk like this! I mean it. I'd be lost without you. You're going to have to start talking and telling me—or *someone*—what's bugging you! What's this self-destruct button you've been pushing? Where did this come from? You've never been like this before…"

"Exactly," he answered tiredly. "Don't you see, Sally? That's just it. I'm not myself anymore."

Sally felt terrible! "I'm sorry. I didn't mean to yell. But you scared me so badly! I don't want anything to happen to you. I've been so worried! Not just the past couple days, but for several weeks. You've got to talk about what's going on with you!"

She realized she was squeezing the life out of Clem's hand and started to let go. But he kept holding on—just not quite as tightly. "You know after I got back from camp and I had that lump on my head?" She nodded. "Well, that doctor that was just in here said that the CAT scan showed some kind of head injury and that maybe that's what's been going on with me."

"I knew it! I talked to that lady cop from Atlanta and then to your mom and that's what we decided! I was coming over to tell you and then…that's when I found you…" She stopped talking, remembering how helpless and scared she'd felt.

Clem saw Sally's eyes cloud over and said, "*You* found me? Sally…I'm sorry." A minute later, he added, "Thanks."

That brought Sally back to the present. She smiled at him. "So," she said, forcing her voice to sound cheerful, "if that's all that's going on, then no problem, right? We'll work through this and when the swelling goes down in your brain, you'll be just fine!"

"I don't know. The doctor said that sometimes it takes a long time to recover if the injury is serious. He said some people never get all the way back to normal. He told me I hadn't fractured my skull, but it can be pretty bad anyway…" Clem began to cough.

"Stop talking so much and have a little more water," Sally urged. "That tube they stuck down your throat will make your throat sore for a while. Just keep sipping the water."

"First you yell at me to talk and then you tell me to shut up!" Clem said after he'd taken a couple sips. He smiled weakly and Sally felt better than she had in weeks. Maybe she'd have her 'old' Clem back before too long!

A nurse appeared and scolded, "Your ten minutes is *way* over! Get out of here and let this boy rest! Go on…!" She shooed Sally out of the room, muttering under her breath, "These kids, they think the rules don't apply…"

Sally joined Clem's parents in the hallway. "They won't let us go back in," Carla announced. "That nurse was mumbling something about 'no respect for the rules' when she passed by. She glared at us and said 'NO MORE VISITORS!'"

"I think she's about to go on break," Sally informed them. "Give her a minute and you'll probably be able to sneak back in. The other nurse said they're planning to move him to a regular room this afternoon, so we won't have to worry about the ICU rules anymore. If that's the case, they must feel like he's doing well enough. So she'll let you bend the rules a little. It's only that one nurse that's such a stickler.

"Oh! I almost forgot. Tell me what the neurologist had to say."

The Tysons described their conversation with Dr. Sanders. The Tysons decided to hang around to see if they could talk to Clem again. Sally announced her plan to get something to eat. She hadn't left the ICU since Clem's arrival.

Clem's parents, who were staying, finally were able to convince Sally to go home. At last she agreed, with the understanding that they would call her if anything happened, good, bad or otherwise.

CHAPTER 35

Conroy High School

Thursday Afternoon

Chief Hayslip, Amy, Carlos and I were still in the vacant office next to the cafeteria and had almost finished going over the Tyson situation when someone knocked at the door. It was the former assistant football coach, Andy Menendez.

"Ah," Chief Hayslip said. "Come on in, Andy. I need to show you something." He passed Menendez a copy of the note that Josh had written about summer camp.

Coach Menendez read through it. Then he looked up at the four faces watching intently. "Well, this is the first I've heard about this. I *do* remember going over to Keith and Josh, asking them to help Clem to the showers. That's all I remember about it. Clem looked hot and his buddies were concerned, but that's it. I didn't know about his fall. That must have happened when I was inside. As I recall, Sam was angry about something, but he wouldn't talk about it. Just stormed around for a while and then got over it, you know?" He shrugged and looked at the group, hopefully.

Then Hayslip passed Clem's note to Menendez. He frowned while reading it and grimaced. "Oh, my God," he said when he was finished and passed a hand across his ashen face. He looked up at Chief Hayslip, speechless.

"The note was found in the boy's bedroom and we're doing some checking. You know he is still in the hospital after what was apparently a suicide attempt. But until he talks, we really don't know what's going on. We're not convinced that Clem Tyson had an opportunity to kill Johnson, but we're checking out all leads. It could be that he's trying to cover up for someone else. We just don't have all the facts yet. Andy, this is all strictly on the Q.T., you know. Not a word to anyone. I think we're close, real close to finding out what actually happened. But as I said, we're still gathering the facts."

"Yeah. I understand. Tyson was dealing with some issues lately and it showed. But killing Sam? That's hard to believe.

"Oh! That reminds me of why I knocked on the door in the first place. I just had a text message from Sally Kim on my cell phone. It seems Clem's awake and able to talk!"

I grabbed my cell out of my bag. Sally had sent me a message as well. The meeting ended abruptly with Amy and Carlos agreeing to stay at the reception that was still going on in the school cafeteria. Chief Hayslip and I raced to the hospital.

CHAPTER 36

Conroy Memorial Hospital

Late Thursday

Hayslip screeched to a halt and killed the engine. He and I jumped out of his vehicle almost before it stopped and tore through the lobby to the ICU Unit. Clem was on a gurney, being pushed down a side hall away from us. I started to panic. It was headed in the direction of the Morgue. I freaked, fearing the worst.

A second man came out of Clem's room, carrying a bag of his personal belongings. He must've seen the look on my face because he said, "Don't worry, ma'am. He's just being transferred to another room."

I stopped dead in my tracks. I allowed myself a minute to regain my breath and get my heartbeat out of the stratosphere. Hayslip commented on my lack of color and told me to put my head between my knees. That's not an easy thing to do when standing in the middle of the hallway! He guided me to a bench and we sat down. I followed his instructions and in a couple minutes the roaring sound in my ears subsided.

"We can't talk to him until they've got him settled anyway, so just relax," he said to me. Then he looked at me and asked, "Are you always like this?"

I almost smiled. "Only when I think someone has just died on us!"

"Okay. I just wondered." He tried, unsuccessfully, to hide his smile.

We gave them a few minutes to get Clem into his new digs and then went to see him. His parents were anxiously waiting outside the room. Carla started to smile at the Chief and then saw me. Her smile faded quickly. Larry never *did* smile.

"Oops," I whispered. "Want me to get lost?"

"No, just let me do the talking," he murmured, not moving his lips.

Fine with me, I thought. *I'm just a chicken. You go right on ahead.*

Hayslip nodded to the Tysons and we both listened while Carla complained that they'd only gotten to see Clem for a second. "Haven't even gotten to talk to him yet." The neurologist hadn't told them much of anything. He wanted to meet with all of them again Friday morning. "And then, to top things off, they tossed us out of Clem's room so they could move him down the hall!"

The orderlies emerged from Clem's new room and stopped short when they saw Chief Hayslip. He stepped aside for a second to talk to the men and I was left alone with Clem's parents. Awkward. I murmured something along the lines of, "Gee, it's nice that Clem's doing better…"

Hayslip returned, saying that he was going to request that the Tysons remain outside for a few minutes longer. They were *not* pleased. And when I followed the chief into Clem's room, they were even *less* pleased!

Clem looked worn out, as though the trip down the hallway had almost done him in. We promised not to stay too long. He needed to visit with his parents and get some rest. But we really needed to talk to him—before anyone else did.

"Son," Hayslip began, "I need to ask you some serious questions and I need to get straight answers. Understand?" He sounded gruff to me. I'd give him all the straight answers he wanted if it were me lying there!

Clem nodded and answered, "Yessir."

"First, I need you to explain yourself."

"I put everything in my note, sir."

"Not everything! I want you to explain exactly how you killed your coach."

Clem stared at his hands. Finally he answered, "Rat poison."

"Where did you get it and how did you get him to take it?"

Clem looked up at the ceiling, his eyes shifting over to the left. *A sure sign he's making this up*, I thought.

You see, if someone is actually trying to *remember* something, they look up and to the right. It stimulates that side of the brain to work. But if a person is lying, that is trying to *make up* an answer; they look to the left to stimulate their imagination!

"I bought it and I slipped it in his coffee."

I spoke up. "He doesn't drink coffee, Clem. Detective Stevens found out from Sherry Johnson that they both drink only tea. They gave up coffee several years ago."

Clem blanched.

Then Hayslip dropped the bombshell. "Yeah, and someone else already confessed to killing the coach. We know that person's telling the truth! So…"

That was a lie, but Hayslip never missed a beat. He stared right through Clem and we both watched him crumble.

"I told her not to say anything else…that when you saw the note you'd stop the investigation! Why'd she do it? Why couldn't she just shut up for once? I had it covered." He closed his eyes and shook his head, mumbling, "Damn it, Mom."

Bingo! That's what I'd been waiting for.

CHAPTER 37

Conroy Memorial Hospital

Thursday Evening

The chief surprised me when we left Clem's room. He merely nodded to the Tysons and told them they could go in. He didn't mention anything about what Clem had just told us. I followed him mutely down the corridor to an empty waiting room. We went in and Hayslip shut the door behind us. I looked at him expectantly.

He was not forthcoming. Instead he asked, "Well, what do you think?" as he sat down in an arm chair.

"For starters," I began, pacing the floor and trying to put my thoughts in order, "we can be pretty sure that Clem didn't kill Johnson—would you agree?"

Chief Hayslip nodded. "Right. And Clem implicated his mother. No need to say anything to her. She's not going anywhere. We can pull her in any time if we need to. To tell you the truth, I'm not so sure what her involvement is," he added.

"Do you think she's totally innocent and that Clem was just trying to cover up for her because he *thought* she'd poisoned the coach?"

"Maybe. Look at what the boy said in his note. He'd 'overheard' his parents talking and heard his mom 'taking things into her own hands' concerning the coach. She could have been talking about anything…from writing him a nasty letter to…going to the school board to complain…to…the list is endless!"

"True," I agreed. "So then when Johnson collapsed, Clem could've added two and two and come up with five."

"Right. However, when Detective Williams and I showed the Tysons Clem's note, Carla turned six shades of white and started to shake. I was sure she'd say something if she'd been the one who'd poisoned Johnson."

"Yeah, that bugs me, too. I can't imagine a parent letting a child confess to something he didn't do." We sat thoughtfully for a moment. "But then again, reading your child's suicide note would make any parent shake. I can't think of much worse than that! Maybe she was reacting to the note in general. I wish I could have been there with you."

"So do I, but with Larry Tyson's volatile nature, your presence would have been a very bad move on our part."

I stopped my pacing and sat down opposite the chief. "The real bummer is that we've got no proof of anything," I complained. "For all we know Carla had nothing to do with Johnson's death, Clem's confession is bogus and the man died from complications of the anti-coagulants that Dr. Sanchez had prescribed."

We sat in silence for a minute. Then I added, "But it just doesn't *feel* right."

Hayslip grunted his assent.

"Why would I keep having visions about an angry woman and the football team if there wasn't a connection?" I asked, more to myself than to the chief.

There wasn't any answer to that, so Hayslip sat silently, drumming his fingers on the arm of his chair, watching me. I felt like he expected me to pull a rabbit out of a hat or something else just as dramatic, but I couldn't. I was feeling more frustrated by the minute!

My eyes wandered and I looked out the glass door in time to see Carla and Larry Tyson heading our way. They were deep in conversation, heads together, eyes on the floor. I could tell they were having a serious discussion. They were arguing about something. Carla was gesturing with her hands and Larry was shaking his head and saying something like, "No, no." I couldn't hear him, but could read his lips.

"Do you see that?" I whispered, nodding towards the pair in the hallway.

"Yeah," Chief Hayslip answered. "I wonder what they're arguing about. Maybe Clem's confession? Do you suppose Mom is having a bit of trouble with that?"

"Could be," I replied. We watched as they exited the building and walked towards the parking lot. Larry held the door open for Carla, cradling her elbow in his hand. "They may be disagreeing about something, but at least he's not angry with her. Did you see that body language?"

"Yep."

We remained silent for a couple more minutes. Hayslip slapped his hands on his thighs and said, "We're not going to get anything else accomplished tonight. Why don't we call it a day?"

I agreed. I was completely burnt out. I couldn't think straight any longer. "Maybe things will be clearer after some sleep. I think I'll stop in to see Dr. Graves at the Morgue in the morning. Maybe he'll have some words of wisdom for us.

"Oh, did you hear what time the neurologist is supposed to meet with the Tysons?"

"Nah," Hayslip replied. "You know doctors. They're independent cusses. He told them to be here in the morning and he'd see them when he could. He'll be making his rounds. You know a doctor's time is more precious than anyone else's," he added sarcastically.

We hoisted ourselves out of our chairs. Hayslip rubbed his hand over his face as we made our way out of the hospital.

Just stepping outside helped me feel better. There's something about a hospital that is so tiring. No matter what time of day or night I'm in one, I feel instantly exhausted. Maybe it's the smell. Or the lighting. Or the hushed voices. Or the worried faces of the visitors. Or the determined looks of concentration on the faces of the medical staff as they hustle past.

I paused before getting into my car just to take a few deep breaths of the night air. Cool, refreshing, autumn air. I looked up, pleasantly surprised to see so many stars. I glanced at Hayslip's taillights as he pulled out of the lot. Then I looked at the stars again. I could see Orion's belt and the Big Dipper. Granted, those are about the only constellations I know, but somehow it felt reassuring. It's rare to see this many stars in Atlanta. I was anxious to get back home, but at least being out of the city afforded me a long look at the vastness of our universe.

In that frame of mind, I made my way back to the Bayside Motel.

CHAPTER 38

Kate

Friday Morning

As soon as I was up and showered I hurried over to the café. I was secretly pleased that Danny wasn't working—I wasn't in the mood for idle chat. I ordered a fried egg sandwich and two large coffees to go, one with some ice added. I wanted to catch Dr. Graves before he got too involved in his daily routine to see me.

I balanced the sandwich and coffees on one hand, the top lid tucked under my chin, while I unlocked my car and opened the door. I was proud of myself for not dumping the whole mess down my front! Depositing the food and drink on the center console, I climbed in and immediately chugged the first coffee—the one with the ice. It was a bit weak, I admit, but at least it was cool enough to gulp. I'd been experiencing caffeine withdrawal!

I drove to the Morgue, munching my egg sandwich. If this had been Atlanta, I'd have had enough time to eat a seven-course meal in the time it would take me to get across town. But here in Conroy, I was in the hospital parking lot before I'd finished licking my fingers. I'd forgotten to grab a napkin. (Grandmother Jeffers would have rolled her eyes and called me uncouth, had she seen what had just transpired!)

I scrounged around in my big black bag. Flashlight, that stupid pair of panty hose…you'd think I'd have some of those wipey thingies…I've got everything else in there! Finally I found a semi-used tissue to wipe the grease off my lips and give my hands the once-over.

I lowered my visor and flipped open the mirror. I smiled into it to make sure there were no stray bits of egg between my teeth. Just a couple. Then I reapplied the dab of lip gloss that I'd eaten off earlier. That little task accomplished, I glanced into my bag again to make sure I had all my case folders and notes, grabbed the hot cup of coffee and made my way inside the Morgue.

Stan Thomas was at his tiny desk again. He must be getting used to me popping in every now and then, because he didn't even flinch when I opened the door.

"Ms. Jeffers…Good morning," he greeted me in his quiet voice.

"Hey," I whispered back. It's funny how everyone wants to be real quiet around dead people.

"Doc Graves got here just a few minutes ago. I'll let him know you're here, but I can't promise that he'll be able to see you. They just brought in an accident victim, so he may have his hands full."

Literally! I thought, my stomach turning.

Hesitantly, he opened the steel door that separated his office from the rest of the facility and turned to me, grimacing. "I hate going in here," he admitted, "even when we're empty!"

Stan Thomas disappeared and the heavy door swung shut with a creak. I opened my second coffee and took a few sips. He finally returned, looking pale. "Gives me the willies!"

The door squeaked shut again and I gritted my teeth. The place wouldn't be nearly as creepy if they'd put a little 3-in-1 oil on those hinges. It sounded like something out of a bad horror flick!

Indeed, Dr. Graves had his hands full, so couldn't meet with me. That was really okay by me. I hadn't wanted anything in particular anyway. I was simply scrounging for any clues at all. ("You're grasping at straws, Katherine," Grandmother Phelps would say.)

"The doc wanted me to tell you that the tox results came back and that he'd been right. He said you'd understand what that meant." Stan Thomas shrugged at me, looking hopeful.

I did. The results confirmed that Johnson had somehow ingested far more warfarin that his regular medication could possibly have provided. This was exciting news! It meant that we had not been wasting our time in Conroy—that someone really had tried to poison him! *But could we prove it?*

I drove around, sipping my coffee, thinking about Sam Johnson's death. Clem Tyson had confessed, but I just couldn't buy it. Who else should we consider? Who else could have had access to both poison and the coach's food?

Of course, my first thought was of the coach's family. Anyone who was in the house would have had easy access to Johnson's food. But with two little kids, would anyone keep poison around? I decided I should pay a visit to Sherry Johnson later in the day.

Next, I considered someone like Shirley, the waitress at Mort's. Restaurant people would have access to rat poisons and other insecticides. Did Sam Johnson eat at Mort's? I doubted it since he was such a health nut. But were there other restaurants in the area where he would have eaten? Possibly. I would need to check that out.

Then I thought of the high school. I kept coming back to that. Johnson ate there on a daily basis. They even prepared special food, specifically for him. Every single staff member wandered in and out of the kitchen all day. Anyone could have tainted his food! That brought Carla to mind again. Always, my little brain ended up thinking about Carla.

I pulled over to the curb and jotted down a few notes. Then I called Sherry Johnson to set up a time to meet. She wasn't available until the middle of the afternoon. When I hung up and looked around, I realized that I was awfully close to the riding stables. I had a couple hours to kill, so I decided to take advantage of the pretty morning and a little free time.

Mrs. Turley seemed happy to see me. She was curious about the investigation, so I shared what little I could with her. I was as reassuring as possible when she asked if I thought there could be repercussions for the stables in connection with Sam Johnson's fall.

We talked horses over a cup of coffee and Mrs. T. decided I should ride Fella. He turned out to be a beautiful bay. I watched as she saddled him for me, noting that she left the girth quite loose. I'd need to be careful.

Matt, one of her trail guides, offered to ride with me, but Mrs. T. said she'd rather go with me herself. It was a slow morning and she hadn't ridden all week. She saddled Winnie, the one Sam Johnson had ridden, for herself.

The morning had become bright and sunny—simply perfect in my estimation. The riding trail was so picturesque! It followed a bubbling little stream that wound through the woods. I mentioned how much cooler it was there than in the city.

"Yes, that's one reason so many Atlantans come out here. They say there's at least a fifteen degree difference," Mrs. T. agreed.

As we rode on, I told her that Gloria and some of my other friends would love the trail. She again offered free lessons to those who would need it and encouraged us all to come soon and often. I felt sure we'd take her up on her offer.

CHAPTER 39

Conroy Memorial Hospital

Friday Morning

Dr. Sanders, the neurologist, glanced over the Tyson boy's test results before entering the room. He closed the file, having glanced at the names once more, then pushed open the door to Clem's private room.

"Good morning, Clem. How are you feeling this morning?" he asked. He nodded to the two concerned-looking adults. "Mr. and Mrs. Tyson…or would you prefer to be called Larry and Carla?"

Mr. Tyson folded his arms across his chest and scowled. "Larry, he's just trying to be nice," Carla scolded. To the doctor, she said, "Larry and Carla is fine."

"I'd hoped to get here a little earlier, but there was an emergency."

Carla hurried to say, "That's perfectly fine. We've only been here about half an hour and it's good just to be able to talk to our boy."

"Good. Let's all sit down and I'll share Clem's test results with you. Then we'll cover what you can expect once he's back home."

Carla sat on the foot of Clem's propped-up hospital bed. The two men took the chairs.

"Will he be allowed to come home soon?" Carla asked anxiously.

"That's not my call, ma'am," the doctor answered amicably. "But I'm meeting with Clem's team of doctors this afternoon. They'll be able to tell you more after that. Let me put it this way. As far as *I'm* concerned, if Clem stays on his medication and sees his regular doctor every couple of weeks to monitor his progress, there's no reason for him to stay cooped up in here any longer." He shot a smile at Clem, who sat up straighter. The boy looked ready to bolt.

"Hold on there, son," the doctor continued. "Before we can let you go, there are some important things that you and your parents need to know. First of all, as we discussed briefly yesterday, your CAT scan showed signs of swelling in the brain. That appears to have been caused by your fall several weeks ago during football camp. From what you've told me about that afternoon, I'm pretty certain that you experienced heat exhaustion as well. It's not *that* uncommon in athletes, but there are still ways to avoid it. You need to drink plenty of fluids—water or sports drinks. Soda pops or iced teas don't do the trick. Certainly not alcohol. You also need to take frequent breaks and rest in the shade." He looked at Clem. "Something tells me that the team didn't follow those rules that day."

"No, sir," answered Clem. "We were allowed to have water breaks, but we were working out at the stadium and there wasn't any shade nearby."

The doctor nodded. "It's also good sense to wear loose, lightweight clothing. Changing the subject slightly, do you recall what the weather was like the week of summer camp?"

"It was in the mid-nineties. And we wore full pads during the two-a-days."

Dr. Sanders sat silently for a moment, staring at Clem's file in his hands. "You know what, Clem?" he said, looking up. "You may not think so at the moment, but you should consider yourself lucky. You were a smart young man to sit down when you did. I know it takes a lot of guts to stand up to a coach, but if you hadn't, your condition might have progressed to heat stroke instead of mere heat exhaustion."

"I wasn't trying to disrespect the coach, sir. I just couldn't stand up any longer. I knew I'd keel over if I didn't sit down."

"Well, whatever the reason, be glad you did. Let me explain a bit about heat stroke. It is much more serious. It can even be fatal if it's not caught and treated immediately. Sometimes a person will have the same symptoms that you had: nausea, vomiting, weakness, fatigue…but other times the person can skip all those and go straight to the symptoms of heat stroke.

"The most serious problem with heat stroke is the elevation of the body's temperature. Normally the body acts as its own air conditioner. A person gets hot and the person sweats. The sweat evaporates and this cools him off. I'm giving you a sixth-grade science lesson here and when you get home, you'll probably want to look up all this on your computer, but meanwhile, keep what I'm saying in mind.

"If you notice someone who is hot and should be sweating, but isn't, consider that a red flag. Instead of the person's skin being moist or clammy, a person who is having heat stroke may have hot, red or flushed, dry skin. His pulse will be rapid. He may have difficulty getting his breath. The person often gets confused, is disoriented or just acts strange. His temperature may reach 106 degrees—*way* above the normal 98.6!"

Nervous, Carla jumped up and walked across the tiny room. Larry got up from his chair and stood by her, their backs to the window.

The doctor continued, "If the victim doesn't get cooled off immediately, he could have a seizure or lapse into a coma. He could even die."

Clem's eyes were wide with surprise. "I didn't know any of this!" he said, a little shakily.

"I'm not telling you this to scare you, but you need to be aware."

Carla elbowed Larry in the ribs. "See? I knew they were working those boys too hard at that camp! I was right to be worried, wasn't I? What if Clem had heat stroke and died?!"

"Okay, Carla, calm down. Just listen to what else the doctor has to say."

Clem spoke up. "How do you get someone who's had heat stroke cooled off?"

"You've got to get him out of the sun. The shade is okay, but an air-conditioned room is even better. Loosen or remove some of his clothes. Get hold of some water and apply it—with cloths if you have them—or dip his shirt in it and hold it against his forehead. Fan the person to get the water to evaporate.

"I heard of one man who turned his backyard hose on his mother. She was furious since she'd just had her hair done. But she forgave him when she realized he'd saved her life!

"Now, ice water would *not* be a good idea. It could put someone into shock. Cool or lukewarm water is best. But you *could* put ice packs under his arms or around the groin area—that would be okay. The idea is to get the person's temperature back down to manageable—say 101 or 102 degrees. Meanwhile, you've got to get him to a hospital, so have someone call 911 while you're getting him cooled off. Otherwise, he's going to have permanent damage. I'm talking brain damage, folks."

Clem gulped. "I guess I *was* lucky," he said weakly. He looked over at his father. Larry had one arm around a quietly-weeping Carla. The other hung loosely at his side.

Dr. Sanders' pager buzzed. At the same time, his name could be heard over the hospital's speaker. He looked at his pager and frowned. Glancing at the three Tysons, he said, "You'll have to excuse me. I'm needed in the emergency room. I've given you plenty to think about for a while, but I got sidetracked. I still need to discuss Clem's treatment with all three of you. You'll still need to deal with the head injury for the next several weeks until the swelling goes down. Are you going to be here later this afternoon? If you are, I'll stop by and go over what you and Clem need to know about head trauma."

They all nodded and watched as Dr. Sanders hurried from the room. Carla wearily sat in one of the chairs. "I had no idea…"

They sat in silence until they heard a knock at the door. Sally stuck her head inside to announce, "Here comes lunch! Hey, why's everyone looking so glum?"

Clem told her what the doctor had said. "Wow! But look at it this way, Clem. You lucked out! You should be sitting here all smiles!"

"We're okay, honey," said Carla. "It's just hard to take in all that information at once. But you're absolutely right, we should be all smiles—and we are." She grinned to prove it. "Larry, let's go to the cafeteria. The kids can talk for a while. I'm hungry and I'm sure you are, too. Maybe I can pick up some recipe ideas from the cafeteria staff!" She pulled Larry away from the window. He sketched a wave before he disappeared out the door.

"Take it easy, son. We'll see you later this afternoon."

A young woman appeared with Clem's tray and Sally suggested he sit in his chair to eat. "Your muscles will wimp out on you if you stay in bed all day."

"I've been walking," Clem argued. "They've had me up and down this hallway fifty times already this morning!" But he smiled and moved to the chair all the same.

"Are you thinking of going into nursing?" the woman asked and smiled. "You're so good with people, I've noticed."

Sally blushed, saying she hadn't really given it much thought.

"Well, you young people can discuss the future while Clem eats. Would you like something?" she asked, looking at Sally.

"Oh, no thank you, ma'am. I'm just fine for now."

"Well then, I'll leave you to it." She winked at them both and went back to her work.

CHAPTER 40

Kate and Sherry Johnson

Friday Afternoon

I checked my cell after leaving Turley's Stables and noticed that Sally had called. As I drove back to town, I returned the call. After a few tries I was able to reach Sally rather than her voice mailbox.

"Sorry," she said breathlessly, "I'm just now leaving the hospital. Carla is here to pick up Clem. They decided to let him come home! I've got all his stuff and I'm following them to the Tysons'."

"Great news! I know how glad you'll all be when he's back home. By the way, do you happen to know where Mr. Tyson is?" I asked.

"Um, I think Clem said he'd gone back to the garage. After their second meeting with the doctor, Mr. Tyson wasn't in a very good mood. Clem said Dr. Sanders told them about the possible long-term side effects from head injuries."

Gulp. I needed to talk with Larry Tyson again and was hoping to catch the man in a good mood for a change. He didn't seem to be having any of those lately. "I'll stop by his garage later this afternoon and then maybe I'll be able to swing by the Tysons'. Will you be there, Sally?" I asked.

"Probably. I'm going to check things at home. I'll probably fix Dad some dinner tonight. That will give Clem some time with his parents. But I may go over later on after my dad goes to bed. I know Clem needs rest, so I won't stay very long, but I'd like to see him anyway."

"I understand completely," I said. "I'm on my way over to visit Sherry Johnson and see how she's getting along. I'll go to Tyson's Garage after that and then I'll stop in at Clem's. Hope to see you there."

We rang off and I got my head together, deciding what I wanted to say to Sherry.

I swung back to the motel for my second shower of the day. I couldn't very well show up at the Johnsons' smelling like a horse, could I?

Sherry Johnson's father was sitting on the front porch when I parked in front of the house. He stood as I climbed up the stairs and wiped a moist hand on his trousers. "How do you do?" he asked politely and shook my hand.

I introduced myself. He nodded and then explained that his hands were damp from holding his iced tea glass. I guess it was his way of offering me some. I accepted and sat with him for a few minutes. He poured from a large pitcher that sat on an end table next to the swing.

The tea was refreshing and we did the small talk thing for a couple minutes. Mr. Smith mentioned how warm the afternoon was for October and said that Sherry and her mother, Mrs. Smith, had filled a plastic pool in the back yard for the boys to play in. "She's trying to keep them occupied, you know. The little one doesn't realize what's happened yet and just wants things to get back to normal. Sean, the older boy, is starting to have nightmares. Things are still pretty much a mess.

"And I've got to get back to work next week. I think Alice, my wife, might stay on for a few more days and help out with the boys, but I'm going to have to leave on Sunday. We don't live far, but it's too far for me to commute every day. Both Sean and Cory will go back to school Monday, so there will be a bit more of a routine for them—and that's good. They need that. As for Sherry…she seems to be coping, but I'm not sure it's even hit her yet, you know?"

I looked into his sad eyes and nodded.

"She's kept up a good front for the boys, but after they go to bed, she cries and cries. It just breaks my heart. I think I heard Sean stirring around upstairs the other night. I'm pretty sure he heard her crying. That's real tough on a kid—to have your mom cry. My theory is that's why he's started having nightmares."

"That could be," I agreed. "Perhaps the two of them should just sit down and have a heart-to-heart about Sam's death. Sean's six, right? He could probably handle it."

"Yep, I guess you're right, kids are pretty resilient. You should suggest that to her when you go back there. Alice and Sherry are sitting on the deck keeping an eye on the boys."

I thanked Mr. Smith for the tea and left him. He continued to swing slowly.

As I rounded the house I could hear the boys laughing and splashing around in their little pool. I yelled a 'you-hoo' so I wouldn't startle anyone. Sherry's mother jumped up to meet me.

I sat on the covered deck with the two ladies, welcoming the shade. I hadn't realized how warm the day had become. I declined more tea, explaining that I'd had a glass with Sherry's dad on the front porch.

Alice piped up, "I just don't know how he sits in the sunshine like he does. A body gets too hot. Me, I'll take this back deck any old day! His blood must be getting thin in his old age! Lawsey-me, since I went through the change, all I am is hot!"

Sherry laughed. "Mom, that's what I call 'too much information'! Goodness, you've just met Ms. Jeffers and you're telling her your life story!"

It was good to get a laugh out of Sherry. I didn't think that's why Alice Smith had made her comments, but…whatever works, right?

"Please call me Kate," I said and smiled. "And don't worry about it," I added, waving my hand dismissively. "I sometimes have that effect on people. They tell me all sorts of stuff. Really, it's good in my line of work."

Alice Smith excused herself to go start dinner, leaving me alone with the pregnant Sherry. We chatted and watched the youngsters in the pool. As we talked about the new baby, I wondered about my brother Dave and his wife Sarah. She was about five months pregnant herself. I began to get excited about becoming an aunt for the first time and asked Sherry all kinds of pertinent questions. (I was proud of myself!)

Then my mind wandered to Papa and whether or not there was any future there. I really would like to have kids some day—and I could hear my biological clock ticking away. It would be cool to have kids about the same ages as Dave and Sarah's. Cousins are so neat. It's instantaneous acceptance—extended family and friendships right at your fingertips!

Whoa! I cautioned myself. *You're putting the cart before the horse, here, Kate! First you need a man. Then you work up to motherhood and fatherhood. And being married in the meantime would be a big plus.*

I shook my head and started paying attention to Sherry again. She was saying something about Sean's nightmares. I silently thanked heaven that her dad had filled me in earlier.

After listening for quite a while, I suggested the 'big-boy' talk with Sean. I hinted that it would probably be a good idea for them to cry together to assure him that it's okay to grieve. It might help him deal with his emotions, since he was old enough to understand that his daddy wasn't able to come back anymore. I cautioned her to be certain to reassure Sean that *she* wasn't planning on leaving any time soon!

"You know, you're right. And they'll both be exhausted tonight after all this horse-play in the pool. I'll read Cory a quick story and tuck him in bed and then I'll have a chat with Sean. I know he'll be upset, but when he finally winds down, he'll sleep like a baby. Maybe he won't have any bad dreams."

We talked about Cory, the three-year-old. Sherry concluded that life as usual was the best way to deal with him at this point. He'd ask questions when he was ready and then she would simply tell him the truth.

I slipped in a few questions on the sly. Sherry confirmed my belief that she'd never keep rat poison around the house. She also said that Sam's idea of a good meal was one that they fixed at home. They rarely ate out. So that blew my theory of him being poisoned at a restaurant. And as far as someone from the family being involved…no way! I agreed with Amy Stevens. Sherry was as innocent as they come!

Cory jumped out of the pool and announced he needed to go to the bathroom—NOW! Sean hopped out too, handing his little brother a towel. "Look, Mom, I'm all pruney," Sean laughed, holding up his hands so we could see.

Sherry clasped the wrapped but still dripping Cory in her arms. Then she hurried him inside before he had an accident. Sean stood next to me, shook his head knowingly, and said, "Little boys!" I burst out laughing.

I asked him to tell everyone goodbye for me, then hustled him in the back door since he was shivering. Not wanting to disturb them further, I walked around the side of the house again.

I called farewell to Mr. Smith, who was still swinging slowly. By the time I'd reached my car, Sean was already on the swing with his grandfather. They were swinging harder and soaking up the warm late-afternoon sun.

The Smiths/Johnsons seemed like a very nice, down-to-earth family. I had a feeling things would be okay for them. As soon as I got in my car, I had a vivid vision of the boys, all grown up, smiling and surrounded by their loving mother and grandparents.

There was another man with them as well and two younger girls. (Perhaps Sherry will marry again. Maybe the current baby will be a girl. Perhaps she and her new husband will have a second daughter. Sometimes having visions is a good thing—especially when everything turns out right. *Neat-o*, I thought, but decided to keep this vision to myself. I wouldn't want to jinx anything!

    I blinked some happy tears out of my eyes and started the car, waved to Sean and his grandpa, and headed down the street. I was feeling pretty good, but had the sneaking suspicion that all that was about to change. After all, my next stop was Tyson's Garage!

CHAPTER 41

Kate and Larry Tyson

Friday Evening

I pulled up in front of Tyson's Garage on Miller Street and killed my engine. I'd put off coming here all day—hoping for a miracle, I guess. Like the place would disappear off the face of the earth or something. I was *not* looking forward to this visit!

Seeing Sherry Johnson and her family had left me feeling all warm and fuzzy. Now here I sat, in front of Tyson's Garage. My warm fuzzies were dissipating quickly!

Larry Tyson gave me the creeps on a good day. And today hadn't been the best for him and his family. Learning about long-term problems from head injuries would be tough for anyone.

True, the Johnsons were going to be all right. And true, the doctors had conferred and allowed Clem to go home and true, Clem seemed to be improving. But Sally had gone on to say that the neurologist had painted a pretty grim picture concerning lingering problems. I could just imagine Mr. Tyson's reaction.

Carlos and Amy had kindly volunteered to come instead of me, but Larry Tyson had become a challenge to me. *Surely* I could have a discussion with the man without totally pissing him off! And I needed to watch his face. I was convinced that he hadn't poisoned Coach Johnson, but had a gut feeling that he knew more than he was letting on.

I took a couple of deep breaths and got out of the car. The men in the green uniforms all looked and stared as I walked through the workshop. I don't think they were checking out my cute body, however. I even caught one of the guys crossing himself. If he wanted to pray for me, that would be just fine. I needed all the help I could get!

Larry Tyson was sitting at his desk in the office, apparently lost in thought. He didn't seem to notice me as I slid into the chair across from him. Suddenly he shook his head, looking surprised. "How'd you get here?" he asked, spooked.

Cool, I thought. *Maybe he thinks I'm a phantom or something. That'll keep him on his toes!*

I nodded and smiled. "Hey! I hear that Clem came home this afternoon. That's great!"

He still looked a bit wary and answered cautiously. "Yeah, Carla and Sally were getting his things together and finishing up the paper work when I left the hospital. They didn't need me, so I thought I'd better check on things here before closing time. We're open till 8:30 on Friday nights…it helps out our clients who work in the city…they can't get here during regular hours, so we stay open late."

"It looks like you've got a lot of clients who take advantage of this." I motioned towards the workshop. "The place is full!"

Mr. Tyson nodded satisfactorily. "Pays the bills."

"Speaking of bills," I said, moving into uncomfortable territory, "do you have insurance to cover Clem's hospital bills? Not that it's any of my business, sir, but I have access to some monies if you happen to be strapped…" I let my voice trail off.

"Nah, we're completely covered. My father started this business years ago and has all the best coverage. When I took over, I kept all the insurance and even upped the liability. We're in good shape."

"I understand that Clem is going to receive some continuing counseling. Is that right?"

I think Larry Tyson actually growled before answering. "Yeah. That damned doctor came back in this afternoon and told us all kinds of things. I think he's full of it! But you know Carla—she wants to make sure her 'little boy' has everything he needs in this world!"

It didn't take any vision to tell he was beginning to get worked up. "What exactly did the doctor say, Mr. Tyson?" I asked innocently.

"Oh man, he said all sorts of things. For starters, he said that Clem's brain was still swollen from that fall he took a few weeks ago. He didn't fracture his skull, but I guess he took quite a hit on the cement steps. And then the guy said it could take months for the swelling to go down completely! Meanwhile, he's going to have trouble concentrating and will still have all this anger to deal with.

"But the thing that really got us was that Dr. Sanders said his symptoms may *never* go away—even after the swelling goes down! I just can't accept that!"

He was beginning to get red in the face. I didn't want the man to have a stroke while I was sitting there! "I've done a little research myself, Mr. Tyson," I said as calmly as I could. "I believe that his counselor will help him learn some new types of study skills. Ways to adapt his current ones so that he'll be able to remember things—almost as well as he did before his accident. And as far as the anger goes, whoever he sees will give him some coping methods for letting off steam. I think we could all use some of that, don't you?"

I gritted my teeth, waiting for him to pounce. He didn't, so I continued, "He's already coping pretty well, you know. I inadvertently made him angry the other day—I didn't mean to," I added apologetically, "but instead of taking it out on Sally or on your wife, he went out to the track and ran a few laps. That was the perfect thing for him to do. You know, he's such a bright young man, I'm sure he'll learn to cope."

"But he tried to commit suicide, Ms. Jeffers," Larry said. I heard the hopelessness in his voice.

"But sir, that was all before he understood what was going on. He was scared. Now he knows what caused all his trouble. He's taking medication to reduce the swelling in his brain. Chances are that he'll be back to normal in a few weeks. The doctors seem hopeful that he'll not have many lingering side-effects at all."

Larry Tyson nodded. "True. All you're saying is true. But then there's Sam Johnson. Clem's note said that he killed the coach. What are we going to do about that?"

"I've been talking to Police Chief Hayslip and we both spoke with Clem that morning in the hospital," I began. I hesitated for a moment, wondering what or how much I should say. "We're both certain that Clem didn't have anything to do with the coach's death."

Larry's face was no longer red. In fact, he blanched so much that I feared he was going to pass out. His face and neck got deathly pale. "Why'd he write that, then?" he croaked.

"We believe he was trying to cover up for someone else." I said, watching him closely.

The color began to come back. Pink, reddish, purple. *Oh boy. Here we go*, I thought.

"I killed him," Tyson blurted out.

I sat, watching and waiting. I figured the silence would get to him. It did.

"The man was driving Carla nuts. And even though I argued with her about Johnson and his coaching methods, I secretly agreed that he'd done something to our boy. So I poisoned him. Simple as that." He lifted his chin and glared at me.

I looked steadily back. I refused to be cowed by this man any more. "I have to admit, Mr. Tyson, that I considered you as a suspect for a short while, but I just couldn't buy it. You see, with all due respect, you're an impulsive man. If you'd thought Johnson had wronged your son, you'd most likely have confronted him and probably punched his lights out." Larry Tyson almost smiled in agreement, but then reconsidered. "Instead, I think you are covering up for someone, too."

That did it. He was on his feet in an instant—that impulsiveness rearing its ugly head. He clenched his fists and gritted his teeth. He hissed at me, saying, "It's time for you to leave, Ms. Jeffers. I'm not covering up for anyone. The damned man is dead. Nothing can bring him back. Nothing will be solved no matter how long you or your friends nose around. It's time for you to leave Conroy. Go back to the city. If you don't, you'll be sorry. Leave us alone or you'll regret it."

"Is that a threat, Mr. Tyson?"

"It's a promise. Now get out of here before I wring that scrawny little neck of yours."

I used my brave voice to say, "Okay, I'll leave…for now."

"Leave me and my family alone." He didn't quite bellow, but I'm sure the men in green heard as I scooted out of the office and across the workroom. I think I overheard someone say something like 'she's got balls'.

Once in the car, I took a couple more deep breaths. A scrawny neck and balls—what more could a girl want?

I decided to pop in at the Tysons'—before Larry closed up shop and returned home! On my way there I called Lieutenant Whitaker to check in.

After I filled him in on all the latest news, he suggested (strongly) that I return to Atlanta for the weekend. I didn't argue. I was tired, fed up, frustrated (on several fronts) and was glad that someone cared about my well-being. Even if it was Doug Whitaker. So after I checked on Carla, Clem and Sally and made sure things were fine with them I went back to the Bayside Motel. I gathered my things and checked out.

The evening was much cooler than the afternoon had been, so I drove back to Atlanta with the windows down and my hair blowing freely. It seemed to help. By the time I was back home, I could no longer pick out any stars, but the cobwebs seemed to have blown out of my brain. The lingering scent of Larry Tyson's anger had disappeared.

CHAPTER 42

Monroe Street Police Station, Atlanta

Saturday Morning

I woke up early and stretched. I'd forgotten how nice my little own bed could be—even if I was alone in it. It seemed like an eternity since I'd been home, but it had only been one week. So much had happened in the interim.

As I lay there, I plotted my day. Of course I wanted to see Papa. He'd told me not to worry about his engagement to Anna. Right. I wanted to kill his mother—but that probably wouldn't endear me to him, so I tossed that idea out.

I needed to check in with Whitaker. I'd promised to stop at the station first thing this morning. I guess my personal issues were going to have to wait a while longer. *Ugh.*

I sniffed the air as I came to full consciousness. Rats—I'd forgotten to program the coffee machine. I rolled out of bed and climbed down the spiral stairs, grumbling to myself. I shuffled to the kitchen. As I passed my desk, I noticed the light on my answering machine was blinking. *Why didn't I notice that last night?*

Had I been that tired? I ground some beans and started the java machine. While I was waiting I retraced my steps and pressed the play button.

"Are you home yet?" It was Gloria's voice. "I didn't want to call your cell phone and leave a message 'cause I figured you'd be in your car and I didn't want you to drive off the road. Sit down. Are you sitting? I talked to Papa. Ronnie and I stopped in at the bar yesterday afternoon before it got too busy. He and Demetri were stocking and…"

The machine clicked off. I groaned. "And…What?!" I hollered.

I could hear the coffee machine giving its final gurgle, so I stomped back to the kitchen and poured a big mug-full. Then I returned to my desk and stared at the phone. It was still too early to call Gloria. She'd kill me if I called before eleven. I glanced at the clock. Four more hours till then. *Crap-o.*

I took my coffee out to my balcony. *Yikes!* I needed to spend some time out here. My container garden looked sick! I turned on the hose and mixed up some Quick-Grow in a bucket. Even though it was October, my mums and marigolds should still have had a few good weeks left in them! Instead, they looked nasty! "You poor babies," I said to them as I gave each one a drink. "I forgot to ask Gloria to come up and water. I'm sorry. This afternoon I promise I'll come back and dead-head you all. That'll make you perk up."

This was getting ridiculous. How could I forget my garden even with everything else going on? I guess it's a good thing I don't have a cat—much less kids. I'd probably go off and forget to feed them! I turned my radio on to a station that was playing classical music. I decided to leave it on for my little flowers. Maybe that would make them happy. The morning was already getting warm, so I left the French doors open to air out the loft. You've gotta love Atlanta in the fall!

I grabbed a second cuppa and headed to the shower. I donned some jeans and a t-shirt and spent a few minutes on my hair. The humidity was pretty low, so I figured I could wear my hair down for once without getting a case of the frizzies. As I was brushing it out, I realized that it had grown past my shoulders. Wow, I hadn't even noticed. I tried, but couldn't remember the last time I'd had it trimmed. Another thing to add to my 'to do' list.

Pete was on duty in the parking garage when I went downstairs to get my car. I waved and he called out, "We're hiring! Let me know if you find anyone who needs a job."

"Is Sally leaving?" I asked.

He shook his head. "No. Gloria!"

"What?" I exclaimed, trotting over to his desk. "What's going on?"

Pete shrugged. "Don't know. She told me when I came on duty this morning. She was going home to sleep, quitting this job and 'moving on'...her words."

He didn't know anything else, so I made my excuses and left. I was *very* curious! I wondered what in the world was happening. I leave town for one week and everything changes!! Gloria, Papa... everything! I wondered what I'd find when I went to the Police Station. Would it have changed too?

The Monroe Street Station looked pretty much the same, but I noticed a big change in Lieutenant Whitaker. A change that made me feel a bit uncomfortable, to say the least. He stood up and came around his desk when I walked into his office. He said my name—kinda funny—letting it linger on his tongue. And he shook my hand—and held on just a little too long. Yuck! *What is* this *about?* I wondered. I felt like backing out of the room and running. But I guess I couldn't do that, so I just sat down, wiping my hand on my jeans. I scooted my chair as far away from his desk as I could.

"Welcome back to civilization, Kate," Doug began. "We missed you! Tell me what went on in Conroy."

I talked, leaving out the part about Papa and Ronnie showing up and spending the night. Strictly business, I filled him in on all the details of the case. I finished by saying, "Carlos and Amy are ready to close the case, but I still have my doubts. I just know that the Tysons are involved. Two out of three have confessed to killing Sam Johnson and they're the two who were probably *not* involved. They're covering up for someone else—maybe the mom. The problem is I've got no proof."

Whitaker commiserated with me. We went over my visions one more time: angry woman, woman with blue eyes, sweaty football players. I left out the one I'd had about Sherry Johnson and her entire family and, of course, the one of the bride (Probably Anna. Grrr).

We chatted about other things that were going on with him and some of the other officers. While he talked, I tried to analyze my feelings about Doug…and Papa.

I came back to the present to hear him say, "I was really worried about you while you were in Conroy, Kate. Larry Tyson sounds like a loose cannon. And now you tell me he threatened you…twice. You're a civilian now. We can't forget that. I can't jeopardize you in any way. You're not to go back there alone, understand?"

I nodded, but my fingers were crossed.

"Anyway, Kate, (There he went, saying my name again! Gave me the creeps.) I don't want anything to happen to you…I couldn't stand it…"

"Wait, Doug," I interjected, holding up my hand to stop him. I knew what he was going to say. He was thinking about his wife, Margo, who'd been killed five years ago. He was just now beginning to move on with his life. He was starting to put his guilty feelings behind him. But now he was trying to put me in the same category with his wife. And I realized that I didn't want to be there—in any manner of speaking.

I had enough issues of my own to deal with. I couldn't handle a relationship with Doug Whitaker. For one thing, there was the age difference. When I'm thirty, he'll be over forty. That doesn't seem so bad, but when I'm fifty, he'll be in his sixties! That seems like a *huge* difference! Me with a sixty-year-old. *Ick!*

And, most importantly, I just don't feel anything for him. I like him; he's a great guy, a good friend and a wonderful man to work with. But that's it. No bells, no whistles. Not even warm fuzzies! Even if things don't work out with Papa, (stomach jitters) I refuse to go into a relationship where there isn't something more than friendship! Now...how to explain this to Whitaker.

"Lieutenant Whitaker," I began, twisting my hands together nervously. "Please don't be concerned about me. I can take care of myself. Even if I have to confront Larry Tyson or anyone else for that matter, I'll be okay. I've kept up with my Tae Kwan Do classes. Not for a while, I'll admit, but I can still hold my own.

"Meanwhile, you've got enough to think about without worrying about me. I love my work. I'm thrilled when I can use my psychic powers to help out whenever you call. I'm learning to balance my work and social life (a lie). I'm able to spend more time with my friends without feeling guilty (another lie, but it sounded good).

"You need to do the same. You're a wonderful person and you need to find someone who truly appreciates every facet of your personality. Someone you can share your free time with. You work too many hours. You need to lighten up a little and play. Margo would want that for you. You and she had such a wonderful relationship. I'm glad you're beginning to accept things and move on. I understand how hard it's been for you to forgive yourself for her death. I felt the same way about my parents' deaths for years. So I sort of know what you've been dealing with. But we can't change what happened. We need to move on. I've begun to and I can tell you have, as well. I'm glad I have a great friend like you. Someone I work well with. Someone I can confide in and share my darkest feelings with. I hope you consider me that good a friend. I'll always be here for you in that capacity."

My voice trailed off. I'd been looking at my hands as I talked and finally had the nerve to sneak a peek at Whitaker's face. He was leaning back in his chair, feet propped up on his desk, eyes closed. His 'thinking' position.

I held my breath. What if he'd fallen asleep while I was rambling on and on? I'd never be able to remember what I'd just said. It sounded pretty good as I talked. I wondered if I'd have the nerve to say it all again.

He opened his eyes and smiled wistfully. "Nicely put, Kate. I understand what you're saying." He put his feet down and scooted his chair up to the desk. He folded his hands and looked at me right in the eyes. I didn't have that uncomfortable feeling anymore. I felt as though the old Doug Whitaker was back. *Whew!*

He began talking again. "I value our friendship. There is no way I'd ever want that to change. We're kindred souls—we've both been through a lot in our lives. We understand each other. We work well together and always have. And you're right. I am beginning to handle Margo's death. I can even talk about her now." His voice caught. "Well, sort of..." he added and smiled, lightening the tension between us.

He stood up again and came around his desk. "Friends and best buddies?" he asked.

"Forever," I said and hugged him.

"Have a good weekend. Go play with your friends," he said with a smile. "If something comes up over the weekend—or what's left of it—I'll give you a shout. Otherwise, touch base with me on Monday. We'll decide what to do about the Conroy situation."

I left the station feeling much more light-hearted than when I'd arrived. I drove past Papa's Lounge. No cars there yet. Bummer. So I went back to the loft to trim back my flowers. It was almost late enough to call Gloria.

CHAPTER 43

Prosciutto's Club

Saturday Noon

I was almost home when my cell phone rang. I'd been mentally preparing a shopping list and almost jumped out of my skin. It was Gloria. Her first words were, "Are you back?" She seemed pleased when I told her I was.

"We're at Lou Mancini's old club, Prosciutto's," she said. "Remember where it is?"

How could I forget? Lou Mancini was Ronnie's boss/surrogate father who we'd watched die just two weeks earlier. It seemed like forever ago.

I told her I'd be along shortly, wondering who she'd meant when she'd said "we". I rerouted my car towards downtown Atlanta. My plants and shopping would have to wait. I was anxious to see Gloria to find out why she had quit her job as security guard. When I pulled into Prosciutto's lot, I noticed several familiar cars. Gloria's, Ronnie's, Demetri's and...*oh, shit!* Papa's.

Oh my god! I didn't want to see him for the first time since his 'engagement' when all these other people were around. But I couldn't turn tail and go back home—I'd already told Gloria I was coming. And she was standing at the back door, waving to me.

My heart started pounding. I had tunnel vision. Maybe it was just the heat. Then again, maybe not.

Gloria was decked out in a short denim skirt and a new t-shirt, bright red. As I walked towards her I wondered how she had poured herself into the skirt. The shirt was rather large, even for her. Right across her (ample) chest was the name MANCINI'S in bold, black letters.

"Mancini's?" I asked.

"Yeah!" she answered, grabbing me by the arm and hustling me inside the dim club. I let my eyes adjust while she babbled. It seemed that after Ronnie'd inherited Prosciutto's, he'd decided to re-name it after Lou himself. "Prosciutto's is lame anyhow," she added. "Sounds like a slab of meat—you know?" I rolled my eyes. "So anyway, we're going to have a Grand Re-opening Gala Event! Ronnie got these new shirts to hand out to the first three hundred people! And Papa and Demetri came over to give Ronnie some pointers…"

I grabbed her and pulled her into the ladies' room as we passed. "I don't know if I can see Papa right now."

"I know what'cha mean," she confided. "But just act cool and everything will be fine. He freaked when I said you were on your way down here. He's really nervous, too. But don't worry."

"I don't know if I can 'act cool' as you put it. He's engaged to someone else!" I wailed. "I need to talk to him in private."

"Stay here, then," she said, turned and disappeared.

I took a couple deep breaths and happened to glance in the mirror. My hair, at least, wasn't frazzled. Couldn't say that much about the rest of me!

I heard the restroom door open and turned, expecting Gloria again. *Gulp.* It was Papa.

"You go in ladies' rooms often?" It was all I could think of to say.

He smiled. Even, white teeth. Glossy, black hair. Deep, dark eyes—ones I'd been lost in for years. I didn't know whether to laugh or cry. *Big sigh.*

"Glory said you wanted to see me alone. Good idea." A man of few words. What did he mean? Was I supposed to attack him? Throw myself at him? Kiss him? Beat on his chest and yell at him for putting me through hell? Run into a stall and lock the door? No visions came my way. *Agggh!*

I finally managed to say, "This is awkward."

Misunderstanding, he answered, "Why? The club's closed. And anyway, who do you think cleans the Women's room at Papa's Lounge?"

I hadn't thought of that. Another big eye roll. "That's *not* what I'm talking about," I said, becoming more agitated.

"Oh. Yeah."

My fingers started twitching. Was I going to have to choke it out of him?

"Kate, don't look at me like that. I told you not to worry. I'm working on it. I've got a meeting with Anna tomorrow when everyone in both families is at church."

"A...meeting?"

"Yeah. She's in love with Demetri—."

"WHAT?" I screeched.

"Oh—didn't I tell you that already?"

"No-o," I answered through clenched teeth. "I haven't talked to you for several days," I added in what I considered to be a very controlled voice.

"Well, she is. And he really likes her. So we'll figure something out. But meanwhile, I can't hang out with you."

I think I raised my voice when I asked, "Why the hell not?"

"It wouldn't be appropriate. I'm sort of still engaged. It wouldn't be fair to Anna—or you either. When I come over to your place, I want it to be only the two of us—no Anna or anyone else. So until I figure this out and set things straight with my parents, I'd better keep my distance from you."

Once again, I didn't know whether I should laugh or cry. Good ol' Papa. Always one to do what's 'right'. Unfortunately, it was one of his endearing qualities, so I couldn't get all pissed off at him, could I?

"We need to get out there," he said, nodding his head in the direction of the main bar. "They're waiting for us. But first…," he added, pulling me into his arms, "This will be our little secret." And he kissed me. Long and slow and deep. My knees buckled. "God, I've missed you," he whispered.

I may have whimpered, but can't really remember.

CHAPTER 44

Kate

Saturday Afternoon

I left Prosciutto's—I mean the soon-to-be Mancini's—a while later. Ronnie and Gloria were bursting at the seams (Gloria literally!) with ideas for the new club. Papa and Demetri had given them several brilliant suggestions while Ron whipped up some sandwiches for us all. Ronnie'd convinced Glory to give up her job as security guard, saying he needed her to be his new hostess at Mancini's. He said a hostess would 'class-up' the place. The other three of us stifled giggles. I wondered how many of the first three hundred Gloria would volunteer to undress in order to give them their new t-shirt. And how many fist-fights Ronnie would get into trying to save her honor.

I had a better feeling about Papa. Maybe he would be able to work things out like he promised. My knees weren't quite as rubbery as they had been. I was glad I'd had my 'conversation' with Doug Whitaker and had gotten *that* over with. But I was still antsy. The thought of spending the evening by myself wasn't very appealing.

I decided to drive up to the estate where Grandma Jeffers, David and Sarah lived.

I phoned my grandmother as I drove toward Buckhead. It was the proper thing to do. Grandma, my father's mother, said she'd open the gate for me. She also said that David and Sarah were coming for dinner. She'd left a phone invitation for our sister, Emily, but hadn't heard from her yet. Grandma assumed I'd stay, too. Since I hadn't made it to the store and can't cook worth a damn anyway, it sounded like a good plan to me!

I arrived just in time for high tea. Grandma Jeffers had long since given up her daily staff. She claimed there wasn't enough room in the gate house for both her and the help. I figured she was really bored. Anyway, she needed the exercise of puttering around, cooking, cleaning and tending to her flower garden.

It was great to see her again. It had only been a couple weeks, but I felt like I'd come home again. The gate house is comfortable and is perfect for Grandma. When David and Sarah married, they took over the big house and Grandma moved in here. She brought most of her favorite pieces of furniture with her. The gate house turned from an empty shell into a wonderful, cozy nest. The dark, wide plank floors were covered with Persian rugs. She had arranged antique chairs and a camelback sofa in front of a stone fireplace. Brass candlesticks topped piecrust candle stands and a couple Chinese lamps finished the main room. The kitchen was small, but functional. A bathroom and bedroom completed the main floor.

Upstairs was slightly different. Two small bedrooms and a bath. Grandma rarely went up there—for a reason. The stairs themselves pose a challenge. One needs to crawl up on one's hands and knees— and has to bump back down on his or her backside. It's hard to be lady-like. I can't quite picture Grandma doing that. She's a very regal person. Kind of reminds me of the queen. She is quite bright, reads voraciously, watches only PBS. She's very formal, but not stuffy at all! Grandma Jeffers has a funny sense of humor and she adores all of us grand-kids.

"Katherine, it's so wonderful to see you again," she said as she hugged me. "You're just in time. I was about to sit down for tea. It's always so much nicer when there's someone to share it with. Will you pour while I get the tea cakes?" She hurried from the living room. I could hear her rustling bakery paper as she set out some goodies. She came back with little lemon and raspberry tarts. "Just something to hold us over till cocktail hour!" And she winked.

I had to smile. Tea was wonderful, but our family has always been best during happy hour. We sipped tea and each had a small tart. We discussed what had been going on in our lives for the past two weeks. We also voiced our concerns about Emily, but since no one had seen her in the past week, there was no update.

Grandma was fascinated about the coach's death in Conroy. "I've read about it in the paper and wondered if you were the 'specialist' they'd called in." I mentioned my reservations about calling the death an accident.

My grandmother was looking forward to attending the Symphony Ball in November and expressed her desire that I join her. "And of course, bring that nice young man you've been seeing." I assumed she was referring to Papa and wondered aloud whether I'd be 'seeing' him in another month. Naturally, she wanted to know what was going on, so I blurted it all out.

"It's not always easy dating someone from a different culture. Give him some space and he'll work it out. I know he's crazy about you—has been for years. You're best friends! But I'm pleased that you've got that spark between you as well. Chemistry is important! Be patient, dear. I have a good feeling about this."

I took her words of wisdom to heart. But baring my soul, even to Grandma, is a difficult thing for me to do. "You just like him 'cause he's a great bartender," I teased.

"There's that," she admitted. "And he's good-looking, too. But seriously, my dear, you and he have a great deal of respect and consideration for each other. You both have wonderful work ethic and have a high sense of what's right and wrong. You're perfect for each other…and he knows it!"

We continued to sit and chat long after our tea was cold.

"Look at the time! Kate, dear, run upstairs and find a dress. Your brother and Sarah will be here any minute and I haven't even begun dinner!"

Grandma graciously declined my offer to help. She knows what a lousy cook I am. "You can help with the salad when it's time. David is going to grill steaks. Sarah was baking bread when I talked to her earlier. She promised to bring a loaf. I'm just going to make some deviled eggs and open the wine to breathe. While you're upstairs, I'll call Emily again to see if she'll be able to join us."

"Would you like me to go get some cheese?" I called from halfway up the stairs.

"No thanks, I've got some already at room temp. Hurry along, Kate. It's drinking-time!"

I checked out the dresses that were hanging in one of the closets upstairs. I keep a few on hand just for instances like this. We are always expected to dress for dinner. Actually, I was rather surprised that I was allowed to have tea while still in jeans. I guess it's because my hair was down—made me look much more formal!

The black dress was too hot. If I recall, I'd worn it last time I was here. The pale blue one was Emily's. Baby blue is not my color! I avoided that one like the plague. I finally found a dark brown knit with three-quarter-length sleeves. It was slightly darker than my hair and I scrounged around in my big black bag and found some blush and lip gloss that would go with it. I'd already popped in some small gold earrings that go with anything, so I was all set. I bumped my way to the bottom of the stairs just as Dave and Sarah came in the door.

"Charming," Dave said and laughed. "Where's the camera when we need it?"

What are brothers for, anyway? I stood, pulled my dress back down to a respectable length and gave him a hug. I hugged Sarah next—a tricky thing to do. She was getting larger by the minute. I patted her tummy. "Hello, little one," I called to the baby bulge. She glowed and I thought of Sherry Johnson.

We all trooped to the kitchen where Grandma blew kisses to everyone. Her hands were covered with deviled egg goop.

"Welcome, all," she said. "Isn't this great? We'll have a little picnic! I just spoke with Emily. She can't make it, but promises to show up next time. She wants me to give each of you a big hug. If you're lucky, I'll wait till my hands are clean!

"David, will you be bartender? And Sarah, let's have just a little of your bread to go with the cheese for hors d'oeuvres. The bread knife is over there."

We carried our drinks and the plate of bread and cheese to the little flagstone patio at the rear of the gate house. We sat for several minutes reminiscing about the fun days we'd had growing up in the big house.

"I just love to sit here, look at the big place and remember," said Grandma, wistfully. "There were some terrible times in that house, especially when Grandpa Jeffers and then your parents died… but the good times more than compensate for any sadness we've experienced. And just think—now Sarah and David will have a new baby to raise and we'll have a whole next generation of stories to tell!"

The evening passed quickly, Dave telling us about the business world. According to him, downtown Atlanta was soon going to be as thriving as Midtown and Buckhead. Both our grandfathers would have loved to hear that news! "Want to make a blue-zillion, Kate?" he asked me at one point.

"Sure! Zillions are good."

"Then live in your loft for another year or so and then put it on the market."

"But I love my loft!" I said. But it did get me thinking. *What if I ended up with Papa. What if we decided to have kids…and dogs…and…hmm?*

So I nodded when he told me to keep it in the back of my mind.

Sarah was still re-doing the baby's room. She'd been reading everything she could on prenatal care. She sipped on her sparkling water as the rest of us switched from hard liquor to wine.

"I really don't miss the booze," she said. I tried a sip once and it just didn't taste good anymore. But I'm sure I'll be ready as soon as the baby is finished breast-feeding."

I noticed Grandma blushing and winked at Sarah and Dave. *So improper to mention the B-word!* "What's-a-matter, Grandma?" teased David. "You don't want to be in the delivery room and get your hands—?"

"Stop!" she said sharply. "Enough, children! I know things aren't like they used to be. And I think I'm awfully open-minded…" We younger people glanced at each other with raised eyebrows and smirks. "…but I don't want to *hear* it! They used to put us out cold when we delivered and we had wet-nurses and nannies to help with our children!" She tried to look severe, but couldn't hide her smile.

"I'm going to be very pleased to do my nursing all by myself," asserted Sarah.

I was impressed. It had taken Sarah well over a year to feel comfortable speaking her mind in front of the grandmothers.

Dave grilled the strip steaks to perfection and I managed to put the salad together. We moved into the dining room for dinner since it was getting dark and the evening was cooling down.

During our meal, I filled everyone in on my latest case. Grandma invited the others to the Symphony Ball. We talked briefly about Emily, our younger sister. She only has one more year at the school of art and design and was starting to send out feelers for jobs—locally, in Athens and in Augusta, as well. She'd been so busy that I was the only one who had seen her for quite a while. I purposely decided not to mention how distraught Emily had been the last time we'd spoken. I mentally put Emily at the top of my 'to-do' list!

We decided to have another family get-together soon. "Or else we could all descend on her at the art institute some afternoon," Dave suggested.

"That'll get her up here for sure," laughed Sarah.

Everyone but Sarah declined dessert. She opted for a lemon tart while the rest of us sipped some port wine.

"I haven't had this much to drink in ages," I commented.

"Then you'll sleep well tonight, dear. You'd better plan on staying here," Grandma added.

Sarah joked that she might need my help rolling Dave home—it unfortunately is uphill to their house. But Dave was fine and was even able to steady Sarah by her elbow as they made their way back up the drive.

Grandma and I finished dishes quickly as she debated whether we all would need new dresses for the Symphony Ball. Sarah, we agreed, would definitely need a new one!

We both yawned hugely (mouths covered, of course). I kissed Grandma goodnight and we made our way to our respective bedrooms. I managed to make it all the way upstairs without hitting my head or tripping on the hem of my dress. That's the true test of how tipsy one is!

CHAPTER 45

Kate

Sunday Morning

I always seem to sleep well when I'm at the estate. Maybe because it's quiet there. I love my loft and being in Midtown, but there always seem to be street noise and sirens. Maybe I sleep well because I know my grandmother is close by and that makes me feel secure. (I guess I still have some abandonment issues.) Maybe it was just the port wine. Whatever the cause, I woke up rather refreshed. I didn't even remember dreaming.

But something woke me up. As I surfaced, I realized that I'd left my loft windows and doors open and the radio on. *Oh, dear!* I'd need to apologize to my neighbor on the eighth floor. But I rationalized that the volume wasn't on *that* high and at least it was classical music—not the rap that I sometimes listen to.

I ended up feeling guilty anyway and decided I'd better get a move on. I put on the same clothes I'd worn all day yesterday and hoped I didn't smell too bad. I checked out my hair in the mirror and grabbed a scrunchie to pull it back. So much for low humidity.

I navigated the stairs as quietly as I could, but Grandma was already up. She beckoned me to join her on the back patio. I grabbed a cup of coffee—in a dainty china cup—picked up a saucer and went outside.

"You're up early this morning, Grandma."

"Indeed. I wanted to see you before you slipped off. And anyway, I love to commune with nature on mornings like this. I'm not much of a church-goer, as you know, so I talk with the heavens right here in my own garden."

"It's a good place to be," I agreed. Then I thought about Papa and Anna's meeting scheduled for this morning while the rest of their families were at church. A tight knot developed in my stomach.

Grandma Jeffers isn't psychic, but she leaned over and patted my hand anyway. "Don't worry, little one. Things have a way of working out." I looked at her, surprised that she could read my mind, but she just smiled. "It might rain this afternoon," she said.

I saw my downstairs neighbor as I was getting into the elevator in my building. She was pleasant and said how much she'd enjoyed my music during the night. I apologized profusely, but she assured me that it lulled her to sleep. She'd decided to keep her radio on at night for company. *Whew!*

My loft was a bit chilly, but it felt good. The humidity was definitely on the rise and the day was going to warm up. I grabbed another cup of coffee—a big honker mug, this time—and headed for the balcony. I sipped quietly, trimmed back the dead flowers and communed with nature just like Grandma Jeffers.

Sometimes I have visions when I'm puttering around in my garden and I suppose it was my lucky day! I could picture Carla Tyson. She was sneaking around. I closed my eyes and concentrated, but couldn't get any more than that. No location, no feeling for time of day. But it was definitely Carla and she was nervous about something.

I finished my trimming and gave the plants another drink. It sure looked like rain, but my poor babies were so dry! They'd soaked up everything I'd given them the previous day. They slurped up this drink as well. (Reminded me of myself one night at Papa' Lounge.) That's one thing about container gardening—especially if one uses clay pots. The moisture evaporates so quickly!

Once inside, I washed my hands and scrubbed my fingernails with a brush. They'd probably never be clean again! My stomach began to rumble. It struck me that all I'd had so far today was coffee. I scrounged around in the fridge. Empty, except for a couple bottles of wine and a lime.

I had two frozen dinners in the freezer, so I popped one in the microwave. I really needed to hook up with some cooking lessons! Maybe Dave and Grandma would be willing after I finished up on the Conroy case.

I ate, standing up in the middle of the kitchen. The cardboard box would probably have tasted better. Definitely a departure from last night's dinner! In my mind I could see Grandma's stern look: 'Kate,' she'd say. 'It's not good for your digestion—eating that frozen garbage and standing up. Sit, relax, masticate.' (That means chew your food.)

I was still hungry, but the other frozen dinner looked even worse, so I gave up. What I really needed was a great big gyro with lots of lamb and cucumber sauce. That got me thinking of Papa—something I was trying to avoid doing.

I hit the shower and felt better after getting cleaned up.

CHAPTER 46

Kate

Sunday Evening

I spent the early part of the afternoon studiously avoiding thinking about Papa. I cleaned my loft, paid a couple of bills, checked and returned tons of e-mail messages. Finally, I ran out of things to do, so I made a shopping list and headed out to the nearest Kroger store.

I considered walking, but decided I wouldn't be able to manage all the toilet paper, paper towels and beer. Not to mention laundry soap. Maybe even some food! Better drive.

It began to rain while I was at the store and I got the giggles picturing myself walking back to my building loaded down with paper towels that were getting wet and swelling up to four times their size, pushing me down to the sidewalk. I got some weird stares from the other patrons.

Funny how stress makes some people get silly. I'm one of them, I'm afraid. The smallest thing will set me into hysterics and send tears streaming down my cheeks.

I kept thinking about Papa. I was scared that he wouldn't call me tonight to let me know how his 'meeting' with Anna went. And I kept thinking about Carla Tyson. How she had to be connected in some way with Sam Johnson's death. Then there was the fact that I had no proof. Yeah, that bugged me, too.

So I giggled. And on my way to my car I dropped a roll of paper towels and it split open and began to swell up and I just stood there in the parking lot, laughing. Of course I hadn't worn a jacket and I got soaked. Then the scrunchie slipped out of my hair. My hair got so frizzy that I could hardly push it out of my eyes long enough to drive home.

Pete was still on duty when I got back. He just looked at me and laughed. "What the heck happened to you?" he called out.

I was still giggling and didn't even bother to answer.

I burst into the loft carrying eight bags of groceries at once. Grandmother would have referred to it as a 'lazy man's load'.

The light on my answering machine was blinking. I dropped everything in a heap, hoping the eggs hadn't broken. I raced to the phone, still dripping with rain. Small water spots littered the desk top. I brushed them away with one hand while I pressed the 'play' button with the other.

It was Papa. My heart started to hammer again and it wasn't due to the fact that I'd just carried a month's worth of groceries inside.

"Hey," his voice said.

I melted into the desk chair.

"I hoped to catch you at home."

My head sunk into my hands. *Awww.*

"I met with Anna this morning and I think things went well."

I stared at the phone. "What do you mean?" I asked. (As though the machine was going to talk to me!)

The message went on: "I still need to talk with my parents and then we all—I mean Demetri, Anna and I—need to talk with her parents. After that, I'll give you another call and let you know how it went. Till then, I'd better stay away from you."

"WHAT?—Dammit!" I yelled at the phone.

Then he finished by saying, "That kiss we had yesterday—it almost undid me. You know what I mean? Talk to ya. Bye."

I almost slid off the chair. How is he able to do that to me? He gets me so agitated I want to strangle him and then ends up saying something sweet and I get all gushy over him again! Burns me up.

I stomped over to my groceries and began slamming them in their appropriate places. When I got to the eggs, I realized that three of them had broken. *Tonight's gonna be omelet night.* At least Grandma had taught me to do eggs.

I decided to put some bacon, cheese, sautéed mushrooms and sundried tomatoes with the eggs, fix an English Muffin (with lots of butter) and pop open one of the bottles of Chardonnay. Maybe I'd end up getting as toasted as my English Muffin! Sounded like a plan to me!

A few hours later I decided that it was time to go to bed. I was lonesome and extremely glad that Papa couldn't see me. I was also relieved that no one else had called. Not Doug Whitaker (a safe guy seemed like a good idea at the moment). Not that arse-end of a guy I'd dated last month (I'd have told him off for sure—and who knows when I'll need an architect again!) Not Gloria—I was thrilled that she and Ronnie were doing so well, but I didn't think I could handle talking with anyone so bubbly. And not my other grandmother, Grandma Phelps. She would have instructed me to put on my big-girl shorts and snap out of it!

So I programmed coffee for morning and stomped up the spiral stairs. It was a good thing that I didn't go out to the balcony. My flowers would surely have shriveled up and died.

I woke up. It was 3:30. I sat up because I was having trouble getting my breath. (No, I hadn't been dreaming about Papa.) It was a different kind of breathing difficulty. Maybe I'd had a vision. I wasn't sure.

I lay back down and took a few deep breaths. *Yep*. It must've been a vision. I closed my eyes in the dark and tried to visualize it again. It was similar to the one I'd had earlier—about Carla Tyson.

I could vaguely see her. She was outside and it was very dark. It might have been raining. I could see some distant light reflecting off a puddle. Carla was creeping—that's the only way to describe it. She was hunched over and sort of tippy-toeing along.

I couldn't figure out where she was, though. At home? At school? There was some sort of building to the side, but it was too dark to tell anything more.

I was well and truly wide awake by then. I decided it was time to take a drive.

CHAPTER 47

Kate: Back in Conroy

Early Monday Morning

I arrived back out in Conroy about 5:30. The morning light was a long way off and it was still drizzling. I thought of my coffee machine. It should just be turning itself on. Damn! I reached into my big black bag and felt around in the dark: deodorant, extra pair of panty hose, several files, a can of Coke. Perfect! Lukewarm, but just what I needed anyway! I popped it open and took a big swig. The fizzies got up my nose and I sneezed. At least I'd swallowed first! That could have been nasty!

I pulled onto the Tysons' street, cut the lights and turned into the neighbor's driveway. I killed the engine and sat quietly, drinking my Coke. I watched the Tysons' house. There was a light in the kitchen, and I could see the silhouette of someone occasionally passing by the window. Clem's truck was still parked way back in the driveway. There was a car I hadn't seen before (maybe Larry's). Carla's little one was parked closest to the street. It appeared that the whole family was present and accounted for.

As I waited, the rain slacked off, which made it a lot easier for me to see. I was able to roll down the passenger's window and had a very clear view of the house and yard.

A shaft of light appeared. Someone had opened the back door. The light disappeared, but I could make out a figure walking back the path to the garage. It looked too small to be either of the guys—it must be Carla. Whoever it was then disappeared through the small door at one end of the garage.

A minute later, the figure reappeared. Definitely Carla. She was carrying something—a box of some sort. Instead of going back in the house, she walked quickly along the driveway and tossed the package into the back seat of her car. Then she looked around. I held my breath and slouched down in my seat, even though I knew there was no way she could see me. Instinct, I guess.

She turned and ran back to the rear of the house and opened the back door again. In the light I watched as she straightened her clothes and walked slowly back indoors.

I glanced at the clock. 5:45. I racked my brain, trying to remember how much time I'd have until Carla left for work. No more than five minutes. Would that give me enough time to run to her car and look at the package? Probably.

I rolled down my driver's window and hoisted myself out. I didn't want to risk turning on the overhead light by opening the car door. I crept around the rear of my vehicle wishing I'd thought to grab the flashlight. I was halfway between the neighbor's and the Tysons' when the back door opened again. I froze in my tracks. I glanced to my right and noticed a bush. I sank to the ground, crawled to it and hid underneath. It had rained hard enough through the night that the ground was damp, even under the bush. I could feel the moisture seeping through my clothes. *Great.* I had only felt a pair of pantyhose in my bag. No extra jeans, no t-shirt. I didn't think I could get away with wearing only panty hose. The mental image almost gave me the giggles again—if I hadn't been so nervous.

Carla walked directly to her car this time and didn't even glance around. Lucky me. And lucky me that I hadn't been any closer to her car than I had been. *That* would have been a bit tough to explain!

I waited until she had turned onto the main street before creeping out from under the bush. I glanced back at their house, but it looked as though no one else was stirring. Dashing back to my own car, I brushed myself off and managed to smear mud all over myself. Pretty. The grandmothers would be so proud!

I was sure that Carla was on her way to school, but I didn't want her to get there too much before I did. I supposed I could get Chief Hayslip to help me talk my way out of a speeding ticket. So I sped. After all, this was official business.

I arrived in plenty of time to see Carla pull into the little lot behind the cafeteria. I drove on and parked my car a block away. I stuffed my phone in my back pocket and carried my flashlight. Then I ran back. It occurred to me that I hadn't exercised in a while. I'd promised myself I would start using the stairs in my building more often. (Not all nine stories, but at least partway.)

I was panting and it had begun to rain again by the time I'd gotten back to the school. Idly I wondered if it would rain hard enough to wash the mud off my shirt.

That's when I saw two things at once. Number one: Carla emerged from the cafeteria. She grabbed the box from her backseat, stuffed it into a big trash bag she was carrying and tied the bag closed. Number two: A Trash Management truck swung around the corner.

Crap! Timing is everything, I suppose. Carla glanced around, but didn't see me. She crept over to the dumpster, bag in hand. Just as the truck turned into the lot, she tossed the bag into the dumpster, turned, waved at the driver and hurried back inside the building.

I stood at the corner of the building, wanting to scream.

"Beep, beep, beep," the TM truck announced itself as it turned around. It got into position to pick up the dumpster.

I ran as fast as I could, flailing my arms around. I think the driver noticed me, but probably thought I was just another lady who wanted to collect the Coke cans before he carted them off. At any rate, I wasn't able to get to him before he'd emptied the dumpster into the back end of the Trash Management truck.

He was finished and about to pull out when I planted myself right in front of him, blocking his exit. I shined my flashlight in his eyes.

"Lady!" he yelled as he rolled down his window. He stuck his head out into the rain. He sounded just a wee bit exasperated when he shouted, "Get outta the way!"

I dashed to the driver's side and yelled up to him, "I'm sorry, sir, but I need to confiscate the contents of your vehicle."

He just looked at me, his mouth agape.

"Police business!" I added.

"Let's see your badge," he said and smirked.

I pulled my cell phone out of my back pocket, juggled it and the flashlight and flipped the phone opened and closed real quickly.

"Nice try, lady, but that was your phone, not a badge." And he raced his engine. I think he was trying to intimidate me. It was working—that was one big truck!

"Hold on," I yelled and huddled over, trying to hold the light between my knees, keep my phone dry and the rain out of my eyes while dialing Chief Hayslip's number. I prayed he'd be at the station.

"Hayslip," came the voice over the line.

"Great! I'm so glad you're there! Jeffers here and I've got a bit of a problem." I explained, briefly, what was going on and then handed my phone up to the now-seething truck driver. I smiled at him, but it didn't seem to help.

"Mother of God!" he exclaimed as he shut down his truck and opened his door. I noticed how large a man he was as he climbed down and stood in front of me and I smiled again, weakly.

"I've got my rounds to make," he announced, angrily. "How long is this going to take?"

"If we wait for the Police Chief, it might be a while. But if you'll allow me to, I'll get started and it shouldn't take too long since I sort of know what I'm looking for."

He gestured to the truck, "Be my guest." And then he smiled—rather nastily.

"Will you hold my phone?" I asked politely. "I don't want to lose it in there," I added, eyeing the mess.

The rain had stopped again, but the rear bumper was awfully slippery. I managed to fall headlong into the garbage when climbing aboard. And I'd been worried about a little mud on my clothes!

CHAPTER 48

Lieutenant Whitaker: Atlanta

Early Monday Morning

"I've got a bad feeling, Carlos," Doug Whitaker said into the receiver. "I woke up in the middle of the night and waited till now to call Kate. I think she's up to something. It's six a.m. and she isn't answering her home phone. I tried her cell and the line is busy. It just goes right into her voice mail."

Carlos sat up sleepily in bed. Fortunately, he is one of those people who wakes up pretty easily and is alert in no time. He stretched his eyes open and glanced over at the sleeping Amy. He smiled, wondering how she was able to sleep like the dead.

Carlos ran a hand through his hair. "I haven't heard from her in a couple of days, Lieutenant. Not since she got back to Atlanta. What do you think is going on, sir?"

Whitaker shared a bit of information that he and Kate had discussed Saturday morning. "I told her to forget about the Conroy case over the weekend and chill out. But you know Kate. If she thinks she's onto something, she just jumps right in with no concern for her safety or anything else. I have an idea that she's gone back out to Conroy without letting anyone know."

"Have you been able to reach Chief Hayslip?"

"No. Can't get through to him either. But I'll keep trying."

Carlos grunted. "I'll get dressed and get hold of Stevens…" Carlos said, sneaking another glance at her. "We'll head out there if that's what you want us to do."

"I'll get right back to you," Whitaker said curtly as he hung up.

"What's this you'll get a hold of me stuff?" Amy mumbled.

"Looks like Jeffers may have gone back to Conroy. Whitaker said Larry Tyson threatened to kill her if she nosed around any more. And Whitaker can't reach her on either of her phones."

"Well, why didn't you say so?" Amy demanded, struggling out of bed and into the jeans that she'd left in a pile on the floor.

Carlos started to argue, "I just *did*," but gave up because Amy was already in the bathroom brushing her teeth. He heard her spit and yell something about coffee as he padded to the kitchen and waited for Whitaker's return call.

"Williams," he answered when the call came through.

"Just talked to Hayslip. She's there and he's on his way to meet her. She's at the high school where she's commandeered a garbage truck."

"She's WHAT?" Carlos asked.

"Just head out there. And give me a call when you're on your way. I'll fill you in then.

"And, uh…did you find Amy? You didn't have to look too far, did you?"

Carlos stared at the phone in his hand. He was glad that only certain places were equipped with visual screens for phone conference calls. He could feel himself blushing. He and Amy had been so careful to keep their budding relationship under wraps. "Well, hell," he muttered and then told the lieutenant that he'd be in touch soon.

CHAPTER 49

Conroy High School

Monday Morning

I heard sirens. Before long I heard Hayslip's cruiser slide across the gravel of the parking lot. I popped my head up over the side of the truck. If Grandmother Phelps told me I looked trashy right now, I wouldn't argue!

Chief Hayslip stood next to the driver who was still muttering about his schedule getting all messed up. He looked at the chief as if to inquire whether or not he was going to join me.

Hayslip chuckled and shook his head. "No way. She knows what she's after. I'd just be in her way if I climbed in there."

"I'm getting close," I yelled and went back to work. Daylight would have made my task a whole lot easier. I was beginning to find cafeteria-type items. That was encouraging. Unfortunately, the garbage from said cafeteria had been sitting in the dumpster since the previous Friday. In the hot sun and then the rain. I won't describe the smell…or the feel. Use your imagination and then double it. Pretty gross!

I poked around for a few minutes before finding the bag I was looking for. It was the only one that wasn't rain-soaked. I'd been in there just long enough to lose my hair scrunchie, get strings from banana peels stuck to my tresses and smell like a land-fill on a really hot summer afternoon. *Lovely.*

"Got it!" I yelled. I popped up into the relatively fresh air for a deep breath. I hopped down from the bumper and didn't even wonder why Chief Hayslip not only refused to give me a hand down, but had actually taken a couple of steps backward!

The two men actually said, "Ew-w," as I approached, my hands outstretched, showing them my treasure.

"Put it down, Ms. Jeffers, and we'll have a look," the chief said, reaching in his pocket for some laytex gloves.

Chief Hayslip then took out a pocket knife and knelt down on one knee. I'd already ripped the bag open. I shined my light on the box. "That's it," I said.

He carefully lifted out the box and placed it on the ground. Then he slit it open and looked up at me. "Rat poison," he announced.

I smiled and hoped I didn't have any garbage stuck between my teeth.

"So?" asked the driver.

Hayslip didn't answer. Instead he said, "Gus?" and looked at the truck driver. I guess everyone really *does* know everyone else in a small town.

"You didn't see anything right there, understand?"

When Gus nodded, the chief continued. "I appreciate you giving us some time this morning and I'm going to need to take a statement from you. I'll need a copy of your scheduled stops so far this morning, but I'm going to let you go on your way for now. I know you've got your rounds to make. And I know you're not going anywhere soon. So I'll catch up with you. Not a word to anyone, all right?" Gus nodded again.

To me, the chief said, "Jeffers, I hate to say it, but we'll need a few more of these bags to prove that this one was in with all the others."

I shot him a sideways glance as Gus started to laugh. But I guessed I couldn't possibly look or smell any worse, so I hopped up in the back end of the truck, held my breath and tossed out three more of the bags I'd opened. "Merry freakin' Christmas, Chief!" I said as I clambered back out again.

"And for *your* holiday gift," Brian Hayslip announced, "I'm giving you a shower and some gym clothes. Follow me." He took off down the sidewalk, keeping himself at a safe distance.

Twenty minutes later, I felt much better. The janitor had let us into the field house where I had a nice hot shower and used a whole bunch of someone's shampoo. The chief threw some sweat pants and a sweatshirt in my general direction. I was ready to go. (Who needs underwear, anyway?) I confiscated a pair of flip-flops from the floor of the locker room and hoped whoever owned them a.) wouldn't mind if I borrowed them for a few hours, and b.) didn't have athlete's foot.

I stuck my head under one of the electric hand-drying machines. I wasn't too worried about the frizzies. I was just happy to be clean. I even found a spray can of deodorant, so I used a liberal amount of that.

"Who says women take forever to get ready in the morning?" Chief Hayslip asked as I emerged from the locker room. "You're quick as all get-out!"

I just smiled. We didn't discuss my underwear situation. I asked, "What do you think of the box, sir?"

Brian Hayslip rubbed his chin. "Lucky for us Carla Tyson didn't stick her head out the cafeteria door and figure out what you were doing this morning."

I nodded in agreement. "This is definitely the box that I saw her take out of her car this morning and place in the trash bag."

"It contains four packs of rat poison," Hayslip noted, "and they contain that old poison that so many rodents have developed a resistance to. So we know that this isn't the new stuff that the school purchased."

"I saw her get the box out of her garage at the Tysons' house."

"Right." We sat in silence, staring at its contents and gathering our thoughts.

"According to the Cafeteria Administrator, Carla'd disposed of all the old poison. Are there serial numbers or some other kind of code on those packets that can be traced to old shipping invoices?"

"Good idea, Jeffers. It may come to that. However, we may get lucky. I've known Carla for a good many years. I have a feeling that if we confront her, she'll spill her guts. At least that's what I'm hoping for. Are you ready?"

I hopped to my feet. "Oh, yeah. This case has been bugging me for way too long!"

CHAPTER 50

Conroy High School Cafeteria

Monday Morning

Other people were beginning to arrive as Chief Hayslip and I entered the cafeteria. Carla was chatting with the administrator in her office, her back to us. We went in and closed the door behind us. The administrator stood and Chief Hayslip said quietly, "Ruth, we need to speak privately with Carla for a minute. Just routine—nothing to get worked up over. May we use your office here?"

Ruth looked at Carla with concern. "Sure, Brian. No problem." She glanced anxiously from one of us to the other. I smiled stiffly. The chief just nodded. She grabbed a couple files, murmured good-bye and scooted out the door.

Carla eyed us nervously and began to perspire heavily when the chief produced the box from behind his back. She sank quietly into a chair, looking rather pale.

I took the other seat while Police Chief Hayslip perched one hip on the corner of the desk. He didn't say a word. Slowly, he opened the box.

If it were possible for Carla to get any paler, she did. Then she began to weep silently. Hayslip handed her a handkerchief.

In the smallest voice possible, she whispered, "He almost killed my boy. He deserved to pay for what he did. He was a bully and he had everyone buffaloed—everyone but me. I couldn't just sit there and let him get away with the things he did."

I looked at the police chief and raised my eyebrows. He nodded and said, "Carla, do you want me to call your lawyer? You might want to have him here, you know."

Carla shook her head. She mopped her brow with his hankie and then twisted it around and around her fingers. "No, Brian. I'm a big girl. I know what I'm saying. And you need to know what really happened. So does Ms. Jeffers, here. So does Sherry."

Chief Hayslip and I sat silently. Carla looked up from her hands—right at the chief and continued, her voice somewhat stronger. "You read the note that Clem's friend Josh wrote. This wasn't the first time that this kind of thing happened. I didn't know the details of this year's summer camp, but I've watched at other times.

"These boys—they're just kids. They don't need this 'killer instinct' beat into their heads. The world's violent enough. And winning isn't the most important thing, you know? Sam had lost the real value of a team.

"They're supposed to learn *good* things from being part of a team. Cooperation, companionship, working together as a group. They come to realize that it's not just about themselves—that it takes everyone doing his own part to make things work. That it's not just the ones who score the points that are important. So are the linemen, so's the center. So are the trainers, the water-boys and the equipment managers and statisticians. Everybody has to work together to make the team strong.

"This carries over long after they're out of school. Once they start working, whether it's in a cafeteria like me or on an assembly line at the plant or even if they go into the business world. Everyone's got their part to do. They should take pride in it.

"Heck, even marriage is like that. What if Larry and I each thought only about our own selves? What if we didn't work together to make our life work? What if he belittled what I contribute or I complained about how many hours he had to put in?

"And then there's Sam Johnson," she continued, "preaching 'fight, kill. Win at any cost'. And to get the boys to that level, he was downright cruel! It was worse than boot camp! He demanded too much. He encouraged the boys to be mean to each other. Win, win, win! He went against so many of the values that we try to teach our kids…he needed to be stopped."

Carla looked down at her hands again. Hayslip's handkerchief was balled up tight in her hand. "So I decided, when we got that new poison in, to keep a few of the old boxes back. I told Ruth I'd thrown it all away. I read up on it and figured I could slip a little in his food once in a while and it'd make him really sick, if nothing else. Then he'd know what it felt like not to be in top form. To need to sit down every once in a while. Then maybe he'd understand how the boys felt.

"And I only did it twice. He was such a picky eater—a health nut. Wouldn't touch a hot dog or any of my potato salad. *No!* I had to fix him special *tofu* burgers and organic crap. *Organic*," she said disgustingly. "—Lordy be! So I stirred some stuff up in his lunch last week—Monday, I think it was.

"And then on Saturday, I put a little in his 'lite' salad dressing. I'm not sure if he even ate any of *that*. But even if he did, I didn't think that'd be enough to *kill* him. When he collapsed at the picnic, I couldn't believe it! I thought, 'Oh Lord, what have I done!'

"So I told Larry, and Clem must've overheard 'cause that's when he started feeling so bad and wrote that note and…everything." She looked up at Chief Hayslip, pleadingly. "You've got to know Clem had nothing to do with it! He was just trying to protect me. He's a good boy—he'd never hurt anyone. Maybe that's why the coach was always so hard on him. He just wasn't aggressive enough."

Finally it appeared she'd run down. The three of us sat there, exhausted. I tried to process all she'd said. She'd meant to teach

Sam Johnson a lesson. There was no way she could have been aware that he'd been seeing Dr. Sanchez in Atlanta. And no way could she have predicted his fall from the horse at Turley's Stables that Friday. Coincidences. Talk about timing! All three of the Tysons had confessed to killing Johnson and I wasn't sure that *any* of them had actually done it!

"Carla," Chief Hayslip said quietly, "you're going to have to come down to the station with me. Do you want to call Larry or Clem before we go?"

"No, not yet. Let's just go and get it over with. Larry will try to stop me if I call him now. And Clem's still too…you know…He doesn't need to deal with this right now."

Hayslip pushed himself up off the corner of the desk and rubbed his hip. I noted that it was probably asleep. Carla stood up and looked at herself in the mirror, straightening her hair and getting herself ready to move on. "You know, I do feel real bad about Sherry and the kids," she said to her reflection. "I'll do whatever I can to help them out. They're good people."

Chief Hayslip gently turned her away from the mirror. "You look fine, Carla," he said. "Let's go." She let him take her elbow and guide her out of the office. She glanced absently around the cafeteria, not really seeing anything.

"It's fine, everyone," Hayslip announced to the cafeteria staff gathered close by. "Everything's okay. I'm just going to take Carla home. Go on about your business."

I was pleased that he was supportive of Carla. No theatrics, no hysterics. I nodded to the workers and followed Carla and the chief out to his cruiser.

She was ready to get in the back seat. Chief Hayslip said, "No, Carla. There's no need for that." He opened the front door for her.

"I appreciate this, Brian," Carla said and smiled. She looked up at me. "Would you go tell Larry where I am?" she asked.

"Sure." I'd been wondering what to do with myself. There'd be no need for me to go to the station right away. So I was glad to have something to do.

CHAPTER 51

Tyson's Garage

Monday Morning

I wasn't in a hurry any longer. In fact I felt completely drained. I slowly drove from the high school to Tyson's Garage on Miller Street. It was still quite early. No one was around yet. Just as well—I needed to think.

I parked in front and got a notebook out of my bag. *May as well keep busy while I'm waiting for the garage to open.* What a mess this was! I felt sorry for everyone involved. Well, almost everyone. I still wasn't sure if Sam Johnson deserved any pity at all!

I jotted down some notes:

> Johnson: age 40
>
>   began medication Oct. 2
>
>   dr. appts. scheduled Sept. 27 Oct. 2, 4, 9, 11, 16, 18, 23
>
>   missed last three dr. appointments (16, 18, 23)

	ate poison Mon., Oct. 15
	fell from horse Fri., Oct. 19
	collapsed and died Sat., Oct. 20
Clem:	head injury August 17
	suicide attempt October 24
	confessed to murder (protecting mom)
Carla:	poisoned food Mon., Oct 15
	again on Sat., Oct. 20
	confessed to murder (guilty?)
Larry:	confessed to murder (protecting family)

As I sat there in the car looking over my notes, it occurred to me that Sam Johnson was the person most responsible for his own death. He'd been negligent. He had cancelled two appointments. He'd been warned by Dr. Sanchez that his INR level needed to be checked at least twice a week to avoid overdose.

Johnson had eaten tainted food once, possibly twice. In a normal person, there would have been no side effects. I needed to talk with Dr. Graves immediately!

But just then Larry Tyson pulled into his parking space. He exited his car, speaking heatedly to someone on his cell phone. Quickly, I stuffed all my notes into my bag. I hadn't had time to consider his reaction to my news. As I got out of the car and swung my trusty black bag onto my shoulder I thought, *this could go well, or this could end up really badly! Kate, you should have taken time to think this through!*

CHAPTER 52

Chief Hayslip and the Detectives

Monday Morning

Detectives Carlos and Amy arrived in Conroy at 8:00. Amy exited the highway, glad to have the sun out of her eyes. The earlier clouds and rain had moved on, leaving the day bright as the sun came up. En route, Carlos had spoken with Lieutenant Whitaker. He had filled them in on the early morning happenings at the high school.

After hanging up, Carlos complained to Amy. He pounded his fist on his leg, annoyed that he'd missed seeing Kate covered with garbage. "Damn! This could have been the 'payback' that I've been promising her! I'd kill for a picture of her coming up out of that garbage truck. Just think—I could've put life-sized posters of Jeffers on the wall in every precinct station in Atlanta!"

"Carlos…" Amy warned. But Carlos noted the humor in her voice. Amy cleared her throat and tried again. "Carlos! Stop being evil. Tell me what Kate found in the truck!"

He explained about the rat poison. Then he told her what the lieutenant had said about Carla's confession. "Whitaker wants us to check in with Hayslip, so go over there first, okay?"

Amy nodded and turned the vehicle in the direction of the Conroy Police Station.

They had to park way down the street because a large tow-truck was in the regular lot. "Morning," a man in a green uniform called out as they approached the station. "Sorry I'm in the way. Give me a couple of minutes. I'll be out of here. Just need to hook up this car."

Carlos answered, "That's fine, man. No problem. Take your time." To Amy he whispered, "Check out the name on that guy's truck. 'Tyson's Garage'.

"Oh-oh! You suppose he saw Carla with the chief?" Carlos shrugged and held the door open for Amy.

"So that's where we stand right now," Police Chief Brian Hayslip concluded. "I'm going to drop Carla off at her house. There's no reason to hold her here any longer. She's certainly not a threat to anyone. And since Clem's back home, she needs to be there with him."

Amy and Carlos both nodded in agreement.

Chief Hayslip looked thoughtful as he stood up from his chair. "I'm surprised we haven't heard anything from Jeffers or Mr. Tyson."

"What do you mean?" asked Carlos, a note of concern in his voice.

"Jeffers was going over to the garage to tell Larry Tyson about Carla. I'd have thought she'd have been back here by now, that's all," he answered.

"She went *where?*" Amy squawked in alarm. "Holy cow! Carlos, let's go!" She jumped up and was out the door before the men could stop her.

"What is it?" Hayslip asked Carlos.

"Didn't Kate tell you that Tyson had threatened to kill her if she showed up again?" When the chief shook his head, Carlos continued. "That's the main reason Whitaker sent us back out here this morning. He was afraid Jeffers would confront Larry Tyson again."

"I'm really out of the loop, here," Hayslip responded. As they pushed out of the front door to follow Amy to her cruiser, he turned to the desk sergeant. "Charlie, have Officer Blake run Mrs. Tyson home for me, will ya? We've got a situation here. I'll be in touch shortly."

As they ran to the vehicle, Carlos filled Chief Hayslip in about the lieutenant's concerns.

CHAPTER 53

Tyson's Garage

Monday Morning

As I watched Larry Tyson's face, I had the sneaking suspicion that this wasn't going to be one of his better days. I stuffed the notes back into my black bag.

"What are you talkin' about?" he shouted into his phone. He shoved his car door open and switched the phone to his other ear. He listened for another few seconds and then said, "You gotta be kidding!"

That's all I heard since his back was to me by then. I wondered who had called him and what they were talking about. He walked rapidly to the garage door, snapping the phone shut. He fumbled with his keys and unlocked the garage. His hands were shaking.

He didn't notice me getting out of my car and following behind.

Tyson was halfway across the work area when he sensed my presence. He spun around and spied me. I stopped. We were about six paces apart.

"You! I told you not to show up here again! Carla left the school with Hayslip! What's he doing—taking her to jail?"

Oops! He knows. I guess maybe that's what the call had been about. "Sir, perhaps we should sit down and discuss this," I said, trying to buy time. I noticed him eyeing the stainless steel workbench. I glanced over, too, and realized there were a whole bunch of tools lying there that could cause a girl like me a very nasty headache. *Ouch!*

"We've got nothing to talk about!" he shouted back. "This whole mess is your fault. I told you not to go poking your damn nose into things. I'm done talking!"

While he was yelling, I was weighing my options. If I turned and ran, he'd be on me in a flash. *So much for option number one.*

I tried to remember some of the moves from my Tae Kwan Do days. I know they're supposed to be so ingrained that they become automatic, but...nothing came to me. *There went option number two!*

It was a shame I was no longer a cop—no weapon! While I was contemplating option number three, he made his move. Grabbing something very long (a tire-iron, perhaps?), he lunged at me, swinging.

I guess instinct *did* kick in. He swung; I ducked. And before he had a chance to recover, I clobbered him with my bag. My trusty big black bag. His head must've connected with the flashlight, because the next thing I knew, he was flat on the floor. I grabbed the panty hose out of my bag. Tossing the tire-iron out of reach, I slapped Tyson's wrists together and tied him up. *I knew I'd need those stockings someday!*

I heard voices behind me and turned to see Amy, Carlos and Chief Hayslip. "She's here!" Amy cried. "And she just kicked Tyson's tail!"

❊

"I let one Tyson go and then I've got to stick the other one in the slammer," commented Chief Hayslip later on. "They've had quite a day!"

The chief, the two detectives and I were sitting around the conference table at the Conroy Police Station. Officer Blake had just led the Medical Examiner in to join us.

"I'm glad you could stop by, Dr. Graves," Chief Hayslip said, welcoming him and offering him a chair. "Coffee?" When the doctor nodded, I poured him a cup as Hayslip continued. "To bring you up to speed, we've been discussing this whole Johnson situation and realize that we've got quite a problem here...We need your opinion."

Dr. Graves nodded and steepled his hands in front of him, elbows on the table.

"Here's what we've got: Sam Johnson was a well-respected coach. He is known all over the state for his winning record, but in Conroy, he's thought of as deity. Larry Tyson plans to speak up about the camp incident with Clem. He's back there now, talking with his lawyer. They may want to file a suit against Johnson or perhaps the school system. Clem's had a lot of difficulties from that head injury. Larry's screaming gross negligence. Just think of the implications!" And he listed them.

1. Conroy and its high school get nation-wide publicity. Negative publicity. We'll be the laughing stock...
2. Johnson's name is dragged through the mud. His reputation is ruined.
3. Our student athletes will be asked to spend months on the witness stand, testifying against their former coach.
4. The people of Conroy are up in arms. Their favorite hero is taken away from them—in more ways than one. (You saw them at his service.)
5. The town is split down the middle: Those who stand up for Johnson and those who trash his name.
6. Our athletic program is ruined. That's huge around here!
7. Sherry and the kids are disgraced.

8. If there's a suit against the coach, any monies will come out of his estate. That would bankrupt Sherry.
9. If the suit is against the district…I don't even want to consider that! Not to mention the boys being dragged into court again.
10. Carla's confessed to Johnson's murder. She goes to prison.
11. Clem and his dad have to live with *that*.
12. Larry's been arrested for assault. Clem's got to live with both parents' mistakes. He's a good kid and has enough troubles of his own right now!

We sat in silence for a bit. Then I spoke up. "Dr. Graves…a question." Everyone looked at me while I decided how to phrase it. "During the autopsy, you found that Johnson had high INR levels. We understand that this was caused by a combination of the Coumadin that Dr. Sanchez had prescribed and the warfarin that was in the rat poison he ingested at the hands of Carla Tyson." He nodded, confirming what I'd said so far. "Is it possible to tell what percentage of the poison came from one source or the other? In other words, would it be possible that the Coumadin, unregulated as it was, could have reached fatal levels by Saturday, October 20th? Even without Carla Tyson's involvement. Especially when paired with the internal bleeding caused by the riding incident on that Friday?"

Dr. Graves rubbed his forehead, thinking. "That's the big question, here, isn't it? Let me think about it. Then Chief Hayslip and I will have a word with the prosecutor."

EPILOGUE

Kate and Papa

The Following Thursday Morning

"More coffee?" Papa asked me as he came out onto my balcony. He carried the coffee pot along with the best-smelling cinnamon rolls in the world. Planting a kiss on the top of my head, he smiled at me and winked. I melted. (Again. Just like I had when he'd appeared at my door the night before.)

I gratefully accepted a roll and more coffee. He had been deeply disturbed when I had told him about my sister, Emily, being attacked and we both decided that I needed to spend the next few days helping her cope.

After sitting in companionable silence for a few minutes, I said, "So, I've told you a lot about what went on in Conroy. I'm exhausted just thinking about it. Let me tell you the rest later, okay? It's your turn. What's been happening around here the past few days."

I watched the man sitting across from me as he talked. I decided I could be content to sit here and look at him every day of my life from now on. I pictured him as he aged: Thirty—the same as now.

Forty—a little heavier. Fifty—a bit of gray? Sixty—distinguished, definitely. Seventy—still mellow. Eighty—a wise grandfather-type. And it would be cool to be there by his side. Aging gracefully!!

He broke into my thoughts when he mentioned a tattoo. "What's that again?" I asked, wiping icing from my mouth.

"Gloria. She's getting a tattoo. She wants to celebrate her new relationship with Ronnie as well as remember her trip to Conroy. Gloria wanted to have 'Ride 'em Cowboy' put on her hip, but Ron talked her out of that. He said that's too suggestive."

I gasped aloud. "Whew! Good Lord, that girl's a trip, isn't she?" We laughed. "Since Ron's the conservative one, what was *his* suggestion?"

"Not sure. But she finally decided on 'Giddyap' instead!"

I blinked in surprise. "Oh, that's *much* better."

"I think you'll get to meet Anna this weekend. Her father said Demetri could take her out on Sunday. (I'll get to that in a minute.) According to Demetri, she's looking forward to getting to know you. He says she's a great cook. Fixes all the traditional meals. And her parents are starting to like Demetri."

Papa went on to say that Amy and Carlos had been into the lounge Tuesday evening. "Yeah, it seems everyone, including Whitaker, knew about their relationship and they were still trying to be real discreet about it. So Tuesday, they said what the heck! We broke out the Ouzo and toasted to their future. It was great! But you weren't there. So since Tuesday didn't really count, we're going to have a *real* party. Both sets of parents will be in town, so this Sunday afternoon we're going to have a barbecue. At my place. That's where you'll meet Anna. Carlos and Amy are going to formally announce their engagement. Carlos spoke with Amy's dad. Carlos wanted his blessing, so he's in on it, but it'll be a surprise for the others! So mark your calendar!"

I was so excited for them! What a wonderful couple! I got tears in my eyes. Papa smiled and handed me a tissue. "For a tough little lady, you're such a softy. One minute, you're kicking someone's backside out in Conroy and the next minute you're crying because your friends are happy! What am I going to do with you?"

I laughed through my tears and shrugged. I honked my nose.

"I have a few ideas," he said, winking again. "But I think I'll wait till your nose stops running." I tried to kick him under the table, but he was too quick. We sat in companionable silence, enjoying the morning. My flowers were making a strong comeback. I'd finally gotten a couple decent nights' sleep. Grandma had promised to give me a few cooking lessons. *Ooh! Maybe I could get Anna to share a few Greek recipes as well!*

My phone rang. I excused myself and took the call. When I returned to the balcony I told Papa, "That was Chief Hayslip—out in Conroy. He wanted to fill me in. It looks like they've made a deal. We've dropped the assault charge against Larry Tyson with the understanding that he goes with Clem to the counselor, who can give them *both* tips on anger management. Larry is not going to file charges against Johnson or the school, but the board is going to take a serious look at their athletic practice policies. Andy Menendez (who's a real nice guy) will probably be made the permanent head coach. He's much more in tune with the needs of the students so there won't be any problems like they had with Sam Johnson.

"And Johnson's name and reputation won't have to be tarnished. His wife and kids will be spared. They and the entire town of Conroy can still have their hero, but he won't be around to hurt anyone else."

When Papa asked if I didn't think things would be tough on Sherry Johnson, I recalled my most recent vision. I merely said, "It'll be hard for a while, but I have a feeling that things will work out okay for them all."

He squinted at me for a moment, his head cocked to one side. Then he asked, "Do you know something about that?" I just smiled. His next question was, "How about the kid's mom—what's her name?"

"Carla! Yeah, listen to this! If she's charged at all, it will be on a way-lesser count, maybe 'assault with intent to harm' or something like that. But since Dr. Graves says we can't prove that what Carla did actually contributed to Johnson's death, her lawyer is pretty sure the charges will be dropped. In fact, they may not charge her at all! Hayslip and Dr. Graves talked with the Prosecutor. He thinks it would be better for Conroy and Johnson's family if the media never get wind of it. And from looking over the facts, he doesn't think he'd ever be able to prove a thing! I doubt Carla will ever see herself in a newspaper article, let alone in front of a judge."

We both contemplated Chief Hayslip's call. "Are you happy with the way the case turned out?" Papa asked.

The sixty-four million dollar question, I thought. "The way things stand now, everyone out in Conroy has been spared years of grief. Everyone. I think justice has been served."